Chapter One – The Slap

SHE WAS GLANCING AT the night's TV listings in the *Standard* when she felt the touch of a hand on her bare shoulder. She turned abruptly, shaking her head, and the man studied her with blue eyes full of mischief.

Greta was furious. It just isn't done. Not on the tube. It's too intimate. While your body's rubbing against other bodies the last thing you want to do is make eye contact.

She looked back at the paper. Saturday night. There was a movie with Jack Black, Channel 5, nine o'clock. Shame about the commercials. She'd microwave something during the breaks. Drink a glass of wine. Or two. She glanced up.

He was looking still. He smiled. Good teeth. She frowned. If she had been in a pub playing pool she would have liked those playful eyes and broad shoulders. She looked down and then back up again, instinctively, as if against her will. He was writing something on his newspaper. He tore off the corner of the page and gave it to her as the train slowed at Gloucester Road.

'My stop,' he said, and squeezed through the sliding doors just before they closed.

His name was Richard. And his telephone number had loads of sevens in it. Was it lucky? For him? For her?

He was watching her through the carriage window, remaining on the platform like a rock in the churning sea of people. She ostentatiously screwed up the scrap of paper and he shrugged with indifference as she let it drop to the floor. The train pulled away and he was gone.

Greta sighed. She had grown to despise the tube in the time she'd worked in the shop. A shop assistant. How did it happen? Why? Two years at drama school. A year in the cattle market hustling parts. And another birthday in October. She didn't even bother to read the trades any more. She was 19. That's almost 20. She'd be looking at comfy slippers next.

She picked up the piece of paper again and looked at all those lucky sevens. Richard. Black jacket. Blue shirt. Dark jeans. Nice tan.

The train pulled in at Hammersmith. She stumbled along behind two girls in grey veils and thought about the crowd at Gloucester Road. Well-heeled. Closer to the action.

As soon as she got home Greta spread the scrap of paper flat on the kitchen counter. She called the number. She let it ring twice. Then hung up.

It was ridiculous to call a total stranger. Then, it was ridiculous not to. What did she have to lose? There were zillions of blokes she could call, well, about six, anyway, but they were all so dire, gabbing on about Formula 1 and football, all after one thing, as if she were a sporting fixture, and, yes, she liked that *thing* as much as the next girl, but she wanted something different, something more ... *oo la la,* more *je ne sais quoi.* She was meant for other things, something better, not that she believed she was better than anyone else, indeed that anyone was better than anyone else. She just thought there was another life out there waiting to happen.

She sighed again. All I do is keep sighing, she thought. She lit a cigarette and poured a glass of wine. The first drag and the first sip are the best. Life's like that. An unfulfilled promise. She had played at the *Royal Court* in Sloane Square when she was 17. She appeared naked every night on stage at the National. She was Polly in *The Raw Edge*, a pilot for a soap that had never got made.

2

A GIRL'S ADVENTURE

A GIRL'S ADVENTURE

CHLOË THURLOW

Published by Accent Press Ltd – 2010
ISBN 9781907761119

First published by Chimera Books 2006

Printed in the U.K.

Cover design by Zipline Creative

For M. Millswan.

You were right, Micky Baby,

it just keeps getting better.

Xcite Books help make loving better
with a wide range of erotic books,
eBooks and dating sites.

www.xcitebooks.com
www.xcitebooks.co.uk
www.xcitebooks.com.au

Sign up to our Facebook page
for special offers and free gifts!

There had been hundreds of girls up for it. But she'd got the part. At 18 she could play 15. They liked that. She looked like the girl next door who gets tied up and raped.

She rather liked being tied up, she thought as she lifted the receiver, phoned again. Hung up again.

Tara had wandered in ready for work in a sparkly silver thong and nothing else. Her flatmate was studying law at the London School of Economics and lap-danced three nights a week to pay the bills. She was holding a silver stiletto with a broken heel.

'If it's not one thing it's another,' she moaned.

Greta smiled. 'A man gave me his telephone number on the tube,' she said.

'Lucky thing.'

'I know.' She paused to take an extravagant drag on her fag.

'Well?' Tara insisted.

'Nothing. He was a stranger.'

'What was he like?'

'Mmm. Tall, wavy dark hair, nice accent.'

'My type.'

Tara stretched her arms above her head and went up on her toes. She had full breasts that were really perky with nipples as pink as a rose.

'You should call,' she said breathlessly.

'What?'

'What have you got to lose?' Tara asked and it was like an echo inside Greta's head.

Greta's bottom lip had dropped and she pulled at it reflectively. Tara had leaned forward to make her point and Greta had to tear her gaze away from the inviting spectacle of her flatmate's boobs.

'Can I borrow your red heels?' she asked, breaking the spell.

'Absolutely not.'

'Thanks, you're a sweetie,' Tara said, and took a puff on Greta's cigarette.

Greta finished her wine. She started to pour a second glass and stopped herself, adding just a touch. She watched Tara slip off back to her room, walking on her toes like a ballerina, and braced herself to make the call again. What would she say? What if she got an answer phone? No problem. She'd hang up.

There was no answer phone. He answered.

'It's me.'

'I knew you'd call.'

'How?'

'Nothing ventured ...' He trailed off. 'Come over.'

'What for?'

'I could say a plate of spaghetti.'

'Mmm. Sounds delicious.'

'You're not a vegetarian?' he asked sternly.

'No,' she said.

'Good, I don't like girls who think they're so precious,' he remarked. 'Anyway, you should never reject what you haven't tried. Don't you agree?'

She had to think about that. 'Yes, I suppose so,' she said.

'It's an awful old cliché, but variety is the spice of life,' he added; he was easy to talk to and she liked his voice.

He now gave her his address. 'I suppose you need to go and find a pen?'

'As it happens,' she said, 'I have a trained memory.'

'I thought you'd be a quick learner,' he replied brightly.

Greta repeated his address.

'I'll be waiting.'

She replaced the receiver. Her armpits were damp. This was insanity. He was an axe murderer. A madman. She shivered and gave herself a little hug. She was just dying to do something different.

Tara wandered in wearing Greta's stilettos; they had been in her room all the time anyway. She gave a little

4

shimmy to show how good the shoes were for lap dancing.

'Just the ticket,' Greta said.

'Why are you looking like the cat that got the cream?'

'I've got a date.'

'With ...'

'*American Psycho*,' she answered, sucking air through her teeth.

'Don't do anything I wouldn't,' said Tara and skipped off in the red heels.

Greta stepped out of her clothes. As she crossed the hall to the bathroom it felt as if it were someone quite different who stood with her face upturned to the shower. She scrubbed away the tube smells, the girlie smells, the reek of other people's cheesy feet. A shoe shop. She shuddered. She shaved her legs. Perfumed her parts, and when she returned to her bedroom it really wasn't Greta May who stood gazing at her reflection in the full-length mirror but someone like her, a perfect reproduction who stretched just as Tara had stretched, pushing out her breasts until they placed on the mirror two tiny kisses of condensation. Her nipples prickled with cold and she rubbed them between her fingers until they swelled and hardened. 'You are naughty,' she whispered.

She slid into black knickers, went back to the bathroom and cleaned her teeth. She lit a cigarette. Smiled at the absurdity of it. Of everything. She put on the black dress that crossed below her cleavage and leaned forward to study her shape; she had lap-dancer breasts according to Tara and she should know. Perhaps she should give it a try; at least she'd be on stage, on show.

Greta shook herself and decided the dress was too revealing. She took it off, tossed it on the bed and tried blue jeans and a shirt. Pretty good hips, she thought, took off the jeans and put on a skirt instead. Clothes help you find the character. Then, when you're up there, out there, you're no longer you, but then you are, even more so.

5

Yes, they really were someone else's eyes peering back as she did her mascara. Someone who didn't work in a shoe shop. She removed the skirt, slid back into the slinky black dress, then swivelled round just quickly enough to catch a glimpse of Polly in *The Raw Edge*.

Greta puckered her lips for the camera and skipped on tapping heels down the stairs to the street. As she was about to enter the tube, a taxi stopped and without a second thought she stepped into the back. She loved London taxis. She didn't like London cabbies. But she did like their cabs. It was like returning to the womb. You were coddled; luxuriated. You learned how to love yourself, your reflection opaque and vaguely surreal in the dark glass, red and amber veins of light crossing the sky. London streaked by, the most beautiful city in the world.

Richard lived in a red brick building divided into five flats. She climbed the three wide marble steps to a blue door. His was the bottom bell. She stood on the coconut mat holding her breath, her finger hovering over the shiny brass button. A tongue of wind had slipped along the street, blowing hair over her eyes. Greta shivered.

The drum of the taxi faded to silence. The street was deserted. *Stage fright*, she whispered. Greta backed away, marched down the steps and only slowed her pace when she turned the corner and reached the newsagents.

She glanced at the titles of the magazines outside on the rack. She pulled out *The Stage* but couldn't face going inside the shop to buy it. She shoved the magazine back into place. If she hurried she'd get home in time to see the movie. She lit a cigarette and blew a long stream of smoke into the sky. The night was clear. Full of stars. The wind had dropped.

Greta was suffering the same old butterfly feeling that came over her every time she went for a casting and, as she had done many times before, she bit her lip, crushed out the cigarette below her heel, cleaned her teeth with her tongue, and set out again for the red brick building. *Come on girl, you can do it.* She took a deep breath and hit the bell.

The blue door buzzed open.

'Come in.'

His voice on the entry phone was deep and seemed to come from far away. Her heels clacked over the black and white tiles in the long hallway, echoing in the confined space. Or was that her heart?

Richard stood in the entrance to his flat wearing jogging pants, a polo shirt. Bare feet. As she stepped inside he pushed the door just hard enough for it to catch, the click loud *like a cell door closing!* They were motionless in the half-light. He leaned forward, placing his palms flat on the wall, her head trapped in the space between them. He wasn't smiling. He just stared. She stared back. His blue eyes were dark like the sea at night. Greta wondered if he would ever be cast as a leading man, but the thought was knocked from her mind as suddenly, shockingly, his hand came down in a swift slap across her cheek.

It stung, really stung. The slap was hard, not so hard as to bruise, but hard enough for her teeth to cut the inside of her mouth, the sound brittle as breaking glass. She tasted blood, and felt the blood race through her veins. Her breath caught in her throat. She would have screamed, but his lips were on her mouth, sucking at her and she responded to his kiss.

They parted, panting for breath, his hands caressing her sides, the curve of her waist, her hips. He lifted her dress and before she realised what he was doing, he ripped the sides of her knickers. Just tore them apart. She heard them tear and couldn't conceive of anyone doing such a thing. It was like being in a play. She played her role, pulling away, but he was strong, calm, in control, and held her still, pinned to the wall. He pulled softly at the elastic at the front of her knickers where they were tight against her belly and she couldn't understand why she eased her bottom forward just far enough to let them slide down her legs to the floor. He brushed the hair from her eyes. Her heart was pounding.

Greta recalled reading in *Cosmo* that women got wet when they were excited. It had never happened to her. Never. But it did now. She could feel a dampness inside her stomach. She felt that dampness grow liquid and leak from her, wetting her thighs. He pulled at the tie holding her dress, peeled the straps from her shoulders and the material slithered like a black waterfall to her feet. He was staring into her eyes and it seemed as if he was looking at someone far away, someone approaching across a clear, uncluttered landscape. Greta was naked but for her suede heels and satin bra. His palms ran down her flanks, up and down, then he turned her around in one quick movement, his weight forcing her down onto the floor.

He entered her in one swift lunge; it was terrifying and marvellous and took her breath away. The cheek where he'd hit her was pressed against the coarse floor covering. She opened her mouth, sucking air in short frenzied gasps. She could feel his breath, hot against her ear. He rammed deep inside her, harder and harder, and she raised her hips from the floor and pushed back, wanting more, wanting to play the part as well as she knew she could.

Greta let the fluids ripple and flow through her arms and legs, from her toes to the tips of her fingers. She spread her thighs wider to take more of him, all of him. She could feel his strong hands gripping the carved handles of her hips, pulling her gently, forcefully, riding her, and she heard little bleating satisfied noises and realised they were coming from her. She used all her strength to push back on to her knees and started waggling her bottom. Air was trapped in her throat. She was panting for breath, a pony after a long ride, and galloped on, hair tossing from side to side, her muscles straining.

Keep going. Keep going. Don't stop. Don't ever stop ...

This is what she had always imagined, always wanted, not a quick shag in the back of a car with some boy who couldn't control himself, not making love like in a story, but the real thing, a good and thorough fucking. She tasted the words: a good fucking. He's fucking me. I'm being fucked. Gloriously fucked. She pushed back, the sound of slapping flesh and oily gurgles reverberating over the walls, the creamy juices gushing from her sopping crack, warming her quivering thighs.

Richard was slowing, stretching the seconds, holding on to something that can't be held. A door was about to unlock inside him and she wanted to keep that door securely bolted. She slid forward on her hands and knees, towing him with her. He gripped her hips more tightly, but she wriggled from his grasp and rolled on to her back, drawing him wet and slippery over her body and taking his steamy cock into her mouth. He sighed as it glided like silk into the soft pink tissue of her throat, her wide curling tongue wrapping it in an embrace. Greta closed her eyes, sucked long and hard on Richard's cock and was overcome by a feeling of complete contentment.

His come exploding across the roof of her mouth was warm and frothy like cappuccino and as he withdrew the sticky warm goo stretched in a trail over her chin and down between her breasts. She savoured the taste, and she pushed her bottom up, supporting herself with her hands, opening herself fully, and his cock was still hard as it slid back into her throbbing sex.

Greta rolled her hips. He tugged at her thighs, thrusting in deeper, and her body became a river as she began to climax, a gushing, tumbling stream of sheer ecstasy, pure sensation, flooding her dripping pussy, completing her, rewarding her, and she knew she'd played her finest role. She gasped and shouted. Richard grew harder, drilling into her, up and down, up and down, and finally came again with a violent jerk that left him spent and exhausted.

Now that he'd finished she imagined he was going to

9

open the door and toss her back out again. But that didn't happen. He did something she had not been expecting. He kissed her cheek. He then lifted her awkwardly into his arms and carried her through to the bathroom.

'You've got to lose a few pounds,' he said, and when she considered the remark a few minutes later in the bath she thought it sounded like a commitment, a promise that there was more to come.

Richard turned on the taps, filled the big bath and added blue crystals to the flow. She was reaching for the hook on her bra automatically, her fingers doing the thinking for her. He turned off the taps and she stepped out of her shoes into the foaming blue water.

He was about to leave the bathroom, but leaned back through the door: 'What kind of pizza do you like?' he asked.

'What about that spaghetti?'

'Takes too long.'

She thought for a moment. 'Spinach with an egg.'

'Anything else?'

'Yes, you can get this week's *Stage* at the newsagents.'

He smiled. 'An actress in search of a role?' he said, and she thought he might be making fun of her.

'Greta May,' she announced and realised with shame that she'd actually had sex with a man who didn't even know her name.

He closed the door and lying there in the bubbling blue water, Greta reached two conclusions: she was at the beginning of an extraordinary journey, and her travelling companion was totally weird.

Chapter Two – Being Spanked

WIDE BLOCKS OF SHADOW like the carriages of a slowly moving train slid over the pale green walls. The sun gave the room's far corners a golden glow. Greta could see her dress abandoned on the back of a chair and recalled with a little smile how much care had gone into choosing it.

She was spoiled and sticky, every nerve ending humming. It was as if something sleeping inside her had opened its eyes and was seeing the world for the first time. Her skin, pulsing faintly beneath her long fingers, was as soft as the petals on the roses on the dresser, and like the flowers she had been designed to give pleasure to the eye, the tongue, the nose, to all senses and desires.

Greta ran her palms over her breasts, across her stomach, down to the gooey pool between her legs. She adored being cosy and warm. She was a bubble of mercury that could take any shape, bow and bend to any position. She arched her back and stretched her long legs. The years of tap and tango and ballet classes had shaped and smoothed her limbs. She took a deep breath. She felt as if she had taken some marvellous drug that made you feel that you had become exactly what you were meant to be. I am Greta May. I am me. And it's ... luxurious.

She glanced towards the windows. It was the beginning of June and through the half-opened curtains she could see wisps of white cloud high on a pastel sky. She had slept like a baby and was fully awake, a feeling she realised that slowly withers with each dull journey to work, with each stranger's foot wedged into a stiff new shoe. Now every line and detail was clear, every object solid, the dresser with its carved gilt handles, the wardrobe, the leather belt coiled like a snake on the chair with her dress.

Greta had been playing roles since she was little. That's what actresses do. You get caught up in the character and your own personality slips through the cracks a bit at a time. Now all the bits had reassembled. She was herself again. Greta giggled. One good servicing and she had become a poet. How silly I am, she whispered, and her voice seemed far away. It's back to selling shoes first thing Monday on the eight-o-something. It's back to being the same old me again.

She snuggled down in the enormous bed, queen-sized, king-sized, it was a downy island, humid and musty, the nub of the starched sheet scratchy against her nipples as she wriggled. She loved being naked in the pale green room with the scalloped ceiling embossed with fleurs-de-lys, the light crisscrossing in prisms as it angled through the leaded windows.

It would be very easy to get used to this, she decided. Luxury. Comfort. Pampering. Richard brewing coffee. She could smell it floating down the hallway, merging with the sweet perfumes wafting up from down under.

Her hands roamed over her body as if she were feeling the wrappings in a game of pass the parcel, over her hips and up to her breasts. I do declare. They have grown bigger overnight. Her fingertips traced circles around her dimpled pink areolae and the pressure made her nipples sizzle and ping. Her ribcage was a musical instrument, a harp, perhaps, where practised hands could coax from her the dulcet tones you would hear in old churches rich with polished wood and dappled by coins of sunlight.

She twiddled her toes, so far away and neglected at the foot of the bed, and decided that her ribcage wasn't a harp at all. It is a keyboard where virtuosos will compose triumphant marches. Greta imagined young soldiers in their multitudes stamping by six abreast as she stood on a high podium quite naked inspecting the parade.

Naked! She liked that word. It was so ... so raw, so rude, so exposed. When Greta was little, the summers were hot and she would run through the big garden without anything on. Her mother would usually be drawing in a pad, sketches for paintings she never completed. She was cool and aloof in ivory kaftans embroidered with moons and stars, long and flowing to protect her pale skin. Mother would watch her from the shade of the apple tree and sometimes she would slip from her clothes, become a child again, chasing Greta through the sea of daisies that patterned the grass, two naked nymphs in a secret garden. Greta would jump in the fish pond and her mother would slide into the slimy water laughing at her own foolishness. Mother had studied art, she wanted to be a painter, but something held her back and Greta didn't know why. When Greta decided at 16 to go to drama school her father had his doubts but her mother had seemed quietly pleased.

Greta was far away in that other world as her fingers vanished into the hollows below her ribs. They crawled ponderously across her tummy to the silky forest of her pubic hair, lush as the grass in the garden at home. A naughty finger popped into her pussy like a dormouse popping out of a hole and had a quick look around. Mmm. Very pretty. All glossy and wet, a place for everything and everything in its place, as the house matron used to say. That naughty finger slid back the hood guarding her clitoris and the bud blossomed into a flower. Her eyes closed involuntarily, her knees moved into an arch and she didn't hear Richard arriving with the coffee brewed and warm croissants with that toasty smell that made her think of Paris.

'You bad girl. You started without me.'

Greta felt as if she'd been caught cheating in an exam at school. 'Oh dear ...

'And naughty girls have to be smacked.'

Greta wasn't sure what to say and did what a director named Jason Wise at the National once told her to do when in doubt and that's say ... ooo, yes please.

'Ooo, yes please,' she murmured.

Richard placed the tray on the mahogany dresser and in his expression as he opened the top drawer was the look of someone doing mental arithmetic. She watched with eyes growing bigger as he withdrew a blue silk scarf that just kept growing longer and longer, an endless blue river of shiny fabric that he passed through his hands like a fisherman at sea and she thought he was probably a magician in his spare time and could do all sorts of enchanting tricks. As he moved away from the dresser the scarf spiralled behind, skipping and dancing over the wooden floor.

He paused and stood motionless for a moment beside the bed and she had a feeling that he had finished doing his sums. Their eyes met and remained locked as if by magnets as in one swift movement he pulled back the sheet, the linen cracking like a yacht sail as it gusted across the room. Greta had straightened her legs, her arms were at her side in a pose that in role playing she had been taught was contrite, obedient. Her mind was a blank sheet of paper waiting to be written on.

He slipped his hands under her back and thighs and gently rolled her over. She felt the soft touch of silk as he tied the scarf around her right wrist.

'Have you been a naughty girl?'

'Yes, I have.'

'And what happens to naughty girls?'

'They are disciplined.'

'And how are they disciplined?'

'They have to be smacked.'

She knew the right lines. It was the sort of thing you do in improv.

As they were speaking, Richard had somehow moved

14

the scarf under the bed and was tying her left wrist with a slip knot that grew tighter if she struggled. Not that she had any intention of struggling. She could roll about if she wanted, but only as far as her bonds would allow and it was such a relief to be lying there without having to think about anything at all. It was like being a baby. Or a pet pussy cat and she purred as he bent to kiss her shoulder blades.

Richard tied her left ankle with another pale blue scarf that he took from the drawer and she thought that was typical. Richard liked everything to be neat, coordinated. She studied his shapely bottom in boxer shorts as he bent to pass the scarf below the bed to tie her right ankle.

Her head was buried in the pillow. She felt Richard straddle her. The boxers had gone. She could feel his hard cock bouncing over her back. He ran his tongue up her spine. He kissed her neck and the spot tingled he was such a good kisser. Her mouth had fallen open and she was surprised to feel it being filled with what seemed to be a rubber ball about the size of a ball on a pool table. Weird, but not unpleasant. The ball was clearly attached to a strap and she could feel Richard dextrously buckling it up at the back of her head. She tried to speak and it came out as gobbledegook, like the sound of water draining from a bath, bubble, bubble, bobble, gobble.

Ohmygod, now what?

Greta realised that a stiff covering was being pulled over her head and it was dark and strange with the morning light suddenly extinguished. She had known Richard for ... what, less than 12 hours, and here she was tied to his bed hooded and gagged and instead of being afraid she felt the blood beating in her nipples, a dewy dampness between her spread thighs.

Swish. Swish.

She heard the crack of what she assumed was his leather belt across her bottom before she felt the pain. And when she felt the pain, like a bee sting from a really

15

big bee, it was too late to scream, not that she could have screamed, and anyway, another crack had followed the first and the air had fled from her lungs.

She panted and gasped. Her skin was damp with sweat. The pain was like a jolt of electricity that shot through her and made her feel more alive than she had ever felt and the feeling was like being a child on those summer days when she jumped into the fish pond.

Swish. Swish.

Her bare flesh fizzed like a firework and it occurred to her that in pain there was pleasure as in all pleasure there is a *soupçon* of pain. She thought this was probably profound and she should write it down on that blank sheet of paper when her hands were free.

Swish. Swish.

She groaned. She was quivering, wet with unknown pleasure.

Richard gave her six of the best and as she lay there with her poor little bum sizzling it occurred to her with sudden horror that what she really wanted most was six more. They didn't come and Richard spent an eternity licking away the pain, his salty tongue dabbing in gentle lines across the weal marks. That clever tongue found its way between the cheeks of her bottom and slipped inside her, in and out like a piston, and she had never realised that this dark illicit passage was alive with such scurrilous sensations.

Richard's tongue moved deeper inside her, an explorer seeking out all her undiscovered parts, and she sucked on the rubber ball like a baby suckling the teat. When he withdrew, she remembered something from Shakespeare – parting is such sweet sorrow, and then he returned, not with his briny tongue but with a small battering ram to beat down the walls of her castle.

Actually, he didn't need a battering ram. The walls had been breached. She had raised the portcullis, lowered the bridge in welcome and like a brave soldier slipping out

16

from the Trojan Horse, the warm head of his cock began to probe her soft centre. Her hips were pushed up, her bottom hole winking lewdly and curious. The head of his cock nestled against the tight ring of puckered flesh and all the nerve endings through her back passage lit up like fireworks and sent shivers of strange pleasure racing up her spine.

He pushed a little harder and she remained quite still. She was holding her breath and sighed as the rounded head of his cock forced its way with a faint pop into her bottom and she felt as if she had been opened like a bottle of wine. The fine delicate skin of her anus was stretched as he marched on and on, deeper and deeper, just slowly, and Greta realised that she did not know Greta at all. There was a whole array of Gretas like the paper people you make from folding a sheet of paper, drawing a silhouette and cutting out a row of figures all the same and all subtly different.

With her head covered and her limbs stretched, her bottom was the focus of her whole body, the star, centre stage, and the very thought of being buggered like this, bound to the bed, arse wriggling, made her dizzy with erotic pleasure and ... something else, something she was beginning to grasp like a stray thought or a new concept ... and then it struck her: she was dizzy with a sense of erotic humiliation as well. She had let a strange man tie her down, gag her and pull a hood over her head. He had beaten her with his belt and she had leaked liquid bliss to oil his way deep into the tight tiny hole of her arse. Wow.

It occurred to Greta at that second that this was a first, her début. She was an ingénue, a virgin. He had popped her arse cherry and she was sloppy and wet, her pink crease slippery with her own creamy excretions, the sac of his balls slapping between her smeared thighs, and even through the hood she could hear a slurping sound as his cock stirred her sticky liquids. I'm being fucked up the arse. Fucked and sodomised. Abused and humiliated. I'm a little whore, a slut, a slag, a tart. She was mumbling incoherently to herself, sucking at the ball in her mouth, her nipples rigidly at attention, her skin bathed in perspiration.

Richard had vanished inside her. Her bottom stung from the beating and her bum hole was filled. She felt complete. He drove into her and she pushed back, forcing her pelvis from the bed, meeting his every thrust. Slap. Slap. The sound of flesh striking flesh in constant rhythm made the same sound as her cheeks sucking on the rubber ball, steady and hypnotic, and again she had a feeling that she was a musical instrument designed for symphonies and choirs of angels.

He has filled my mouth and he has filled my arse. I am a very fulfilled girl. Her pussy was sopping and her clitoris from pure friction was ready to burst. Greta did wonder for a moment if Richard might be drilling to find something lost and precious, myrrh perhaps, or ambergris, but then he froze in mid thrust and went rigid. Rigid Richard. And Grateful Greta. His cock erupted and she felt his orgasm bloom into a bouquet, whitewashing the walls of her well used arse.

He shimmied and shivered across her back, a fish out of water, and it felt to Greta as if there had been a terrible yearning inside him and now it was purged. She had done that and she was proud to have such a wondrous gift. He slithered out on a gushing tide of creamy come. It swelled through the crack in her bottom, slurped warmly down into her pussy, and at that moment the force building up for so long inside her finally did explode and she quaked sobbing through a long rippling climax.

When Richard rolled off her, Greta instantly missed the weight holding her down. He removed the hood and pushed his head under hers so that he could rub the tips of their noses together.

'Do you like having things in your mouth?'

She nodded.

'And in your butt?'

She nodded, slowly at first, then more vigorously.

'Are you going to be obedient?'

She nodded again and she thought he's such a tyrant, just like Jason Wise at the National.

Chapter Three – The Game

IN THE CAB TAKING them to Camden Market the driver had already admitted that he was *infatuated* with Margaret Thatcher and was now drawing an improbable connection between rude cyclists and failings in education.

'Bring back the bloody birch,' he hissed in well-oiled alliteration.

Richard made informed comments but she could tell that he had no interest in politics at all. She had no idea what interested Richard – well, that's not true, she had an inkling; she had six perfectly spaced pink lines across her bottom and a feeling that she was finding the role nature had craftily intended.

Strangers on a train. She had never done *anything* like this before and it was liberating. She had hungered for adventure. That's why she had left her friends behind and gone to drama school in the first place. Acting had been her passion since she was little but it did grow tiresome always being typecast.

When she looked at herself in the mirror she saw clear, sparkling green eyes, a wide mouth with sulky full lips and neat features framed by a curtain of chestnut brown hair, a shoe-in for *A Midsummer Night's Dream*. She had, full dome-shaped breasts (designed for lap dancing!), wide shoulders, long slender legs and a little tummy that pouted in a saucy curve.

It must have been the mirror's cruel trickery that in her reflection Greta perceived the leading lady while the casting agents and directors saw the girl who is forever being slapped and smacked and tied in chains. She had never quite understood why and appreciated now that those agents and directors had been rather more astute than she'd cared to realise.

She flicked through *The Stage* Richard had brought back with the pizza. There was simply nothing for leading ladies! It was amusing for a moment to consider giving Jason Wise a call. After all, her old boyfriend had only craved what Richard had roundly taken. A buzz zinged through her as she pictured herself being lashed to his bed, her bottom mooning up to meet his belt, her silky flesh being thrashed.

I've been thrashed and buggered. Well and truly buggered. She just adored this word. It rolled off the tongue. It was like smack. I've been smacked and buggered. Buggered and smacked. Gagged and hooded, stretched like a starfish and taken a big throbbing cock deep into my cute little arse. Mmm. She wriggled and leaked and remembered she wasn't wearing any panties.

Now, what was she thinking about?

Oh, yes. Jason Wise. Jason who was all mouth and trousers, or a lack of them, all promises that never came to pass, the part that never happened, the LA director who never appeared. He was the dust on a bookshelf, a relic from the past best left undisturbed. To escape his clutches she had left working in theatre but it was only temporary. On a journey it is the diversions that make life interesting.

Greta turned to look out the taxi window. The sun was putting a sheen on the shop windows and she had an intuition that the drive across London was taking her into the future, not to a minor role, but something bigger, more important, that everything until that moment had just been a rehearsal.

The road was bumpy. She bobbed up and down, the slaps against her buttocks giving her the same warm coddled feeling that she'd had when she sank into Richard's blue bath. He held her still, his calming hand

21

moving up her thigh and she felt her blood grow warm, the breath catch in her throat. She was leaking still and the pungent aroma that rose from under the hem of her black dress made her blush. She slid forward as his hand vanished into the valley between her legs. A finger parted her labia, stroking the swollen petals in a beckoning motion, and she was disappointed when his mobile buzzed and he pulled away to answer.

'Gustav,' he said brightly. 'You're in town?'

Pause. For some reason, Greta was holding her breath.

'Listen, I have found something with a *lot* of potential.'

Pause. He was rolling the goo between his thumb and first finger like a gardener with the earth. She was fertile soil waiting to be ploughed and sown.

'Young. A bit ungainly, you know, the usual.'

Pause.

'They always need training, Gustav. This one's a quick learner.'

It sounded to Greta as if they were talking about a racehorse and she thought Richard was probably a trainer and spent a lot of time outdoors; he had a sun tan already and it was only June. While he was listening, he slid his sticky finger into her mouth and the taxi driver was watching in the rear-view mirror as she sucked it.

'... OK, we'll be at the gallery,' Richard said finally and glanced at his watch. 'Say 12 o'clock.' He paused again. 'Yes, that's an idea. Bring it along.'

He closed the phone and turned to her. 'Good,' he added with a thoughtful expression.

'Who was that?' she asked.

He narrowed his eyes and rubbed the end of her nose with his wet finger. 'Let's play a game,' he suggested. 'It's fun.'

'I like games,' she said and really meant it.

'OK. Listen very carefully: you must do everything – everything I say. And not ask why.'

'That doesn't sound like much of a game to me.'

'But there's a prize.'

Her eyes brightened. 'What?'

'You mustn't ask,' he said.

'Meany.'

'Or it won't be a surprise.'

She tapped her bottom lip with a finger. 'But what if it's not a very good prize?' she asked.

'The best prizes are like unicorns. They don't appear unless you believe in them.'

That didn't make much sense to Greta so she just shrugged.

'A deal?' he asked.

She pretended to think about it but she had already made up her mind. 'A deal,' she replied and they shook hands.

The streets were crowded as they stepped out of the cab. The sunshine was warm on her bare shoulders and the air smelled of ripe peaches. Richard reached urgently for her wrist and dragged her in a mad dash to the last available table at the street café on the corner beating two other couples in the process.

'You're quick,' she said breathlessly.

'You've got to grab *every* opportunity,' he told her. 'Grab it and hold on tight.' He was holding her two hands across the table, he squeezed hard, then let go to snap his fingers for the waiter.

The morning croissants had been tipped down the waste grinder and Greta was starving. She reached for the menu, wincing as she changed positions on the metal chair, a blush colouring her cheeks and neck. She was learning new things about herself and knew that, of all knowledge, it is self-knowledge that matters most. If she were cast now in *Macbeth* or *Titus Andronicus* she would willingly submit her flesh to the ravages of madmen. She admired excess in others and was discovering an untapped well of excess in herself. She even liked the word excess.

23

It was like sex only backwards.

Richard ordered a full English breakfast.

She looked up from the menu. 'I'll have the same.'

The waiter ignored her and Richard glanced at her with raised eyebrows as he continued the order. 'And the lady will have the wild oats with strawberries.' *Oats*, she was thinking, as the waiter wrote it down. 'Two fresh orange juices and a double espresso.'

We're already playing the game, she realised. 'You can never be too rich or too thin,' she said with sarcasm when the waiter had gone.

'Or too obedient,' Richard added.

Then he smiled and it occurred to her that she liked this game, whatever the prize. She was going to ask Richard if he trained racehorses but it was more fun not knowing anything, his job, his surname, his hobbies.

She focused on his blue eyes. 'People hate being looked at on the tube,' she remarked.

'Not everyone.'

'Everyone,' she said emphatically. 'How many girls have you given your number to?'

'Very few as it happens.'

'I bet that's not true.'

'They are always *very* carefully selected.'

She didn't really believe him but was pleased anyway. 'I was chosen?' she asked.

He tapped the end of her nose. 'Questions. Questions. Questions,' he said, and he wasn't smiling.

She tucked into her oats and strawberries. It was surprisingly good and it seemed as if even her taste-buds had had awoken like Snow White after a long interminable sleep. She glanced up. He was studying her, watching her lips.

'Selected,' she said, and he wiped milk from the corners of her mouth. 'Even I didn't know I was going to call you.'

'Saturday evening and you're looking at the TV

listings in the paper.'

'All the boys my age are so boring.'

'You're ... 20?'

'Almost.'

'What kind of school did you go to?'

She didn't answer.

'A boarding school. A convent,' he suggested and she frowned because he was right. 'With nasty little nuns.'

'Vicious, actually.'

'You miss the discipline, Greta May,' he said. 'It is the secret of being a great actress.'

'That's what they said at drama school.'

'And they were right.'

He carried on eating and Greta thought back to the brief conversation when she was in the bath; she'd had a feeling as Richard was leaving to get the pizzas that he knew exactly who she was, that they weren't strangers who had met by chance on a train. She'd thought it then and she thought it now. She had been selected, as he put it, chosen for a role and, if that were so, she intended to give the best performance of her life.

Greta wriggled in her chair and the lightning flash across the marks of discipline made her wriggle even more.

The two couples they had beaten to the table were still waiting, each glaring at their partner, blaming them for the delay, and when she thought back to those months when she'd lived with Jason what had lodged in her memory was the pettiness of it all, his reprimands *to make her better*, his smelly socks, the sink full of saucepans and grey stubble in her toothbrush.

In a relationship there is always tension but with a stranger all those pressures are forgotten and you can just give in to your fantasies. Her mind stretched back over the three years since she'd left school and what she recalled most was doing things she didn't really want to be doing, learning her craft with dull repetition, reading for parts that rarely came, the incessant ennui. She wasn't exactly sure what ennui meant but it was from a play by someone wicked like Jean Genet or Guy de Maupassant and she knew it was something intolerable.

Richard stirred his espresso.

'Why didn't you get me one?'

He didn't reply and she remembered she wasn't supposed to ask.

'Coffee bleaches the calcium from young bones,' he then said.

'What about my cigarettes?' she asked hopefully.

'Ah, yes.' He had insisted that she leave her bag at his flat, she didn't need money or her mobile phone, he explained, and carried her Camels in his pocket. He gave them to her and she slipped one between her pouty lips. It waggled as she spoke.

'Do you have my lighter?'

He took it from his pocket and held it up between two fingers, but instead of giving it to her, he pushed the ashtray across the table. 'Take the cigarette out of your mouth and break it into small pieces.'

The cigarette froze.

'What?'

'I don't need to repeat myself, do I, Greta?'

The game, she thought, and reluctantly did as she was told, breaking the back of the Camel and discarding it.

'Now take them all out of the packet, one at a time, and break them into the ashtray.'

She sniffed haughtily but it was for her own good she realised and obeyed his instructions. He watched the pile of ruined cigarettes fill the ashtray and then crushed the empty packet.

'Smoking is strictly against the rules,' he said.

'I didn't know there were other rules as well.'

'Then you must learn, mustn't you,' he said firmly and she nodded tamely because she knew he was right. Richard pushed the ashtray to one side. 'Come on,' he added, 'you need a new dress. That's for evenings.'

He paid the bill and the girls who had been waiting for the table gave her a dirty look as they passed. Richard took her hand as if it were a part of him and they crossed the road to wander among stalls of glittery tops and turquoise jewellery, healing crystals and flak jackets. She slowed to watch a cartoonist drawing sketches but Richard tugged on her hand and she trotted along like a pony, clip-clopping in her backless black suede shoes behind him.

She could smell Indian spices and ice cream, the sharp tang of petrol as the fire-eater blew streams of flame from his blackened lips. Richard tossed her lighter into his hat. Everything was going, going, going. She had left *The Stage* on the table at the restaurant. She didn't need to search for a part. She already had her role.

Boys were taking off their T-shirts and tucking them into the backs of their jeans and girls were wearing less and less and she thought one day a clever designer would come up with the ultimate design and dress them in nothing at all.

As they moved into the heart of the market the crowd was more dense and people were staring at her as if they knew her from somewhere but couldn't quite recall where. It puzzled Greta that she was getting so much attention and decided not to think about it and just enjoy it. She was seeing herself as if from outside herself, her aura faintly glowing. Like her bottom.

She gave it a little wiggle and at that moment her line of vision was struck by a sulky brunette in a silver dress, her body moving amorphously, her velvet eyes as she lowered her dark glasses full of energy and secrets. She ran her tongue over her lips and there was something carnal in the way she slid her fingers across Greta's bare arm as they crossed.

Greta straightened her shoulders and swung her hips. Richard was still holding her hand when they stumbled

27

upon the perfect stall where white cotton dresses swayed above on a line like clouds in the breeze. They went through the rail and Richard found a Little Miss Muffet outfit with puffy sleeves and a high neck. It was truly awful. She pulled a face and then shrugged when his stern look reminded Greta there was a prize at stake.

'You have to try it on.'

'What?' she said. She couldn't believe it ...

'Here,' he said emphatically.

'Richard ...'

He folded his arms.

'Don't you remember,' she whispered, 'you ripped my knickers off. I'm not wearing anything.'

He held up his palm as if it were a paddle and showed how it could be put to good use. Greta looked around her.

'There are like ... loads of people.'

Sweat prickled her armpits. Her cheeks coloured. He wanted to see her naked in the busy market and the scary thought struck her that she wanted it too. She had a craving like thirst or hunger – or for nicotine – an irrepressible desire to expose her breasts that tingled, her moist pussy, her bottom with its pink stripes like a badge of obedience and humiliation. She wanted to take her clothes off in the market place just as she had done all those years ago in the garden.

Richard was staring into her eyes as she reached for the thin black straps and slid them one at a time over her shoulders. She hesitated. There were corrugations on his brow, a look of impatience about his lips. She continued, peeling the material from her breasts. She paused for just a second, pulled at the tie and let the dress fall shimmering about her ankles.

As Greta stepped away from the black pool of material she was overcome by a surge of contentment. The tingle that crossed her bottom as it was exposed to the air tempted a squirt of moisture from her lower lips and her flush turned crimson as she reached for the Little Miss

Muffet costume. Richard was about to give it to her but suddenly changed his mind.

'No, it's not you,' he said, and gave it back to the stallholder.

Greta was so disorientated by Richard's ability to turn the normal world upside down, she hadn't noticed the stallholder trembling slightly, his mouth ajar. A crowd had gathered as if they were at a slave market in ancient Athens and a few words from a play slipped into her mind: It's not a woman's beauty that bewitches, but her nobility, a line from Euripides, and she threw back her head and stood proudly naked for everyone to see.

Richard pointed at another dress hovering above on a wire coat hanger and she'd had her eye on that one all along. The stallholder lifted it down using a hook on a long pole and she remembered the sulky-eyed brunette as the soft cotton received her curves, the bodice tight, hugging her stomach, revealing the chasm between her breasts. The skirt was embroidered in the same pattern of fleurs-de-lys that decorated the ceiling in Richard's bedroom and Greta wondered if this were more than mere chance, that the chain of events were like the links of a chain all connected and binding her to her true destiny.

As she stood straight again the silent audience spontaneously put their hands together in applause before merging back into the crowd.

'There. That wasn't difficult, was it?'

She shook her head and smoothed down the fabric.

'One day, Greta, you'll demand it.'

She wasn't exactly sure what he meant but couldn't ask. Richard considered her carefully before nodding to the stallholder. He took out his wallet and when the man folded her black dress, Richard waved it away before he could place it in a carrier bag.

'She won't be needing it,' he said, and again she bit her tongue to stop herself asking why.

Chapter Four – The Object

GRETA FELT RATHER SMUG as they wandered away from
the stall. She would never have dreamed of taking her
clothes off in a crowded market before, her breasts
exposed, her pubic hair damp and faintly smelly, her
bottom bare and criss-crossed with the geometry of her
first thrashing.

She had a suspicion that Richard had a taste for
corporal punishment and there would be more to come.
The thought made her both shudder and tingle at the same
time. She had reached the conclusion, at least
subconsciously, that it was good for her. She was wet clay
on the potter's wheel. Each slap and spank was moulding
her, making her, each strike of the belt turning her into
something symmetrical and perfect.

Then, there was something else, something utterly
amazing. After the strapping she had taken, her orgasm
reached new heights, new depths, new tones and textures.
Richard had burnished all the nerve endings in her little
bottom, illuminated that mysterious dark place that her
own fingertip had petted gently and buggered her
mercilessly. Magnificently. She slowed for a second to
consider the game, the sense that she was taking part in a
theatrical casting, and wondered what the role really
entailed.

Her hand was jerked and her heels drummed a tattoo as
she hurried like a geisha to catch up.

Richard tightened the grip on her hand, not with
affection, but as if he were a strict parent with a child, or a

teacher with a disobedient girl. She knew there was no future with Richard ... like in Richard & Greta, Greta & Richard, but what made the smile widen across her full pink lips was the realisation that she didn't want to be a part of something, one half of a whole, the other shoe in a pair. She just wanted to be herself, explore her own potential.

Potential? The word came into her mind like an echo and she wondered where it could have come from.

'Come along,' he said.

Talk about a slave driver!

At the end of the market two plump girls in bondage were stepping from a taxi and Richard held the door for them before ushering her in.

'The Serpentine Gallery, please,' he said in his nice accent and the driver tooted his horn as he pulled rudely into the traffic.

Richard turned to take a close look at her. He removed her lip gloss from his pocket, redrew her lips and gave her a tissue to blot them. He straightened her hair with his fingers and then used the same tissue to flick the dust from the toes of her shoes.

'They don't really go, do they?' he said and she couldn't help feeling that she'd let him down.

'Sorry,' she murmured.

He sat back with a cross look. Greta almost asked what was troubling him but knew she mustn't. Was it the black shoes? The worry lines creasing her brow? Was she looking like Medusa with her wayward coils of hair? The No Smoking sign on the glass partition made her desperate for a quick puff but her cigarettes had gone, even her lighter, and it had been a present from Tara. She felt a sigh rise through her bones and entwined her fingers in Richard's hand for comfort.

'How am I doing?' she asked.

He fluttered his hand in an iffy gesture and she felt terribly disappointed. She was trying to be good and

31

resolved to try even harder.

The taxi stopped at the gallery and she stood quietly to one side as he paid the fare.

'Don't let me down now,' he said.

'I won't, I promise,' she answered and really meant it.

He walked quickly ahead and she tripped along the path into the gallery. It was warm inside, the light softened. A few people were moving like dancers below the high domed ceiling. On display was a collection of mixed media sculptures, smooth voluptuous objects in wood, steel and stone, each form so seductive you wanted to reach for them and, so rare in a gallery, you were invited to do so. She ran her palm over sweeping curves of white stone, across fans of shiny copper, over stiff carved phalluses of grained polished wood.

She closed her eyes and all the little scenes from the coarse floor in Richard's hallway to the hood being pulled over her head were joined as if by a film editor, the whirl of images warming the oils of her insides and she had an awful urge to touch herself.

They had reached the far end of the long chamber where the diffused glow from lights set in the floor embraced two figurative sculptures in two different shades of marble, pink and pale green, each locked like a lover to the other by reversed shapes of evocative forms, breasts, a penis, lips, a lock of hair. The artist had joined the figures into one form and together they resembled a curling heart.

Richard retreated behind the sculpture, his head visible in the v-shape between the raised shoulders of marble. She hurried to join him and he placed her where he had been standing.

'Be good,' he whispered, his breath tickling her ear.

He lifted the back of her dress. A finger slid into her pussy, then another, and she shuddered as he manoeuvred them back and forth inside her. Sex in public. It was so rude. So cheeky. So fab. She was doing what nature had intended and realised with Zen-like awakening that she had never had sex before. Not really. The breathless grunts of Jason Wise had been as clumsy as a car running on three wheels, his little jack handle always trying to force its way up her bum. Those quick knee-tremblers with gauche boys, no sooner in than out with a syrupy splash of spunk on her belly. The rare glimpse of an orgasm like a soap bubble that vanishes the moment you reach for it. So fast. So furious. So disappointing. Boys just don't know what to do and Richard wasn't a boy. He was an artist and in his hands she perceived herself transforming into something divine and magical.

Greta was clenching her muscles, rolling with the movement, enjoying the sheer audacity of what they were doing when she noticed a man in the far corner filming her with a digital camera.

'Richard ...'

'Be good now.'

He maintained the same steady motion and she gripped the marble carving for support. The man with the camera moved closer. She could see her face mirrored in the lens.

The people in the gallery were losing interest in the other exhibits and were stopping one after the other to watch and listen. Richard's clever fingers were going faster, her pussy throbbing, all slippery and hot. The camera panned in on her open mouth. Greta was trembling, ready to come, and it was like the ripples on a pool stilling as Richard withdrew his hand, the feeling ebbing away and leaving her like a skydiver when the parachute opens and you fall gradually, unremittingly back down to earth.

'Gustav,' Richard said. 'This is Greta.'

'Agh, agh, agh,' she sighed.

All that she had taken in was that Gustav was tall and broad like Richard with the same blue eyes, a thick wave of messy bronze hair, a pale linen suit and a striped shirt. He moved to the back of the sculpture and Richard placed his hand on the middle of her back to indicate that she should remain exactly where she was. Richard took the camera and continued filming.

Gustav was carrying a tripod with the telescopic legs folded away. The long rubber handle was ribbed in raised finger holds and was finished in a rounded tip that he flicked at the hem of her skirt. She felt the rubber handle run up her legs and pause at her pouting cleft. Greta was in new territory and felt uncertain. She knew she had to be obedient, but Gustav was a stranger, not Richard. Richard had become – what? What had he become? Greta wasn't sure and clinging to her uncertainty shuffled her feet fractionally apart. God, she whispered to herself, I really didn't know I was such a slut!

The handle was twisting one way, then the other as if Gustav was screwing and unscrewing the cap from a bottle, the head prying open the wet lips of her vulva before drawing the shaft smoothly up inside her. Her knees shook. She gripped the v of the sculpture so she could take more, and she wanted more, her drenched sex sucking on the hard rubber until she toppled over the brink into wild wanton frenzy, hips thrusting, head thrown back, a line of sweat like hot lava running between her breasts.

She thought at first that she was doing this for Richard, but she wasn't. She was doing it for herself, riding the rubber so hard the sap drained from her, swimming down her thighs and calves. Her face flamed as he eased the handle up to the hilt and the crowd stood mutely, awed by her performance. The rubber cock, bigger than any man, teased and punished the swollen protruding lips of her oozing sex and she gasped as she bent her legs to absorb the last turn of the screw. Her hips were lifted high, her back slightly arched, and though she tried to be quiet, little sobbing groans left her parched throat, slowly building, growing in volume until she exploded in a dramatic crescendo, her sighs turning into a scream that shook the glass in the domed roof and traumatized the cracks in the veins of marble.

Gustav slowly unscrewed the handle from her sopping hole and she continued to cling on to the marble figure. She wasn't sure if she could stand on her own two feet. Her breath came in snappy gasps and through the ringlets of hair veiling her eyes the people were motionless as if far away and lost in thought. However aesthetic in form and metaphysical in concept, she had brought life to the sterile carvings, her vast roaring orgasm giving the works on display the memorable quality the artist had no doubt set out to achieve.

Wow, she thought, I've had the biggest orgasm ever. And in public!

Greta took a deep breath to compose herself. Then, on shaky legs, as she followed Gustav out from behind the sculpture the most extraordinary thing happened. The people in the gallery clapped and she instinctively placed one foot behind her and bowed the way she'd been taught.

'You're doing OK,' Richard whispered and she felt inordinately proud as he led her through the crowd back into the sunshine. She had been applauded twice in one day and that's really something.

Gustav led the way to a red Range Rover, the sides coated in dried mud, and while he drove the short distance to Gloucester Road, Richard studied the film in the viewfinder.

'Lighting's not very good,' he said.

'It's only a try-out,' Gustav responded testily.

Richard wasn't convinced. 'I thought these things were state of the art,' he continued, waving the camera about.

'Perhaps it isn't the quality of the camera?'

Richard closed the viewfinder and Greta sat dazed in the back, hands in her lap, knees together, her whole body one giant erogenous zone. Gustav watched her in the mirror. He wasn't smiling. He was assessing her and she realised he resembled Richard, a little older, and just as tanned. She realised, too, that their little spat was a display of sibling rivalry but had no idea how competitive they really were.

Gustav lived in the same building as Richard, occupying two floors among an eclectic array of oriental rugs, chaises with high backs and drapes patterned with hunting scenes. Like the sculptures in the gallery, the large abstracts on the pale lemon walls were erotic and vaguely feminine. She looked at them all but her eyes kept returning to a square canvas with a simple grid of six brilliant red, randomly placed lines, one crossing the almost parallel arrangement of the other five, the edges bleeding into a plain of pale pink, the combination sensual and hypnotic.

She had sunk exhausted into a pale brown leather armchair, kicking off her shoes, and watched Richard and Gustav wire the camera into the television with the brusque impatience men have with electrical things.

When her image flickered on the screen her green eyes seemed brighter, wet and sparkling like algae in water. The worry lines that marked her face when she was on the tube had gone. Her skin was smooth and she looked so awfully young, a convent girl with the future spreading endlessly before her. Her features changed as the spasms began. She became anxious, breathless, greedy for each new assault on her senses. As her mouth fell open it was so embarrassing watching herself have multiple orgasms and it occurred to her that when you throw back your head to come it doesn't look like you're enjoying pleasure but enduring pain. Had the same thought gone through her mind this morning? Or yesterday? Time had taken on a new dimension. It had stretched, every moment growing as vibrant and surreal as the paintings on the walls.

The film came to an end and she lifted her shoulders in a modest shrug. Richard beckoned her out of the chair and took her hand so that she could stand on the glass coffee table in the centre of the room. He gestured for her to remove her dress and she did so automatically. She was born to be naked, admired, fondled, fucked in every hole and in every way. Richard knew that. Gustav knew that. He was nodding, stroking his cheek. He turned her around as if he were inspecting an *objet d'art* at an antique market. He lifted a lock of her hair.

'Natural?' he asked, and she nodded.

He traced his fingers over the lines decorating her bottom. She bit her lips. The pain had gone but the sensation made her tingle and it was hard to stand still. His palm ran down her legs, feeling her muscles. She raised one foot at a time so that he could inspect each sole. He looked between her toes. Greta shivered and held her breath as two fingers journeyed down her spine and came to rest in the dimples in the small of her back.

He pressed, as if pressing two buttons, then told her to go down on her hands and knees. He motioned for her to lower her shoulders until her head rested in her cradled arms, exposing her in the most submissive way but it seemed perfectly natural and she didn't feel humiliated at all. He inspected her bottom, her pussy, glistening still, always wet, the puffy lips peeled back to reveal the little shining star of her distended clitoris.

As Gustav looked at her various bits she closed her eyes and couldn't help remembering the rubber handle on the camera tripod reaching new parts of her undiscovered universe. Her breasts hung low, abundant with their own weight, her nipples unashamedly erect. He tested them between his fingers and gave them a hard squeeze that sent little sprites of pleasure racing through her veins. Everything seemed to be in order. She sat cross-legged, opened her mouth as wide as she could and Gustav examined her teeth. She was pleased that she'd never needed a filling. He ran his fingers around the curve of her mouth, then pinched her bottom lip and kept squeezing until it swelled and drooped in a pout.

'Might do,' Gustav said in a serious tone.

'I think I've got you worried.'

'Worried,' he repeated haughtily. 'If I may remind you, dear boy, you have never won.'

'There's always a first time.'

'That's wishful thinking.'

'We shall see.'

'We shall see what we see, Richard,' said Gustav.

Greta remained cross-legged on the glass table looking from face to face: they had set jaws, the same intense expression and she just wished she knew what they were talking about.

Gustav pulled her ear playfully and she came to her feet. He stood back, his hand nursing his chin. He leaned forward, ran his palm over the curve of her rounded tummy, then took her hand in a gentlemanly fashion to help her down from the glass table.

'Good girl,' he said and gently slapped her bottom.

She sat back in the chair. Richard had tossed her dress over a sofa and it was so far away across the room she couldn't be bothered to go and get it. Richard had said in the market that she wouldn't be needing her black dress any more and there was no reason to think that she would need the white one either. She had been *selected*, and it was exciting not knowing what for.

Chapter Five – The Whipping Stool

GUSTAV PUSHED A VIDEO into the machine. The screen came to life and Greta watched a girl riding into view bareback on a pony. The girl, too, was bare except for the leather straps around her neck, wrists and ankles. The pony slowed and the camera moved in for a close-up, the girl's hair glittering like copper in the sunlight, her tanned skin freckled over high cheekbones.

'We have stables in the country,' Gustav said.

His voice was far away and she barely heard him. Greta was transfixed. The girl was dazzling, ethereal, flawless. She had the most startling eyes Greta had ever seen, as shiny as polished brass, and in them she perceived both knowledge and serenity. Beauty carries its own burden, guilt over unmerited good fortune, or irritation at being admired. But as the girl slipped smoothly down to the ground, naked, as free as the wind, it seemed to Greta that she must have gone through those feelings and submitted to the understanding of who and what she was. Greta noticed that the pony had practically the same colour hair as the girl. Its eyes were pure amber.

The film cut to another scene inside the stable. The girl was towelling down the pony, her pretty bottom peeking back at the camera, her svelte slender body moving like a well-oiled machine. She was tall, strong, perfectly formed, an unspoiled, diamond-cut girl brimming with refinement and grace. The camera operator must have called because she turned with a smile, shook her auburn hair and stood with her head erect, hands loose and motionless at her sides. The scene went blank.

'Wow, she's really come on,' said Richard.

'You still think you can compete?'

Richard glanced at Greta. 'Actually, yes I do?'

'It's your money.'

'*Our* money,' Richard corrected.

He glanced at her again. She didn't understand. She didn't understand anything, but couldn't ask because that was the rules and she was wondering about her prize.

Richard must have read her thoughts. 'Do you ride?' he asked her.

'Yes, of course. Since I was little,' she replied and was so happy to see the look of relief cross his features.

'Would you enjoy spending some time in the country?'

'Yes. Yes. Very much.'

'It will be a ...' he looked for the right words. '... an education. You'll learn all sorts of new things.'

'I like new things,' she said and blushed.

Greta stood.

Richard looked for a moment at Gustav, then back at her. 'We'll need a few weeks and we really should make a start,' he said and paused. 'Next weekend?'

'I'm sure that will be all right,' Greta answered and shrugged. 'I don't think they'll mind at work.'

Richard glanced back at Gustav. 'Well?' he said.

Gustav thought for several moments. Greta was biting her lips.

He spoke first to Richard. 'I'll make all the arrangements,' he announced, then turned to stroke her bush affectionately. 'Good luck ...' he paused, as if searching for a word, 'Pegasus,' he then said, and his stern expression became a rare smile.

Greta was so relieved to see Gustav smiling she was suddenly a little girl and uncontrollably happy. She stood, clinging to his neck and he swung her round in a circle. He put her down again and led her back to the chair where she'd been sitting. There was a sticky puddle on the leather seat and she went obediently down on her knees to lick it all up.

She stood feeling a bit silly and Gustav nodded with approval as he grabbed his keys.

'Let battle commence,' he said and high-fived Richard as he left the room.

Gustav had to return to the country and after he'd gone, Richard took her by the hand and she skipped barefoot up the stairs to the loft below the eaves. She really adored having nothing on. It made her feel more feminine, her full breasts rolling with her movements, like the girl in the film, her nipples hard, burning with the blood rushing into them.

She shook herself and tried to stop thinking about her breasts as she glanced around at the modern pieces of equipment, running and rowing machines, wall bars, a weight press and an odd-looking wooden bench with the two front legs slightly higher than those at the rear. Straps with buckles were attached to the legs and the leather top was sloping at such an angle that it would be most uncomfortable as a seat.

Richard was studying the bench as he spoke. 'Did you like our game today?' he asked her.

She nodded thoughtfully. 'Yes, yes I did actually.'

'We shall play lots more games in the country,' he added and she smiled.

He walked around the bench, patting the leather top in the firm tender way you would stroke the flanks of a horse. Greta looked more closely and could see that the deeper colour at the centre wasn't part of a pattern, but was stained from use, although from what use exactly she couldn't be sure.

'It's an ancient design copied from a drawing in a book of fairy tales by the Brothers Grimm,' he told her. 'Do you know the story of Polly Flinders?'

She was running her fingertips over the leather surface and paused to shake her head. Richard recited the poem:

Little Polly Flinders,
Sat among the cinders,
Warming her pretty little toes.
Mother came and caught her,
And whipped her little daughter for spoiling her nice
new clothes.

'Gustav had it built in Canterbury,' he added. 'It was used in olden times to discipline girls.'

Goosebumps prickled her skin and her armpits felt damp. She swallowed hard. Richard had been speaking in a friendly voice, but now he looked stern and she really did want to be good.

He patted the top of the bench again. 'Come,' he said. 'Let's make a start.'

She didn't know what he meant, but was coming to see that it was better to just be obedient and trust Richard. He knew what was best. She was standing with the high side of the bench in front of her, at the level of her belly button. He took her shoulders and she leaned forward, her stomach resting perfectly over the dark stain on the angled top. She spread her feet for balance. It came as no surprise that in this position it was easy for him to strap her ankles. Her breasts hung low and heavy below the bench and her arms fell naturally against the back legs, her wrists at the level of the remaining two straps which he tightened securely. It was quite comfortable, her bottom forced up in such a way that she knew it was going to receive some attention.

Richard crossed the room and she saw his reflection in the long mirror as he removed something from a drawer. He returned with the same sort of gag that he'd put on her that morning. She took the ball into her mouth and he tightened the buckle at the back of her head. Her hair was hanging over her face and he tucked the obstinate curls below the strap.

'Pegasus,' he said. 'That's really quite clever.' He stood back. 'Are you ready?'

She nodded. She was ready. She was going to be strapped or smacked or flogged and her bottom was ready, pushing itself forward, perky and curious.

She watched out of the corner of her eye, through stray locks of hair, as he opened a tall cupboard and spent a long time peering inside. She had no idea what he was peering at, but he reached a decision, removed something and closed the door. As Richard drew closer she saw a short-handled whip coiled in his hand and tears slipped one after the other down her cheeks. She had been telling herself that discipline was good for her, it's what actresses need most. She thought the strapping with the belt had been a bit of a lark, and it's all very well being brave and brazen after the event. But the whip in Richard's hand looked deadly serious. So did Richard.

'How many do you think you need?' he said.

She couldn't answer through the gag. She shook her head.

'Shall we start with six?'

She wasn't sure what to do. Six lashes with that horrifying whip seemed such a lot. Was he suggesting more? Would he settle for six? She just didn't know. It was all new to her. She nodded her head hopefully and he looked pleased.

'So you want six?'

She nodded firmly.

Richard disappeared from view. She listened to his footsteps on the wooden floor and then she heard the whip lash the air, once, twice, three times. He was flexing his muscles, checking the angle of descent, getting into practice. A chill ran through her. She closed her eyes and bit down on the rubber ball.

And then it came, slicing through the still room and searing her white bottom just below the small of her back. The sound was tremendous, a terrible crack like a jet taking off into the sky. The pain was shocking, electric, totally beyond any pain she had ever felt or imagined.

'One,' she heard him say and braced herself.

Her body broke into a sweat. She sucked hard on the rubber ball. Spittle was rolling from the corners of her lips, snot ran in files from her nose. The second strike fell just below the first, just as painful, just as fiery as it bit into her creamy soft flesh, and the whip she realised was fiercer than a belt, the leather finer, sharper, cutting deeper, and she panted for breath and waited.

'Two,' he said.

Four more, she was thinking. That's not a lot. I can take that. I'm Greta May. I can do anything.

Number three fell in the same pattern just below the first two, right across the indentation at the top of the crease between her cheeks and she felt an oily trickle ooze from her pussy. It had opened like a flower. The pain of those three stripes was so intense it was almost a pleasure and she pushed her arse out, spreading her cheeks still wider to receive the next.

'Three.'

And then four, the lash so hard, so uncompromising she felt the sting across the ring of her anus and she found the word bugger floating through her mind. I've been fucked and buggered and whipped. I'm a slut. And I've been whipped because I've been bad. I've been disobedient. I deserve everything I get. Her arse was on fire and her vagina was a swamp, a sopping drenched quagmire of sweat and pussy juice, pushing open and winking crudely between her thighs.

'Number four,' he said. 'Two to go.'

As if she needed reminding. The fifth crossed the bottom half of her split bum cheeks, the tender flesh of that neat little curve screaming as every nerve ending caught fire. Liquids were pouring from her mouth and nose, from the inflamed lips of her vagina. Her white arse was the centre of her body and concentric circles of intense pain radiated out across her back, down her thighs. Greta was beginning to understand why she needed this.

She needed to prove herself, show Richard that his trust was justified and Gustav had no reason to doubt her.

'Five,' he said, and his voice had changed, grown muffled.

One more, she thought, and pushed her hips out, showing him her split gash and puckered arse that he'd buggered so methodically that morning. The pain was transforming to pleasure and she didn't understand the weird alchemy of this but with the pride rising in her body was an irrepressible desire to feel the weight and hear the cracking sound of number six. She clamped her teeth on the rubber ball and braced her legs.

Then it came, harder, cutting deeper, roaring through the air, the pain barrier exploding, taking her in its embrace. It was excruciating, unbearable. There was a snake uncoiling inside her tummy, its head rising as the sixth whiplash crossed the soft petal flesh of her labia. The snake hissed and roared and raced screaming through all her curling corridors and passageways, wet and creamy, licking over the walls of her anus and across the slippery cavern of her burning vagina.

'Fuck me. Fuck me. Fuck me,' she mumbled, her voice lost, and she heard the whip drop to the floor.

'Six,' he said, and it was such a relief when she felt his cock sink deep inside her, completing the thrashing in the best way, the only way. This is what she craved. She wanted to be fucked and fucked and fucked again. Fucked hard and long. Beaten and strapped and stropped and fucked in the arse, in the mouth, in the cunt. She was a wild creature born for fucking and like a thirsty animal she lapped up every drop.

He started to come immediately and so did she, the force of their orgasm extinguishing the pain and she rocked back and forth across the leather bench, her body singing.

Richard withdrew with a sucking sound and spunk ran in a stream down her legs. He stepped round the whipping stool, removed the gag, and she thought how brilliant the design because his cock, stiff still, was at the exact level of her mouth. She stretched forward to slip it between her teeth and tasted her own fear and juices, sweat and sperm. She lapped over the silky skin, pushed the tip of her tongue in the fine furrow at the crown of his cherry red helmet, and as she gave it a thorough clean it occurred to her that once you've been tied up like this, lashed to a stool and flogged, there was no way back. This was the beginning. She was reborn, a new being in a brave new world.

He slid his cock from her mouth and whispered. 'Six more?' and she wasn't sure how to react, whether he was just testing her, teasing her, seeing if she really was obedient.

She nodded timidly.

'Next time,' he said. 'I don't want to spoil you.'

He disappeared and she breathed deeply, appreciative of his kindness. She was panting for breath, sweating on the leather top, her face streaked with tears, her bum stinging and contented. When he returned he was unscrewing the lid from an old-fashioned jar of ointment.

'Witch-hazel,' he said, 'it's going to hurt but it's good for you.'

That came as no surprise to Greta. He rubbed the unguent on to her burning cheeks in gentle, circular movements and although it hurt like hell as he promised, the whipheat weakened and the pain faded to a candleglow.

'Thank you, Richard.'

'I have to go away, Pegasus, just for a few days,' he said. 'Are you going to be good?'

'Yes, Richard.'

'What I want you to do is ... everything.'

'Everything?'

'When a girl has been properly disciplined her impulse is to feel grateful and loyal to the one who carried it out,' he said.

'Yes, of course.'

'Don't be. You mustn't be grateful Greta. I want you to be free. Don't think. Do. Just follow your instincts and intuitions wherever they take you. Can you do that?'

She nodded and he unbuckled her from the bench. He held her by the elbows.

'Everything,' he said again.

She was looking up into his eyes and it was strange the way he bent forward and kissed her.

They crossed the room to the mirror. Greta turned to look over her shoulder at the tartan pattern decorating her bottom, the six raised pink weal marks above the darker blush from the strapping.

'It's rather pretty,' he said and she smiled.

Chapter Six – The Taste of Girls

THIS COULD HAVE BEEN the longest week in the history of the universe but as she hurried for the tube that Monday morning Greta determined to make the most of it. Richard had taken her home in another Range Rover, a dark green one, and just as muddy, and she felt quite abandoned as she watched him drive away.

When she arrived at work, Madame Dubarry was sipping coffee with small hissing noises and listened distractedly as Greta explained that she was going on a riding holiday in the country and wanted to take her summer leave starting Friday. Madame Dubarry studied her through the steam rising in curls from her cup.

'You had a ... good weekend,' she said, fluting her brow.

It was more a statement than a question and Greta swallowed the little lump in her throat and nodded.

'Yes, yes I did.'

'And what did you do?'

'Well. You know ...'

... I was fucked senseless on the floor by a complete stranger, I was beaten with a belt, thoroughly buggered, I stood naked in public for all the world to see my striped bum and shameless breasts ... oh yes, I had a glorious orgasm in an art gallery, I was strapped to a whipping stool for a good thrashing ... and fucked mercilessly.

'... just the usual things,' she said with a little shrug and was sure Madame Dubarry could read her dirty mind.

'Go. Go. You must make the most of every

48

opportunity.'

'Thank you, I will,' Greta replied, and wasn't aware of Madame Dubarry's fingers rising to touch the spot where she kissed her powdered cheek.

The first customer of the day had entered the shop, a man with a leonine quiff of silvering hair and the brisk movements of someone who, while in no hurry, anticipates immediate service. Greta pulled in her tummy, straightened her shoulders and, just as Madame Dubarry had taught her, slid like a masked guest at a costume ball languidly towards him.

Being an extremely expensive shoe store there were very few shoes on display, the suggestion being that prized objects are rare and precious. The man was considering a brown suede loafer with a buckle across the instep.

'They're beautiful,' she said.

She gave a little shimmy as he turned.

'Indeed, they are,' he replied, staring openly down her cleavage.

'What size?'

He raised his eyebrows. 'My size?' he repeated, a mischievous glint in his blue eyes. He glanced down. 'Quite big,' he added with a soft, Mediterranean rhythm to his English.

She sat on the low stool wielding the shoe horn as he slipped his long foot into a size 11, his eyes following the antics of her playful breasts as they reached like two puppies over the v of her black suit jacket. He strolled up and down the burgundy carpet, swept his hand over his hair as if to show her how lush it was and she sighed contentedly as he withdrew his Amex card from a snakeskin wallet.

'*Buono. Buono*. Now we shall be well shod,' he said in an oddly familiar way as he signed the slip.

Greta put the shoes in a bag. 'Here we are,' she said, but instead of taking the bag, he cupped her hand in his

49

long fingers and stared into her eyes as if he were in search of her secrets.

'I shall come and see you again. Soon,' he said and Greta felt a tingle of fear run up her backbone. He squeezed her hand and she thought about Richard as she plunged into his hypnotic blue eyes.

'*Buono*,' she replied.

The lion strode out on his long legs and Greta unpopped the top button on her jacket as a young American entered with the look of someone lost on their way to Piccadilly Circus. She persuaded him to purchase a pair of black brogues for winter as well as the fawn slip-ons that had first caught his eye. When his map appeared from his pocket she accompanied him outside and pointed the way.

'Gee, thanks.'

'It's my pleasure.' And she thought it is so easy to please Americans. They are just like children.

The air smelled fresh, even in Bond Street, and Greta was overcome by a feeling of joy and optimism. Just one week and she would be going on holiday.

When she came back inside the store, Madame Dubarry nodded with approval and gave her bottom a friendly slap.

Mmm, that's new, she thought.

Greta rolled her hips like a mambo dancer as she snaked down the narrow stairs to the stockroom. Something had happened to her. It was weird. Nice. But weird. Suddenly everyone wanted to touch her. Even on the Underground from Hammersmith that morning Greta had played a cameo role in a minor fantasy.

The carriage had been packed to bursting point, the wage slaves being shunted to work like farm animals to the abattoir, and there was a balding, middle-aged man with a bulging briefcase resting his hand gratuitously on her buttocks. It's the usual game, the innocent hand holding the newspaper, his curled fist as if by some perverse fluke bridging the gap between them.

Greta had always made it apparent by pulling away and glowering that these sly advances were unwelcome, but after the experience with Richard decided to have some fun and gave her arse a tantalizing little wiggle. After all, Richard had told her to do everything her instincts told her to do.

The man's breath stilled. His fist froze for a second, then he upped the pressure, his knuckles kneading the soft flesh of her tender bottom. It wasn't until the lights flickered out between Knightsbridge and Hyde Park Corner that he abandoned the paper and turned his hand to cup the swell of her cheeks in his open palm. They remained like that, as rigid as the marble sculpture at the Serpentine Gallery until she stepped out of the train at Green Park.

The hand was still mentally glued to her backside as she bent from the waist to pick up empty boxes, blushing as she planned to dress the next day in a shorter skirt. She mounted the ladder to reach the shoes on the high shelf. Greta was aware of her body's every motion, as indeed was Madame Dubarry who watched her as people watch celebrities.

During her lunch break, Greta fought the urge to buy a packet of cigarettes. *Smoking is strictly against the rules.* She found a gorgeous little silk bra with teeny tiny panties like the wings of a butterfly and wondered why something quite so small should have quite such a large price tag. You only live once, she said to herself, parading through the store for everyone to see, and drank bottled water with her sushi at Pret.

In the tabloid she found on the table there were stories about hurricanes in Florida and blackouts in France and it all seemed far away and unimportant, a world that had nothing to do with her. Greta had been a reflection of other people's desires and expectations. She had been moulded by her parents, by convention, by the nuns at

Saint Sebastian.

As she sat watching the people streaming by like worker ants outside the window she was aware quite suddenly of her own individuality, her own sense of self. She felt renewed, free, young again. It was heady stuff and she understood that only when you have a firm grasp on your own identity do you bring that special quality to the stage. She had always set out to shape herself around the character, when a great actress will mould the character to herself. This was a revelation and Greta knew intuitively that whatever role she played in the future she would perform with unnerving passion.

She strolled back to work in the afternoon sunshine, the new underwear in layers of tissue in a shiny black bag, as big as her new purchases were small, another of their tricks, she thought, and when she smiled, people in the street smiled back at her.

There were customers waiting, two squat, turnip-shaped women with accents from Eastern Europe who bullied her with strident voices and whom she served with the charm and equanimity of the girl in the riding video until they parted with great wads of red £50 notes.

'You have a gift,' Madame Dubarry whispered, her tongue fluttering across her ear and Greta was sure it wasn't selling shoes.

It's really weird, but when you work hard time flies; *Tempus Fugit*, as she'd learned in Latin at school, and was shocked when she noticed the big hand reach for six o'clock. She had sold 37 pairs of shoes in one day and that was a record.

No one reached for her arse in the tube back to Hammersmith but after the long day bending and stretching her panties, by the time she arrived home, were moist with girlie excretions. The aroma brought back memories of pony club, the feel of a throbbing warm animal between her stretched thighs, the piquant whiff of the stable, the girl in the video riding free, tanned and naked.

She took her knickers off, pressed the white cotton to her nose and ran the damp crotch over her lips. Greta liked her own smell and dropped back across the bed, the pearl of white cotton over her face, her fingers reaching for her pussy. The little nub of her clitoris was aching for some attention. She was so juicy down there she could feel the vibes of early orgasm and made herself stop, delaying pleasure in pursuit of greater pleasure. It was all very Shakespearean. She pulled off the rest of her clothes and in the bathroom her eyes lit on the economy-sized bottle of supermarket shampoo.

Just the job, she thought, teasing and tickling the mouth of her pussy as she stepped back across the hall into the bedroom. She inserted the rounded bottle top with a soft sucking pop as she fell back on the bed. She had forgotten to close the door and the thought of Tara strolling in at any time sent wild fantasies galloping like carousel horses through her dirty mind. You are such a slut, Greta May, such a slapper, you should be punished, smacked, strapped, whipped, beaten. She tasted the words and nearly wet herself.

She drove the bottle in deeper and remembered how Gustav had screwed the tripod handle slowly, patiently in and out of her wet pussy. The memory was delicious. Her free hand massaged her breasts, slipped down her side and under her bottom. She nursed the rubbery ring of her anus with its little muscle like a valve before sliding her index finger inside. She gasped for breath. Her right hand was pumping away on the bottle and the finger in her bum nursed the pattern of spiralling pleats and creases, all so neat and pretty like a snowflake. Her arms moved robotically and, as her legs arched, she pictured herself in a hazy black-and-white photograph depicting a disobedient maid bound to a whipping stool. She could still feel the sting of the whiplash across her backside, her insides were churning and as she reached her climax she levitated clean off the bed.

She collapsed down on the sheets and the shampoo bottle slid like a boat leaving shore from her well-oiled pussy. She sniffed the bottle and couldn't quite work out the smell, and she licked at her own creamy juices and was unable to pinpoint the taste. She lay back, legs straight, and as she stroked her nut brown bush she imagined having sex on the tube train with hundreds of people moving like formation dancers to the beat of her urgent thrusts.

The door slammed at the end of the hall and she carried on stroking her sticky pubes even when Tara put her head around the door.

'Greta ...' Tara's mouth fell open.

'Can I borrow your pink suit tomorrow?' she asked in response.

Their eyes met. 'Don't you have anything to wear?' Tara asked.

'Not a thing.'

Tara giggled. 'You are becoming such a pervert, Greta. What happened with that man on the train?'

She had to think for a minute. 'Everything,' she answered.

Her eyelids flickered and closed. She was still on a high from getting herself off and just as if she were scratching an itch on the end of her nose, a fingertip slid unconsciously to sooth the bud of her burning clitoris.

Greta was so ashamed with Tara watching but it was so much nicer than doing it on your own. Her legs lifted like two halves of a swing bridge, her hips rose from the bed and the little animal noises escaping from her were stilled unexpectedly by Tara's pink lips.

Greta opened her eyes and smiled.

Tara's head was the other way round, upside down, and it was awkward as her tongue slid into Greta's mouth. They kissed. They kissed again. They kissed some more, so soft and sensual it was like being back at boarding school, the first tentative touch of her best friend's lips, the first clumsy hand down her big cotton pants, her swelling breasts inflamed with new sensations. They changed positions and it was so much better than kissing boys with their sharp teeth and whiskers. Tara's lips were full yet firm, soft and sweet, like a mango, or a juicy peach. Or a strawberry picked in the fields, smelling of sunshine. Greta licked her cheeks and kissed her eyes and fluttered her fingers in the air with loss and abandon as Tara rolled from the bed and landed on the floor. She tried to reach for her but Tara stood back.

'Wait,' she said, and pulled her T-shirt over her head. She unzipped her jeans and looked like an Indian dancer as she wriggled to get out of them. She unhooked her bra and ran her pants down her legs. Tara's pussy was shaved clean and looked like a toy fresh from its box, a mysterious sea creature Greta wanted to savour and taste. An aphrodisiac. She was spellbound. Tara moved close to the bed and Greta ran the tip of her finger gently through the pale pink gash. It opened like a waking eye and leaked minute bubbles of oily liquid like tears, so soft and sensuous Greta was impatient to tend those tears with her tongue.

She slid her hand around the curve of her hips and drew Tara towards her. In one nimble movement she dropped back on the pillow with Tara's vulva glued to her face, spread over her hungry mouth. She had tasted sperm a few times, not many, but enough to know that it has the slightly sweet-and-sour tang of lychees, but Tara was syrupy like sticky treacle pudding, so sweet and seductive you feel impelled to lick the plate clean. She cupped the globes of Tara's bottom as Tara gyrated above her, then she stiffened and the spurts of Tara juice on her tongue were like little sneezes or kisses, precious as jewels.

Tara slithered down the bed into Greta's arms, her silky lap-dancer body soft yet firm, ripe yet fresh, young and healthy and so eager, so wanton, Greta had the odd sensation as she touched Tara that she was touching herself. Their hands were explorers finding cheekbones and hipbones, shoulder blades and precise little knees, the swell of thighs, the pattern of ribs that Greta thought of as a musical instrument and Tara plucked at her strings until she sang. She sucked at her lips and made her sigh with new pleasures as her pointed tongue bathed the hollow of her throat, a neglected wee place that Greta was glad was finally receiving some attention. Tara moved slowly down and down until her tongue wormed its way through the damp undergrowth into Greta's heaving sex.

Tara lapped at her pussy like a pussy cat lapping milk, licking and sucking, a hot gooey puddle appearing beneath Greta's bottom as the oils flowed from her. Greta spread herself as wide as she could. She wanted Tara to spiral up inside her body until she disappeared and they were one. Tara had manoeuvred her way in a circle and now clamped her naked pussy back over Greta's lips. Tara's syrupy dew trickled down her throat and Greta's mind went back again to those pyjama parties at school when everyone took off their pyjamas and she recalled nostalgically that there is nothing like the taste of girls.

They sixty-nined until Tara went into spasm and when she climaxed once more Greta felt all the tension flowing from her friend's stiff young body. She turned and they snuggled under the covers like two little animals in a basket. Tara had small, pert, pointed breasts with nipples that were hard and hot to the touch.

'You needed that,' Greta said.

'And how.' Tara licked Greta's little sea shell ear and whispered. 'I didn't know you were like that?'

'Aren't we all like that?'

'We are now.'

They kissed and giggled and played with each other's breasts. Tara slid back down again below the duvet and drank like a pony from the well of Greta's chalice. Greta shuddered and sighed.

'That's so nice.'

'I've wanted to do it for such a long time,' Tara murmured.

'You only had to ask.'

'But how was I to know?'

'I would have thought it was obvious,' Greta said.

'Greta May, you're getting so conceited.'

Greta thought about that, but quite the opposite was true. She'd been living in a daze, unconscious, unaware of her ... potential. She stroked the top of Tara's head and, when Tara had taken her fill, she slithered like a creepy crawly up Greta's body and kissed her again, a long, silky soft kiss like only girls can. The room was hung with carnal smells, with girlie scents, with oestrogen, and Greta was suddenly starving.

'Let's eat,' she said, and swung her legs from the bed.

She put some water on to boil and cooked spaghetti à la puttanesca while Tara ran out to the corner store for a bottle of Italian red. Greta didn't bother to get dressed and enjoyed the cold air hardening her nipples as she reached into the refrigerator for sparkling water. She scratched her matted pubes while she stirred the pasta.

When Tara got back, the bottle of wine nearly slipped from her fingers. She screamed at the top of her voice and pointed at Greta's bottom.

'Oh my God, what's happened?'

'What?' Greta turned. 'Oh, that.'

'Your bum, Greta. Has someone been hitting you?'

Greta nodded. 'Twice, actually.'

'Oh, no, was it that man?'

Greta licked the pasta spoon. 'Mmm,' she said. 'And how.'

Tara looked confused. 'Poor thing. It's all red. Doesn't it hurt?'

Greta nursed her bottom cheeks and then turned to take a closer look. 'Not really,' she said. 'It does at the time, it hurts like hell, but it doesn't last long.'

Tara bent to take a closer look. There were six crimson stripes evenly spaced across Greta's cheeks, the first six from Richard's belt fading as if they had been written with invisible ink. Tara sewed a row of kisses across her bottom and stood again.

'But why, Greta, why did he do it?

Greta had to think about that. 'Pleasure,' she said finally.

'That's all very well, but what about you?'

'I mean me,' said Greta. 'The greater the pain, you know, the greater the pleasure.'

'I thought pleasure was all in the mind.'

'I think pleasure's a bit like unicorns. They don't appear unless you believe in them.'

Tara stared sceptically back at her friend as she searched in the drawer for the corkscrew. She opened the wine with a lusty pop and poured two glasses. She drank hers down as if she needed it.

'You will be all right?' she said.

'Course,' Greta replied. 'I'll never do anything I don't want to do ... but I do want to do *everything*.'

'I was right, you are a complete pervert.'

'Oh, God. It's true. I let a man touch me up on the train today.'

'Another one?' Tara screamed.

'He was quite old and very bald.'

'What did he do?'

'You know, the old knuckle game.' She demonstrated on Tara. 'First the back of the hand, then, when he's more confident, he cups your bum with his sweaty palms.' She squeezed gently and Tara let out a tiny squeal.

'Yuck. And?'

'You're getting into this,' Greta said and swivelled round to lower the gas. She turned back and carried on with the demonstration. 'Then he rubs his finger between your cheeks, digging into your arse ...'

Her hand was up Tara's short skirt and she was wet

still.

'Mmm?' Tara said.

'Quite nice, all in all.'

And they both burst out laughing.

Greta mixed the sauce with the pasta and put it back over the flame with a knob of butter. Tara had set the table. She lit a candle and they clinked glasses as they sat.

Greta watched her flat mate turn the strands of spaghetti in a neat cone on her fork and it occurred to her that all people really need is more sex. More excess. When Tara had arrived home from the LSE with her bag of books she was lined and grey, the world on her shoulders. Now, she was young and fresh, her brown eyes glowing with moons of candlelight.

Hot sauce dripped on Greta's bare breast and the fiery moment of pain reminded her that she was naked, she was alive, she was being herself. Modesty was impractical, a handicap. She would cast it out like a devil and pursue sexual pleasure wherever it led her, however extreme.

'Nothing succeeds like excess,' she said, and Tara raised her glass to make that a toast.

'You really should come to the club,' she urged, her gaze focusing on Greta's full breasts.

Greta shrugged. Her mouth was full and she had no intention of becoming a lap dancer. It seemed such a waste of energy getting men all excited when they were only allowed to touch the girls as they stuck money down their pants. Greta liked being touched. She wanted to be touched. She was a sculpture still forming on that potter's wheel. A wet one.

'I'm going to the country for a holiday,' she announced, suddenly remembering. 'With the man I met on the train.'

Vino trickled from Tara's mouth as it fell open.

'No. Not that one. The other one.'

'The spanker?'

'Mmm.'

Tara wiped her lips and leaned on her elbow. 'What's he like; I mean, what's he really like?'

'A bit scary,' Greta answered. 'I know he likes bottoms, and sex, of course.'

'Does he like you, though?'

'I think he does, but not in the usual way. He wants me to be myself.'

'A complete tart, in other words.'

'A complete something.'

'I'll drink to that,' said Tara, and they clinked glasses before downing the remainder of the wine.

After dinner while Tara got on with an essay, Greta washed the dishes. She took a shower to scrub away the day's smells: other people's feet, the tube, the lingering perfume of Tara Scott-Wallace. Thanks to the witch-hazel, even the second set of pink stripes on her bottom were fading and she missed them already.

In bed she opened one of her favourite books and came across a line highlighted in yellow: *The only way to get rid of temptation is to yield to it.*

Oscar, of course. Who else?

And there was another line that jumped out at her: *There is no such thing as pornography, just bad writing.*

'Absolutely,' she said out loud, and if Oscar Wilde had been there that moment she would have kissed him, whatever his predilections.

The bedside lamp made a spider web on the ceiling and she was still reading when Tara appeared in the doorway with a tub of Ben & Jerry's chocolate nut Chunky Monkey. She wasn't wearing any clothes.

'I've always had this ice cream fantasy,' she said and Greta pulled back the covers.

Chapter Seven – Dirty Bill

THE BALD MAN WAS waiting at the centre of the platform, briefcase between his feet, his gaze fixed on the entrance. Greta took this in with one sweeping gaze and was aware of the relief crossing his features.

She passed without looking in his direction again, and stopped with the pointed toes of her pink shoes touching the danger line. There was a voice on the speakers, a man who seemed to be gargling with water. The blast of subterranean air running over the silver rails was cold on her face and she listened as the tube raced like a screaming banshee from the dark heart of the tunnel.

'Excuse me. Excuse me,' she heard the man say as he barged his way behind her into the carriage.

They clung to the same pole, eyes never meeting, bodies swaying as the train lurched carelessly around the curves to Barons Court. He waited for the appropriate moment, a particularly violent lurch, and his palms slipped over the rounded domes of her arse.

To push back or not to push back. That is the question.

Greta pushed back, rolling her cheeks like an elephant having a good scratch against a tree. She was wearing Tara's pink suit; they were the same height, but where Tara was lean and muscular, Greta was more shapely and slices of herself were erupting like ripe fruit from every fold and crease, her tummy from the skirt's waistband, her breasts cupped in the new bra from the jacket, her long creamy legs that the bald man caressed. His hands circled her thighs under the skirt when the lights dimmed, only to fall away when they brightened again.

He edged to one side to let a woman pass with her shopping trolley at South Kensington and scurried back to his position as a fresh wave of travellers pushed into the carriage, young men with floppy hair and striped shirts like striped toothpaste squeezing back into the tube, the girls in grey suits reading the *Financial Times* with that anxious look people get when something sharp touches a raw nerve. Their mission was to succeed in a man's world and Greta thought it much better to succeed in your own way, in your own world.

During the blackout as the train dawdled its way from Knightsbridge, Greta found two wet palms moving from the base of her thighs and up over the curve below her bottom where they came to rest.

It was only a bit of fun but the drips leaking into her panties were so sweet and intoxicating she was sure that if all the business girls would only dig down into their innermost fantasies, they'd revel in doing the same. She could see it in their eyes, in the melancholy twist about their tightly sealed lips. The City boys with their floppy hair were ready for anything and the business day would be far better served if the girls abandoned their attaché cases and dropped their hands down somebody's trousers. It would be good for the economy. Good for the country. Greta wanted to spread the word like a missionary, not in the missionary position, actually, not as such, she wanted to be touched and used in every position and wanted her sisters on the train to get down on their knees for a great life-confirming gang bang.

The daydream made her giggle. The bodies swayed as the lights flickered and turned them into performers in a shadow theatre. Greta closed her eyes and gasped for breath as a lone finger stroked the swollen lips of her vulva. It was hot in the tube, the sun beating down through the pavement, the earth, the metal roof above her head. Sweat ran between her breasts. The wheels screeched and pounded. The train reeled, tearing the finger from her wet lips, their bodies asunder. The lights flickered again as if they were in a thunder storm and the man with hopeless fervour pulled her back against his caged erection, her thighs jabbed by a bulging sheath of cotton as the train slowed into Hyde Park Corner. He remained like that, immobile, locked in unfulfilled passion until she spilled from his grasp on to the platform at Green Park. Her stop.

Her taut bottom was damp through the crack and she was sure she could hear squelching noises as she clipped along Bond Street swinging her shoulder bag. The weather was lovely and she wished she had her mobile phone so she could call Jason Wise and tell him her knickers were wet.

Madame Dubarry had always been strict about her dressing in black as if the buying and selling of costly shoes was vaguely funereal, but didn't say a word when she walked in all pink and breathless.

'Coffee?' she asked.

'I've given it up,' answered Greta.

'Smoke?'

'No. No thank you.'

'No vices, Greta?'

Greta rolled her eyes and watched Madame Dubarry gazing at her breasts rising and settling with each cycle of breath, her nipples wantonly erect and pushing into the soft silk of her uplift bra. Stretched to breaking point, the top button on her jacket had given up the fight and hung on broken threads.

'That looks untidy,' Madame Dubarry said, pulling off the offending button, and Greta ambled out of the staff room to greet a woman dressed from head to toe in Burberry. An American.

She bought two pairs of summer sandals in tan and dark brown, like two shades of chocolate in a tub of

Chunky Monkey, and while Madame Dubarry snapped her credit card through the machine two young men with the moist eyes of puppies followed her as she led them like a museum curator along the display of brown loafers, black loafers, the new blue slip-ons with a golden crest on the toe. They gazed spellbound up her skirt as she unpacked boxes and brought out shoes from their maroon cotton bags. She wriggled and jiggled and realised the admen were right, sex sells, the flash of her breasts and thighs like a personal guarantee that the young men were leaving the store shod to perfection.

By lunchtime Greta had sold so many pairs of shoes her head was spinning. She was too revved up to eat and caressed the curve of her empty tummy as she wandered into the winding maze that led to Soho. There was a man just in front of her, glancing over his shoulder, whistling as he walked, and she was sure she had seen him peering in the window a couple of times that morning. The man's tune was oddly mesmerizing and Greta felt like one of the lost children being led by the Pied Piper from Hamelin. The streets became narrow, confusing, a maze of film companies and prostitutes, night clubs looking sordid in daylight, a neglected church in a garden of tombstones.

Boys in saffron were ringing cymbals and chanting, and outside the music store men with dreadlocks sat in the sunshine beating drums, the sound sensual and rhythmic. Greta felt hot in the pink wool suit. She passed through a warren of sex shops with their arrays of whips and latex costumes, crotchless knickers and uniforms. She saw in a window something called a ballgag and now she knew where Richard did his shopping.

Her feet took her into the pink neon interior and she tried to imagine herself dressed as a nurse, a school mistress, a dominatrix with metal tits and a devil mask over her face. She was trailing her fingers over the leatherwear when she sensed someone watching her. The man she'd unintentionally been following was studying her reflection in the mirror and she turned to meet his eyes.

'A'right there, darling?'

She dropped her hand to her side. 'Yes. Yes thank you,' she replied.

'Got some nice stuff here, ain't they?'

'Very nice.'

'Like that sort of fing, do you?'

'I'm not exactly sure,' she answered, although she thought she probably did.

'What's your name, then?'

'Greta May,' she replied.

He nodded knowingly as if her name were familiar to him and she wondered if he had seen it on a playbill.

'I'm an actress,' she added.

'I bet you are. And I'm a set designer.'

'Really?'

'Bill Longman, innit,' he declared, and looked Greta up and down as men do with horses and used cars.

She held out her hand. 'How do you do?' she said and he stared down at her extended fingers. He was scratching himself below the medallion lodged in the mat of dark hair on his chest and concluded these ministrations to take her by the wrist.

'Not bad at all,' he answered, and jerked her towards the door. 'Listen, I fink we might have a little rehearsal. What do you reckon?'

She was going to reply but didn't get the chance and pattered out of the shop, her legs driven by Bill's unseemly confidence and by the notion that Richard would clearly approve. They turned into a narrow alley lined with horse posts, the buildings leaning drunkenly together and blocking out the sun.

'Got a place here, dead central,' he said with a sniff.

He ducked to enter a shadowy porch with innumerable bells and tawdry postcards with telephone numbers offering random services. She heard a key turn and followed him up a rickety staircase, the reek of lavatories and cheap perfume sliding under doors on each landing. She heard thumps and muffled cries, the distinctive snap of the whip, the urgent beat of colliding flesh.

Her back was clammy with fear. Greta was tempted to turn and run back down the stairs, but she had become the girl in the horror flick who hears noises in the night and goes out to investigate with a dead torch and nothing on but a nightdress and knickers. She was watching the movie and had to see it through to find out the ending.

The hollow sound of their footsteps made the hairs on the back of her neck rise as if from an electric shock and an icy tremor ran up her spine as Bill came to an abrupt halt. He jangled his keys and opened the door leading to an attic where half the space was taken up by a mattress covered by a stained rubber sheet.

Bill took something from his top pocket and tossed his jacket over a cane chair with a sunken seat. It was a roll of five £20 notes held by an elastic band. He showed her how much was there, re-rolled the money, put the elastic band back in place and stuck the £100 in her pink jacket.

'Ooo,' she said.

'That's just for starters, Greta May,' he told her. He sniffed again and his tone changed. 'Now, come here.'

He crooked his finger and she went obediently towards him. He undid the remaining two buttons on her pink jacket and it slipped from her shoulders to the bare wooden floor. Her full breasts were shuddering with the beat of her heart and he weighed them in his palms, nodding professionally.

'Nice, very nice. Skirt,' he said.

She unzipped her skirt and wriggled it down to her feet. She removed her little Cartier watch, a gift from her father at Christmas, and placed it on the window sill. She folded the skirt and jacket because they belonged to Tara and put them neatly on the chair.

When she stood before him again, Bill turned her

round in her new bra and panties and she remembered being inspected by Gustav in his lovely apartment, so different to the attic with its smell of sewers and hospitals. The wallpaper had lost any sense of pattern and was held in place on the edges by packing tape and drawing pins. She could see glimmers of light through the roof tiles and the golden dust that hung in the air was the microscopic scales of dinosaurs.

Bill had finished his examination. 'Down,' he now instructed.

He reached up to take a clump of hair and forced her down on her knees. He unzipped his trousers, pulled his cock from his pants and pushed it unceremoniously between her lips. 'Start slow and easy, you know what I mean, then build up to a climax,' he told her like he was giving a violin lesson.

Greta bowed her mouth up and down the stretched rubbery skin, her taste buds assaulted by unwashed towels, the tip of her tongue flicking and tickling his cock, pressing down with her lips and teeth, slow and easy, just as he said, teasing the thing like a cat with a mouse. She thought with practice she could be really good at this.

Greta was aware of her own scent as vaginal fluids oozed from her, dewing her thighs. Sweat ran down her back and chest, her bottom was wet, her nipples throbbed and tingled. The ring of her anus popped gratuitously and she took the smelly cock deeper into her mouth, wrapping the meaty shaft in her curled tongue. She bobbed backwards and forwards, eyes pressed shut, oblivious to everything except that fleeting moment and it occurred to her that she was completely and hopelessly addicted. It was a drug. One fix and you're hooked. I'm a sex addict. A nymphomaniac. How astonishing. How marvellous.

If the nuns could only see me now.

She smiled at the thought, and it wasn't easy smiling in that position, and at that same moment she felt a tiny drop of liquid touch the roof of her mouth, just a speck, and he withdrew his throbbing cock, spraying her face with a thick frothy squirt of come, over her eyes and nose, back into her open mouth, the gooey stuff coursing down her chin to drop in globs on to her breasts. He was panting for breath.

'Don't move. Don't move,' he gasped.

He shook the last drop of semen from the end of his cock and it landed on the curve of her tummy.

'Don't you dare move,' he said again.

He tapped his cock on her chin and cheeks as if he were playing a drum and she remembered the drummers in the street with their curling dreadlocks and lusty rhythms. He pushed out a pall of smoky breath and took a fresh gasp of air with a sigh. He then leaned back, legs apart, and an arc of hot beery urine splashed into her cleavage.

Greta remained motionless, unable to move, shocked and sickened and strangely thrilled, gripped by the very repugnance of what he was doing.

He changed the angle, the flow rising up across her chin, into her surprised mouth, in her ears and nose, across her hair and it ran in trickles over her shoulders and down her back, an endless cascade of steamy bitter-tasting piss that soaked her bra, seeped into her knickers and mixed a cocktail with her own flowing juices. This was disgusting, outrageous. She was beyond redemption and she adored her own sense of complete and utter abandon.

Bill shook off the last drips and stuck his shrinking cock back in her mouth. 'Lick the tip,' he said, and she ran her tongue scrupulously over the dimpled groove with its vinegary taste of stale lemons. When she had finished, he pulled out and stood back with a furious expression.

'Look at the mess you've made here,' he said. 'You'd better get it cleaned up, then clean yourself, you dirty bitch.'

He kicked a filthy towel across the room and she patiently crawled over the hard floor on her hands and knees to wipe away the puddles of pee. She wrung out the towel in the loo, and when she went back to start again it felt as if she were in a play yet to be written but she could visualise the scene clearly on stage at the National. When she had done a thorough job she stepped into the bath. There was no hook for the shower and she sat under the meagre trickle of water holding the shower head. Bill put the lavatory lid down and scratched his grizzled chest as he sat.

'I'll tell you what I'm going to do, Greta May, going to set you up in a little flat, Hackney, somewhere up and coming, or Brixton. Somewhere with a bit of class.'

Greta just listened. She knew Bill was enjoying his fantasy even more than he'd enjoyed pissing over her. She ran the water through her corkscrew curls and when she took off her knickers her pussy was so sticky it took all her will to resist nursing the throbbing little rosebud aching to be touched. The hot piss when it had first touched her skin had come as a surprise, a bit like the slap of Richard's leather belt, but there was no aftershock to enhance the sensation, no follow through, just a glorious sense of decadence and not altogether unpleasant.

She dried herself as best she could on a threadbare towel. She washed her bra and wrung it out with her knickers. She didn't have a bag and put them on wet. She dressed in the pink suit and slipped into her pretty pink shoes.

'Well, I really ought to go,' she said.

'Go? Go? What you talking about?'

'I have to get back to work.'

'Work? You're going to be working with me now. We're partners, ain't we.'

'I'm sorry, Bill, but I can't. I'm going on holiday Saturday, and if I don't get back to work I won't have a job when I come back.'

'Do what? You mean...' His voice trailed off. He was shaking with anger. 'You snotty bitches are all the same, coming down here, leading me on. You've taken my money under false pretences.'

At that he leaned over and grabbed the roll of £20 notes from her pocket.

'Ooo,' Greta said. She'd thought that was going to come in handy for her holiday money.

'Now bugger off. Go on.' Bill opened the door and shouted at her as she clopped her way down the narrow stairs. 'Coming up here, pissing me about. I feel like a right berk, I can tell you. It's all a big con.'

Greta wasn't sure why Bill was so angry. I mean, she hadn't pissed all over him!

'I've been done up like a kipper ...'

His voice reverberated down the stairwell, his words sounding as if they were from a script, from the same mystery play, and he was improvising, finding the poetry in his role.

She wove her way around the horse posts and hurried back through Soho, the drummers steadily drumming, the boys in saffron chanting, Bill's gruff voice ringing in her ears. She had allowed herself to be humiliated with such ease she couldn't help wondering how far she may have let him go, how far she wanted him to go. Is there a limit, she asked herself, and answered readily that she really didn't think there was. She had been repressing her natural instincts for so long she was like a coiled spring about to be sprung, a rocket primed and ready to fire. She glanced up as if in search of herself flying across the heavens. The sky was pure blue like a sheet of silk, the day sweltering, and she arrived back in Bond Street sweaty, hot and 20 minutes late.

She rushed off to the lavatory, hung her soiled undies on a hook and that feeling that had come to her when she stood naked in Camden Market came to her again as Madame Dubarry watched her climb the aluminium ladder in the basement in search of a size 7 summer lace-up that was on the stock list but had vanished amongst the

70

untidy shelves.

'We're going to have to stay behind and sort this out,' Madame Dubarry said and Greta noticed as she looked down that Madame's carmine lips had been freshly painted.

The short man requiring a size 7 was to be disappointed but he grinned from ear to ear as Greta leaned forward and let his nose slip for a moment between her warm breasts.

She steadied him on his shaky legs. 'Why don't you try again tomorrow,' she whispered. He nodded like a bird dipping its bill into a lake and Greta thought it's so easy to make other people happy and, when you make other people happy, you feel happy yourself.

She discovered during the course of the afternoon that if she went down on her haunches, instead of sitting on the low stool, her customers had a much better view up her legs. If they wavered, she opened her thighs until they could see the pink fruit nestling in the fleece of her pubic hair and, mesmerised, they reached like Pavlov's dogs for their credit cards.

By the time the clock reached six, Greta had sold 48 pairs of shoes, a new record. She checked the time with her wristwatch and realised it wasn't there and she would never be able to find her way back through the labyrinth to Bill's sordid attic.

Madame Dubarry locked the door with a decisive click and Greta followed her down to the basement. You would think that the more shoes you sell the easier it would be to find the sizes you need, but the very opposite occurs. The boxes topple over, you hurriedly put browns in with the blacks, a 9 mismatched with a 10, and if you don't sort them out you get into a terrible muddle.

Greta didn't wait to be asked and mounted the ladder. She reached for the untidy boxes, passed them to Madame Dubarry who in turn made sure they were correctly labelled before placing them in neat piles on the floor behind her. The work was slow. It was hot in the basement. Greta climbed further knowing she wasn't wearing any knickers and felt such a tart.

She was a slut, a slapper, a slag.

She savoured all the words beginning with an s: sexy like a spider, a snake, a serpent, so sensuous as she stretched up on her toes. She could feel Madame Dubarry's warm breath running up her legs to the pouting cleft of her wet pussy. The lips were rudely open, a glossy eye winking lasciviously down over the rungs of the ladder. She cleared the second shelf. Her skirt rose up over her back as she climbed on to the top shelf and found the missing size 7 lace-up, the cheeks of her bottom pushed out like a white flower around the velvet whorls and pleats of her puckered arse.

Once all the shoes had been sorted, Madame Dubarry passed the boxes back up to her and Greta descended the ladder with the sense of a job well done. There was a single chair in the stockroom and Madame Dubarry made herself comfortable before gently tapping her lap.

'You were late back from lunch, Greta. What are we going to do?'

'I don't know, Madame Dubarry.'

'What happens when girls are disobedient?'

There was that word again: disobedient; obedient. It was such a catch-all, such an invitation. It was like saying are you still beating your wife? The question implies the answer.

'They have to be punished,' Greta said, and it sounded like a line from a film by Luis Buñuel.

The other woman nodded as if the obvious had been clearly established and Greta approached, dropping her head to one side as she came to a stop. Madame Dubarry slipped the two big pink buttons on Greta's jacket from their hasps and pulled at the sleeves until it fell to the floor. The sound of the zip on her skirt being lowered was loud in the confined space and Greta swivelled her hips obligingly until the little item of clothing dropped away. Except for her shoes, Greta was completely naked, her underwear drying still on the back of the bathroom door, and she raised her hands to cover her breasts because forbidden fruit she knew tastes sweeter and that's what she would have been told to do on stage.

Madame Dubarry sat back to study Greta's heaving breasts, her ribcage that fluttered as if a little bird were behind the bars. She ran a fingertip down between her breasts to her pubic bone, then patted her lap once more. Greta took a deep breath and, as she stretched herself over the woman's knees, it seemed as if this were really the proper position for a naked girl to be in, her white bottom open like a Faberge egg with its surprises and secret gifts. She wriggled and pushed out her bottom as if it were just one of a multitude of bottoms and she was anxious for it to be the one selected.

'Just as I thought,' Madame Dubarry said, inspecting the fading stripes that ran in parallel lines over her soft, smooth flesh, an inquiring fingertip tracing a path along the length of each stroke.

She slipped her inquiring finger into the wet cavern of Greta's open vagina, then turned her finger in a spiralling motion like a corkscrew. Greta turned with the motion and was most put out when it came to an end. Madame Dubarry removed her sticky digit and Greta heard a slurping sound as she slipped it between her lips. She began stroking her perfectly rounded cheeks. The ring of her anus like a dark eye was winking crudely up at Madame Dubarry, and she answered the message by shoving her finger deep into Greta's arse where it performed the same churning dance around the soft clinging walls.

Greta sighed and arched her back, thrusting out her bottom in readiness for the first slap of Madame Dubarry's hand and, when it came, the sting made her leak like a hose full of holes, tears welling from her eyes, warm liquids escaping from the wet gash of her pussy, everything glistening, the plump juicy lips of her vulva open and pink like a healthy dog's nose. She wriggled and felt ashamed as she pushed her bottom up further and a firm hand rested on the small of her back to prepare her for the next slapping whack that was harder and louder and echoed over the bare walls. Greta opened her legs wider and a searching hand gathered the oils from her pussy and that same hand came cracking down once more on her bare arse.

'That's three,' said Madame Dubarry, the breath caught in her throat. 'Three more, I think.'

Greta was curious why six was the standard. Why not five? Or ten? Or seven – lucky for some, like Richard's phone number. She thought it was probably just tradition and girls had been taking six of the best since time began.

Madame Dubarry rested long enough to get her strength back and put all her effort into the next one.

'Number four,' she announced and the pain shot up Greta's spine and made her grip the legs of the chair more tightly. A small screech left her throat and she bit her lips until the sweet coppery taste of blood filled her mouth. Her body was damp and slippery. Madame Dubarry's skirt had ridden up and she felt like a freshly-caught fish slithering over the woman's bare legs.

Greta braced herself against the side of the chair. She pushed up, ready for number five, and it came down like a flash of lightning, the sound resounding off the walls, the aftershock sending fire crackers fizzing over her back and thighs. Her breasts prickled with pins and needles and she reached up to nurse her pink nipples, squeezing, soothing, tormenting, rolling the fine, tender flesh between her tingling fingers. Greta didn't know why she adored being smacked but she did. Some people don't know why they adore chocolate and no matter how hard they try they cannot stop themselves popping it into their mouths. She liked chocolate, too.

Madame Dubarry paused once more, building herself up for the final triumphant parade across her little bottom and used the moment to explore more thoroughly between her legs. Greta stretched her feet wider and rocked on her toes.

'Stop wriggling, girl.'

'I'll try,' she replied but she couldn't promise.

Greta had opened herself completely, and Madame Dubarry's slender fingers slowly parted the brush of her brown triangle of hair before peeling back the curtains of her swollen labia. Greta could sense the salty tang of her own arousal and panted for breath as those clever fingers slid through her oily excretions to the magic button of her sex. She sighed as if her whole body were a singing, stinging, hopelessly needy clitoris.

She rocked back and forth, biting her lips, and it seemed as if all the day's odd encounters had led as if preordained to her being stretched naked across her boss's knees in the basement below the purring strips of neon, her bum being spanked. Madame Dubarry dipped her fingers back into the reservoir of creamy discharge and Greta bobbed anxiously, the magic button demanding attention. The padded tip of an index finger slipped back under the hood, worked its way into the sensitive grooves of her hot sex and, with a sudden rush of pressure, the feelings itching between her legs snatched the air from her throat.

Tears filled her eyes. She was coming, coming, reaching down into the wells of her body. It was like a serpent was sleeping inside her and when it was awoken it would spit out spurts of her precious juice. The creature had opened its eyes. Not yet. Not yet. She gasped breathlessly, her mouth gaping, the beat of her heart making her breasts swell and she squeezed her nipples until they stung. Sex and pain. It was a drug. She wanted more. Waves of pleasure surged through her, from her burning buttocks, up her backbone, down through the looping crevices and cracks of her sopping pussy. She was being spanked and fingered. Finger fucked and spanked. She was naked, legs spread, everything slimy and slippery. The waves grew stronger. She was approaching her climax and just then Madame Dubarry extracted her hand and brought it down with a mighty crack that ricocheted over the walls and Greta exploded, screaming in glorious orgasm, the sound making the shoes rock and tremble in their boxes on the shelves.

They remained motionless, Madame Dubarry trembling a little as she began to stroke Greta's bottom and Greta realised that there wasn't any pain, just a warm, spoiled, comfy feeling like when you sit in front of a log fire.

'There now. Is that better?'

'Mmm,' said Greta and she could have stayed there for ever being coddled and spanked.

She pushed herself up on her feet and Madame Dubarry held her sides and ran her tongue over her belly button.

'You will go ...' she whispered, '... as far as you want to go.'

Greta dressed and they turned out the lights, set the alarm and entered the warm London evening. They were silent now, unsure what to say to each other, but it didn't matter because Greta only had one word in her mind and she yelled it at the top of her voice.

'Taxi!'

A cab with the yellow light burning was cruising Bond Street and she stepped in the back with a little wave over her shoulder. Greta May liked being luxuriated. She thought it would be very easy to get used to it and had no way of knowing that quite the opposite was being prepared for her in the not-too-distant future..

Chapter Eight – Training Girls

A LINE OF SUNLIGHT was creeping through the curtains to put a fresh perspective on the print of Dali's *Persistence of Memory*, a gift from someone and Greta lay there all warm and sticky trying to remember who.

Tara was making sleepy noises at her side and in the air was the musky smell of a thoroughly spoiled girl. Two thoroughly spoiled girls. Greta grinned as she breathed in the aroma. Along with the tang of girlie juices was a hint of raspberry ripple. It was smeared on Tara's forehead and cheeks, there was a smile on her faintly parted lips and a shiny glow on the tip of her nose. *You are a clever little nose*, Greta whispered, slipping finally from the bed and across the hall to the bathroom.

Her mouth dropped open as she studied herself in the full-length mirror. She was a work of art as original as anything by Salvador Dali ... no, not Dali, he was more figurative: she was a Jackson Pollock, her body a collage in shades of pink and vanilla. The ice cream was dotted with fiery stars, or horror of horrors, nasty red pimples, and she ran a wet finger over the pattern to make sure. They were strawberry pips and she popped them in her mouth.

Mmm, delicious.

She turned, glancing over her shoulder at the swirls curling down her legs and suddenly understood why people decorated themselves in illustrations and piercings. It might be fun, she mused, although nothing permanent remains fun and, anyway, Gustav didn't approve of girls with filled teeth, so he certainly wouldn't appreciate tattoos.

Greta had a good look at her bottom. It was rosy cheeked and she wasn't sure if this came from traces of raspberry ripple or the spanking she'd taken from Madame Dubarry. She ran her hands over the curved arabesques of warm flesh. The sting had gone, it only lasts about half an hour, but the memory made Greta so moist her ears pricked up when her name murmured sleepily from across the hall.

'Greta ...' the voice cooed. 'Where are you?'

Greta stepped back into the bedroom. Tara was hiding under the duvet.

'Is there anybody there?' Greta asked.

A hand appeared, the fingers dancing. 'I'm all sticky and yucky,' Tara said, raising the covers. 'And there's a funny smell ...'

Greta crawled back between the sheets. She slid her tongue the length of Tara's body, all the way up from her wriggling toes to her shiny nose, into her eye sockets and across her forehead. She cleaned her ice creamy ears, her long neck and the warm groove of her throat. Their lips met and Greta knew that she would always prefer kissing girls. Their lips are softer, smoother, more inventive.

Tara rolled over. She was dominant, ambitious. She liked to be on top. She lapped the raspberry ripple from Greta's cheeks and chin, her pointy tongue like a feeler leaping into the hollows below her collar bones before running down between her breasts. One after the other, she took the firm peaks into her mouth, squeezing them softly between her teeth until they swelled and grew so hard Greta thought she was going to burst. Tara continued her journey over Greta's tummy, her tongue pausing to consider the little well of her belly button, and down into the humid nest of her pubic hair.

Tara spun round in a flowing lap-dancer move and lowered her dripping sex into Greta's mouth. Greta took

Tara's bottom and did the same, Tara's engorged vulva opening juicy and slicked, so gloriously naked. Greta wanted to submerge herself in Tara's ocean and changed position, opening her thighs, the tips of her fingers spreading back the outer lips of her vagina in order that she could plunge in, her face buried in the oily warmth. Tara was a fount of silky liquids, a magic potion that made Greta forget everything except that solitary moment. She was one giant erogenous zone, a pulsing g spot, all sensation and thoughts about nothing. Except the next sensation.

A pulsing surge of pleasure coursed through her body and Greta was unsure if *she* were about to come, or Tara? Were they coming together? Their bodies were a ball of glossy smooth flesh slipping and sliding into new shapes, the tip of Tara's tongue moving slower now, feather-like across Greta's swollen clitoris. She did the same for Tara, the same action, the same motion; they were *yin* and *yang*, each the opposite of the other, completing the other, pink tongues in wet pussies moving in perfect harmony. The pressure kept building, the air grew still, then Tara tensed as the dam burst and they both climaxed, the circle broken as the ripples became two crashing waves that rocked through them and they collapsed, panting for breath, the eight quivering limbs of a beached octopus, the bed steamy as a swamp.

Tara curled into Greta's arms and nibbled her ear. 'I got an A for my essay on copyright law,' she murmured.

'You are a clever girl.'

'Two more weeks and it's over, no more work.'

'Lazybones,' said Greta.

'I wish,' sighed Tara, and gave Greta's nipple a hard pinch.

'Ouch!'

'I'm going to end up squatting on erections all summer,' she complained, and then paused. 'I'm just dying to do something different.'

'If you *really* want to you probably will.'

'Optimist,' said Tara.

'Pessimist,' said Greta.

Tara was massaging her breast now, kneading it softly like pastry dough. The breath caught in Greta's throat, then her eyes caught a glimpse of the luminous face of the alarm clock.

'Ohmygod, I've got to go,' she said and Tara gave her nipple another good pinch as she slipped from the bed.

'Sadist.'

'Masochist.'

'Lazybones,' Greta screeched from the bathroom.

She turned on the shower and lathered the sponge. As she was soaping the remains of the ice cream from her legs it occurred to Greta that she had only laundered the bed linen the night before and if Tara persisted in her fetish she would end up forever washing sheets like that woman in mythology condemned for eternity to carry water in a vessel that leaked so artfully it was always empty when she reached her destination. Who was that now?

She couldn't remember. She couldn't remember anything. Sex had opened the door to her inner self and closed her memory banks to all thoughts except the next adventure. And there was something weird. It truly was a drug: the more sex you have the more you want. As she stood there with the hot water raining over her, Greta was absentmindedly caressing her nipples.

Ohmygod. The time.

She threw a big white towel around her shoulders and ran her palm over her cheek. That night when Richard had slapped her in his hallway it was as if the old Greta May had flown away, gone into storage, a musty wig, or a taffeta dress from a costume drama, and the new improved version was now smoothing sun block down her long legs, over her arms, her breasts with little raspberry ripple nipples always so tingly and overt, always anxious

80

to be touched. She kissed a fingertip and planted the kiss on each of their little noses. *Be good*, she said, and turned quickly to the mirror to see if she could see herself as others saw her.

'Slut,' she hissed.

Tara had rolled under the covers and had gone back to sleep. Greta decided not to disturb her, opened the curtains in Tara's room, and raided her closet instead. Greta was caressing the moist opening to her sex, her eyes running over the piles of books, the sweaters and knickers leaping from drawers, the dresses like phantoms fleeing from the wardrobe. Tara was always so busy lap dancing and writing essays Greta felt positively exhausted as she slid into a silver thong, a matching bra and a shimmering metallic dress that flickered with rainbows where it caught the light. The sky was clear blue, the sun moving in a veil of mist like a belly dancer. It was going to be another scorcher and that always made people happy. Greta studied her reflection.

The dress was completely unsuitable but she had a feeling that there was something right in getting it wrong. Tara was stick thin and toned from all that dancing, all those essays, and the dress on Greta was so stretched it was as if she were bound in shackles. She shivered and tossed her mane of brown curls. The thought of being bound made the blood bloom on her cheeks. Greta was getting to know herself, her needs and desires, and just wished that what she was becoming aware of now, in the last few days, she'd been aware of when it could have informed her acting, helped her career.

In one of the scenes in *The Raw Edge,* she'd been bundled into a car by two men, then tied to a bed in a gloomy basement. She had reacted with classic hysteria, hammering her fists, wailing at the top of her voice, and this might be true to life, but it lacked subtlety, subtext, a space for the imagination. If she had the chance to play Polly again she would give her an air of tragic mystique, that mixture of strength and vulnerability that leaves audiences wondering if she is truly a victim or if there is a dark side to her character that encourages cruelty.

Greta sat pondering these thoughts as she painted her eyelids pale blue. She had not given up her career. *I'm only 19, for heaven's sake*, and it didn't seem quite so old any more. She was, as actors say, just resting and would return better equipped when the time was right.

She slicked mascara over her long lashes and as she opened and closed her eyes she looked like a pony about to be taken for a long ride. The image was silly and slipped away as she rouged her cheeks below high, prominent cheekbones and added pale pink lipstick, all very demure and inviting. She pursed her lips and blew a kiss.

'Slut,' she said again and giggled

Greta stepped into silver heels and the dress rattled like spare change as she walked. She borrowed a silver evening bag with a long chain and it occurred to her that she was dressing for a date. She glanced about for her cigarettes and lighter, her mobile phone, the little Cartier wristwatch. All gone, vanished for ever, and she made do with some lippy and Tara's Ray-Bans. Her tummy grumbled but there was no time for breakfast.

Tara was making sleepy noises, and Greta brushed a lock of hair from her brow. She dropped her keys in the silver bag, closed the door and strode along the busy street passing the lines of baked cars locked in a metal chain across London, the drivers sweaty and anxious, the exhausts pumping clouds of purple haze into the ozone.

The man with the shiny head was waiting on the platform. Like Greta, he seemed to have taken care with his appearance. His white shirt was freshly ironed, he wore a green tie with hunting dogs running down its length, shiny brown brogues and an off-white linen suit, as unsuitable for the Underground as was Greta's attire for the shoe shop. She was glancing over the top of her shades and noticed the customary look of relief in his beady eyes as she made her entrance.

The platform was full. She walked its entire length, almost to the end, heels clacking, heads turning, and stood like a long thin needle really much too close to the edge. The wind was charging over the glittering rails. The crowd swelled about her like moons to a silver sun and the train was an angry demon roaring from the tunnel. The doors opened and the bald man made sure he was right behind her as they shoved their way into the carriage.

People wishing they knew how to fold a newspaper on the tube were engaged in origami. Two schoolgirls in short navy skirts were talking in loud voices, and the hand that ran like a frisky animal under Greta's skirt quivered with pleasure as it came into contact with her bare flesh.

She reached for the hanging strap, swivelled her hips and her lips parted as a finger ran over the gusset shielding her crack, up and down, slowly, softly. It was so decadent being fondled in public it made her wet and breathless. She closed her eyes and thought about the cold ice cream melting under the eager laps of Tara's tongue, her pussy sticky and dripping. Greta could feel a prickling in her thighs and went up on her toes, up and down, up and down, in counterpoint to the caressing fingertip, the movement releasing a creamy trickle between her legs and she had an awful urge to rip her knickers off.

The papers kept rustling like dry leaves. Further down the carriage a drunk was singing and it was only 8.30 a.m. The lights flickered. There was something sensual about flickering lights. Greta was sucking for breath through parted lips. Pushing down on the dancing fingers. Air was trapped in her body like the air chasing through the Underground. She was going to cry out. She couldn't control it. It was coming, coming, something glimpsed on the horizon. Her body was damp and slippery. Oh yes! Oh yes! She gritted her teeth. She was there, nearly there, vagina throbbing, muscles pulsing, contracting, she arched her back, bit her tongue, stretched her legs apart, *Ohmygod ...*

... when at that very moment the carriage tilted and they were torn viciously apart.

The train leaned into the bends and one of the schoolgirls yelled ...

'Like. Excuse me ...'

... as the bald man was thrown against her.

'Perv,' said her friend, curling her lips with distaste.

And Greta knew that it wouldn't be long before she was proffering her little arse to strangers on the train. You could see it in her saucy eyes, in the swell of her breasts peeking from her unbuttoned blouse, so soft and tempting. She was ungainly with long limbs like a pony and it dawned on Greta that Richard and Gustav didn't train horses, they trained girls. She had been discovered, harvested, selected for something and the fact that she still wasn't entirely sure what made it all the more exciting.

She smiled at the girl and the girl smiled back. They were conspirators. The lights dimmed and during the prolonged moment of darkness, her travelling companion manoeuvred his hand back over the globes of her bottom. He was like a small boy with a marvellous toy. He adored her arse. He wanted to take it home with him, nurse it, caress it, bring it presents. Keep it safe. In the air was the scent of her own arousal, the sweat of hot bodies rubbing together, the sugary perfume of schoolgirls.

The bald man was anxious now, worrying at the strip of material running tightly and damply between her legs. She was clammy from the ripples of an unfinished orgasm, vaginal oils slicking her panties, glossing her thighs. The train had built up speed, a knife plunging through the tunnel, rattling and screeching. The noise grew louder and, like a key entering a lock, a finger finally lifted the thong and was about to slip into her gaping crack when the driver stamped down the brakes and they were torn apart again.

The schoolgirls screamed. Sparks bounced across the windows, the wheels squealed and the passengers were pitched forward like earthquake victims as the train careened to a halt at South Kensington. The sudden jolt shook the man from his feet. He tripped over his briefcase, slipped to the floor and the schoolgirls cried out with renewed passion as he peered up their navy blue skirts.

'Perv.'

'Pederast.'

'Disgusting,' added a man in an old-fashioned bowler hat.

The looks the girls exchanged with Greta included her in their secret club and the bald man lost his confidence as the toffs and City girls squeezed in with their freshly-washed hair and bulging shoulder bags. He stood forlornly at her side and Greta cheered him up during the remains of the journey by running her knee between his thighs. It was the least she could do.

She skipped from the carriage at Green Park, bought a hot bagel that scolded her fingers and strode along Piccadilly shedding crumbs along the way.

Madame Dubarry was just unlocking the door as she arrived and the man with small feet who had been seeking out a pair of summer lace-ups was waiting with his nose pressed against the window.

'You're here,' he said when he saw her. 'Thank God.' His jacket was rumpled and his hair stood out in points.

'Size seven, white,' she said and his eyes glowed like a lottery winner.

He followed her inside. She went straight to the stock room and returned with the box. Greta sat on the low stool, her skirt riding over her legs as she slid the shoes from their cotton bags like a diamond dealer with precious stones. The man was wearing the intense look of a schoolboy and it occurred to Greta that men are instantly boys when there's a hot pussy around. They go into rut and it was thrilling to have this power. She had power over men and Richard had power over her. Perhaps her power came from his power? She thought about that as her customer shuffled his feet into the lace-ups and she tied two bows.

'There,' she said and he took the shoes for a test run along the burgundy carpet, flexing his toes, peering down as he walked.

She strolled slowly up the aisle towards him and he clutched her arms when she stopped.

'I have to paint you,' he said. 'It's a matter of life and death. You must, simply must be committed to canvas ...'

He spoke fast in a funny accent and Greta couldn't quite understand what he was saying.

'I beg your pardon?' she said.

'I have to paint you. I just have to.'

She smiled. 'Ooo, yes please,' she responded and the man gripped his hands in prayer.

He looked up to heaven, well, the chandelier actually, and Greta was sure there were tears misting his grey eyes. 'Thank you, thank you, thank you,' he repeated and looked back at Greta. 'I was up all night preparing ...'

'Preparing?'

'*Everything*,' he said darkly and she trembled as she tried to imagine things beyond her imagination.

He decided not to change back into his old shoes, the new ones were so comfortable, and while she was running his credit card through the machine he wrote down his name and address. Greta promised to get a taxi after work and he galloped out with a spring in his heels, the old shoes in a maroon bag with long string handles.

Four minutes past nine and she'd made her first sale.

Greta served a man with two wives, the newscaster with dyed hair she had seen on television and a footballer who pinched her bum as she bent to open a box.

'Cheeky,' she said.

'Don't shake it about then.'

And she gave it another provocative wiggle.

Madame Dubarry seemed glazed that morning and watched Greta moving through the store as if she were seeing an apparition, the ghost of herself, perhaps, in the age of her namesake. She had exchanged her usual dark attire for a white suit that clung to her curves and Greta was aware of the firm slender body moving below the folds of white linen.

Madame Dubarry was smoking a gold-tipped cigarette in the staff room during a quiet moment and stabbed it out as Greta entered. She reached for her hand and pulled her on to her knee.

'Just a few more days, Greta, and I'll never see you again.'

'Course you will. I'll be back ...'

'No, dear, you're never coming back,' she said emphatically. She ran her hand over Greta's shoulder blades. 'I can feel your wings. They're just beginning to grow. You're going to fly away and have the most marvellous life.'

'But how can you be so sure?'

'Experience,' she replied. 'Be yourself and you will be everything.'

That sounded like good advice and Greta marvelled at how each decision we make is so important. If you take one wrong turn, it's easy to take another and you could end up going round in circles. She had at first thrown Richard's phone number away and had she not picked it up again, she probably wouldn't have been sitting there right now on Madame Dubarry's lap with Madame Dubarry's hand running up and down her bare thighs. Greta turned to kiss her forehead and, at that same moment, the doorbell chimed and she hurried out, her heels like heartbeats muffled in the thick weave of the carpet.

The tall man with the lush flowing locks had entered.

He smiled warmly, greeting her like a cherished friend.

'Ah, there you are,' he said. 'What a pleasure.'

'Hello,' she replied. 'How are you today?'

He thought about that for several seconds. 'I'm quite well. Under the circumstances.' He didn't explain those circumstances but stood there openly studying her and she felt like a mannequin in a shop window.

'Is there anything I can show you?' she finally asked.

'I'm sure there is, but that wasn't what I had in mind.' He paused again and smiled. 'I'd like to invite you to tea.'

Greta replied instantly. 'That sounds super,' she said. 'I'd like to come.'

He looked serious now. 'When you've finished work?' he suggested.

Greta drew breath through her teeth to show she was disappointed. 'I can't today. Someone's going to paint me ...'

'Tomorrow?'

Now she smiled. 'Brilliant.'

He produced his card. There was no address or telephone number, just the name Count Leonardo Ruspoli in finely etched gold letters on a grey background.

'You don't look like a girl who eats cake and biscuits,' he remarked.

'I'm afraid I am,' she replied.

'What's your favourite food?'

Greta raised her shoulders as she thought about it. She didn't have a favourite food. She ate everything.

'Fruit salad ... and ice cream,' she finally answered because she couldn't think of anything else.

'Perfect, Greta,' he said, and she was surprised.

'You know my name?'

'I must have heard your colleague using it the other day.' He smiled. 'Am I right?'

She nodded. 'Greta May,' she said and they formally shook hands.

He gave her directions to his hotel, which was just

around the corner, and told her to show the card to the doorman. He ran his long fingers through his hair and was about to turn away when Madame Dubarry appeared from the staff room. The Count bowed, just slightly, in the chivalrous way of Europeans from another time.

'Fruit salad happens to be my dish *de choix*,' he whispered and Greta watched him stroll unhurriedly along Bond Street.

Greta showed Madame Dubarry the card. 'He invited me to tea,' she explained.

'Ah, Count Ruspoli,' she said, her eyes bright. 'Didn't I tell you?'

They had to stand back right then because a large woman with pendulous breasts and wearing tweeds barged in rattling her handbag.

'Ah, Mrs Maddox,' said Madame Dubarry. 'What a pleasure.'

'I saw those little kitten-heels in the window. They're fabulous. I must have them. I simply must,' she cried and stared at Greta. 'Well, come along then, girl, what are you waiting for? We haven't got all day.'

Greta was breathless and stared back at the woman, at her gigantic breasts clanging like lead bells against the shimmering silk of her white blouse.

'Size?' she mumbled.

'I don't know, let's have a look, shall we?' she said and Greta had a feeling they would be bringing out every pair of shoes in the store before the woman's feet found happiness. Madame Dubarry raised her plucked eyebrows, gripped her hands behind her like a trusted courtier and accompanied the woman to the velvet sofa below the soft lights that made everyone look their best.

Greta ran up and down the stairs perspiring and the woman watched her as if she were a clever monkey as she slid the shoes from their bags and on to the plump waiting feet.

'Come along, girl, come along,' she kept saying.

'You've brought the wrong size, haven't you. Let's start again shall we.'

She grew hotter, the silver dress crinkled like tinfoil, and the woman slapped Greta's flanks in encouragement, her toes wriggling merrily in the spotted pink kitten-heels.

'There, now you're getting the hang of it,' she said and Greta noticed her nod towards Madame Dubarry with that look of approval she remembered the house matron giving the games mistress when a girl was about to be slippered.

The woman finally selected two new pairs, the kitten-heels and some high pointy sling-backs that made her feel all fluffy and good about herself. Shoes can do that. She stood and arranged the shoulders on her tweed jacket.

'Come here, girl,' she said, slapping her thigh. She pinched Greta's cheek affectionately but it really hurt.

'Ouch!'

'You're going to do very well,' she said. 'Very well indeed. I can tell.' She glanced at Madame Dubarry.

'Very well,' she said.

How very confusing, Greta thought, and left for lunch as the woman searched for her credit cards.

She sat in Pret with her sushi and carrot juice feeling oddly content. She was wondering why during those six months at the shoe store everyone had virtually ignored her, then not one, but two different men had made dates and they both seemed terribly interesting, not boys but men. One of them a count, for heaven's sake!

People were passing the long window that looked out on Piccadilly. Greta had heard on the radio it was going to be the hottest June on record and girls were shedding their clothes like sweetie wrappers, like mannequins on a runway with the summer collection. There was so much bare flesh being offered for bronzing it made her positively giddy. Bare waists, bare legs, bare breasts. One girl who passed was wearing a hipster mini that was so low you could see wisps of pubic hair. Greta nodded out of respect as their eyes met.

At least she wasn't alone in her impulses. Girls want to take their clothes off. She wasn't sure why but she knew it was true. Girls' clothes aren't just designed to be provocative, they are designed to be taken off: look at the black dress she had chosen that night to go and see Richard, one pull of the bow and she was virtually naked, on show for a perfect stranger. You get dressed in order to get undressed, and while dressed, it's the way in which you conceal the bits that are covered that makes it interesting.

She had never thought about these things before but it made sense. When you see stars on the red carpet at Cannes, the men are tightly buttoned in their dinner jackets while the girls glide by in a few square inches of chiffon, their bodies offered as if in competition for the Palme d'Or. Men keep their shoes on as they stroll along the beach, but girls like to feel the wet sand between their toes. Girls when they really try can get in touch with their deepest instincts, their innermost desires, their true selves. Give any girl two glasses of champagne and the slightest excuse and she will become a striptease artist. It's just fun. Greta pursed her lips and sucked on the red and white striped straw stuck in the carrot juice. Her knickers were damp. Her nipples tingled. She loved being a girl.

As she was leaving Pret it was quite astonishing because she bumped into the saucy schoolgirl she had seen on the tube and they both screamed and threw up their hands smiling because it's always a pleasure when you see someone unexpectedly in the City. The girl's name was Bella. She was nearly 18 and was just finishing her A-levels. She was supposed to have spent the morning at the Portrait Gallery but after half an hour had marched her long legs and perky breasts into Soho to check out the sex shops.

'Be careful,' Greta warned her. 'There are some weird people about.'

'I shouldn't think there's anyone weirder than Miss

Birch in classics,' she said and Greta laughed. 'She's always getting us to stand on the desks so she can explain how the Greeks built their temples.'

'You go to a girls' school?'

'Unfortunately,' Bella replied.

'Me, too,' said Greta, 'least I did,' and they grinned with secret knowledge.

'I need to get a job in the summer and I want to find something, you know, interesting for a change.'

Greta tapped her lips thoughtfully with her finger and studied the girl in the same way as Count Ruspoli had studied her. 'You know something, I might be able to help.'

'No?'

'Come, we should hurry,' and they gripped hands as they skipped along.

Greta felt like a schoolgirl herself as they rushed back to Bond Street and it only occurred to her now as she glanced up at the sign that Bond Street was such a cool name.

Madame Dubarry agreed to give Bella an interview on the spot and Greta noticed the girl unpopping an extra button on her blouse as they descended the stairs to the stockroom. The door closed behind them with a muffled sigh.

At that moment, the bell tinkled and she watched Jason Wise stride in behind his pointy beard. Greta wondered with all these weird coincidences occurring if she were in the midst of an elaborate game of snakes and ladders and here was the stretched gaping mouth of the anaconda.

He stopped, hands held up in mock surrender. 'I will,' he said, 'accept only one answer ...'

'I don't know the question.'

'... yessssss,' he hissed.

'Only if you buy some new shoes.'

He grinned.

She smiled.

He'd got her.
Or has she got him?
'Size 8,' he said.

Chapter Nine – Greta Abstract

THE SKY WAS BRIGHT and clear, even the Albert Bridge was freshly painted, but as the taxi turned into the back streets of Battersea it was like going back in time and she imagined Jack the Ripper prowling through the shadows. Everything was dark and gloomy, the winding terraces so densely packed she found it hard to breathe. She clutched her bag, as if for comfort, but Richard had taken her mobile. She didn't know why and was suddenly dying to go away to the country.

Greta heard fire engines bells in the distance and then saw a blazing car beside the road. The driver's eyes in the rear-view mirror flamed as they fell on her. For some reason it brought back to her mind the brief conversation with Jason, that wicked cast in his eye.

What's he after? There has to be something.

Perhaps, that's not fair, she thought. After all, he'd been very complimentary. He had bought a pair of suede slip-ons and his invitation to go for a drink at the club on Friday with Marley Johnson reminded her that she was on sabbatical and the smell of the greasepaint still beckoned.

Greta had appeared at the National with Marley in a play where, in the lead role, he had played a black slave who had gained his freedom and now had a throng of white people as his slaves. She couldn't recall what point the play was making, but every night and two matinees for six weeks she was hauled from a circle of cowering women and led to the front of the stage where he ripped her dress from the neck to the hem. He pulled the rags from her shoulders, gripped her wrists behind her and thrust her naked body at the startled audience. Her cheeks would bloom with shame but she remembered feeling totally alive at every show and was praised in *The Observer* for her 'selfless performance'.

It was her best review.

The taxi stopped at a gap between the buildings and she gave the driver a generous tip.

'Fanks, darlin',' he said, and sounded just like Dirty Bill.

Greta made her way down the silent passageway, glancing over her shoulder at the pursuing footsteps until she realised it was only the echo of her own heels on the cobbles and she felt silly for being such a worrier. The passage opened on the river bank. The sun was bright again, the reflection on the water making the same shifting pattern on her metallic dress.

She showed the address she'd been given to an old lady walking her dog and the woman sucked her dentures as she pointed to the grey building immediately behind her.

'Looking for that artist, are you? Bloomin' nutter if you ask me.'

Greta nodded. 'They usually are,' she said, and the woman carried on clucking.

Her little dog was snapping merrily and Greta bent to stroke its head.

'Right one for the girls, he is. Come on, Angus. Come on. Leave her alone.'

Angus licked Greta's leg and the taste of her bare flesh drove both the dog and its owner into paroxysms of hysteria. Angus started frothing at the mouth and howling, chasing its tail in circles, and the old lady was suddenly whipping the animal's flanks with the lead.

'Bloody fing. Come here,' she was screaming. 'We know what you need ...'

Finally she got hold of Angus by the throat, attached

the lead and gave it a good few whacks on the backside with the leather strap. The dog howled and Greta watched in horror.

'It's all right. They like a bit of discipline,' she said, and owner and dog wandered off completely satisfied.

Greta looked up at the building. It was an old factory with the words *Allon & Goldman* in ancient lettering fading on the brickwork. She climbed the iron stairs to the loft and was surprised at the contrast when she pushed through the door into a modern studio with a polished beamed ceiling and a long glass wall facing the Thames. The space was ringed with numerous canvases that recalled the abstracts on Gustav's walls.

The name on the slip of paper she had been given was Vanlooch and she didn't know if that was Mr Vanlooch or just plain Vanlooch, but it was the sort of thing painters go in for. He was speaking on a mobile and she was sure she heard him say, 'She's here,' before closing the machine. He watched her approach, the dress jingling as she moved through the big squares of sunlight that patterned the paint-dappled floor. Even the floor was a work of art.

'This way,' he said, and led her to the far corner where there was a bathroom. 'You can hang your clothes in there. I want to make a start while we've got the light.'

A nude portrait, she thought. What else? She started removing Tara's silver dress.

'Everything,' he said.

Vanlooch had appeared timid in the shoe store but standing there in his new shoes he was on his own territory and occupied the space like the captain of a ship, the studio with the water outside having a vaguely nautical air. He watched her undress, scratching his cheek while he made an appraisal of her body. Greta was entirely confident being naked, especially after that day in Camden Market, and only blushed at her own wantonness.

They crossed the studio to the windows and Vanlooch studied her in the light, her breasts, her arms, the tilt of her chin. He turned her round and, as Greta watched the people across the river washing their houseboats, he slipped to his knees as if in prayer to the holy orifice. He squeezed the cheeks of her backside, moulding her flesh like he was making a sculpture, and she wondered why men were so obsessed by bottoms, with her bottom. They were fixated, spellbound, overcome. They wanted to touch it and smack it, lick it and beat it with whips and belts. It was a pretty bottom, she'd always thought so, and while he nursed it in his palms she felt so ashamed as an oily teardrop leaked into her pubes. He ran the side of his finger like a saw between her legs and the breath caught in her throat as she grew wetter. Greta adored being touched, being fondled and fingered and it was frustrating because she hadn't had sex since first thing that morning and it was already getting on for seven.

'We ought to make a start,' he said, and stood with a sigh.

Immediately behind them, flat on the floor, was a framed canvas, about six feet by four feet. It was pale blue like the sky outside, and around one end on the stained floorboards were numerous bowls of paint in every conceivable hue.

'It's acrylic,' he said. 'Washes off in a jiff.'

Vanlooch wasn't looking at her. He was gazing at the bowls of paint as if in all those bright colours was a clue to the meaning of life. His hands, she noticed, were well shaped, his long slender fingers that were knitted together uncoiling as he came to a decision. He took a plastic cup, scooped up some pink paint and poured it into an empty bowl. He added a dash of vermilion with the tip of a wide brush. The pink was shot through with spirals of red, the paint darkening a tone as he stirred them together with a wooden spatula.

'Come here and bend over,' he said sternly.

97

Greta thought for a moment he was going to slap her arse. In fact, he did, but gently, and it tickled as he coated her bottom in the dark pink mixture with a wide brush.

'Ooo,' she said.

'Don't wriggle about. This is vital.'

He painted her bottom with infinite care, over the two plump cheeks and into the crease. She then had to sit on the top left hand corner of the canvas.

'Stay there. And don't move.'

He watched her like he was reading a foreign menu, waiting for the print to set. She began to get cramps sitting still for so long, but at that moment he reached for her with extended hands. 'Easy now,' he said, and pulled her slowly to her feet. He smiled for the first time.

She stood away and studied their handiwork.

'Angel's wings,' Vanlooch said contentedly.

Dipping a fine brush into black paint, he skirted the outer edges of the print she'd made with narrow, fluttery chevrons. Greta was amazed as the picture emerged. The cheeks of her spread bottom had stamped two perfect wings, the contours from her flesh leaving a gauzy, diaphanous effect. Vanlooch's swirling flicks with the brush created a feeling of movement, of flight. He was very clever.

Vanlooch took her hand and they stepped away. There was a bucket with a sponge and he used it to wash off the dried paint, over her cheeks, deep into the crack, the water running down her legs. She tilted forward as he swept the sponge between her thighs and worked it scrupulously into the runny cleft of her pussy. He wiped her dry and for some reason Greta remembered the girl in Gustav's video towelling down the amber pony.

He started again, painting her bottom, squatting her down carefully beside the first set of angel's wings and creating a matching pair, almost, but not quite identical. He produced the same feeling of movement with the black scribbles and washed her bottom and pussy, the sponge sliding over her distended clitoris and making her giggle.

They made 12 sets of angel's wings, five along the top, with five making a mirror image facing them, and two more to fill in the gaps on each side. The outside edge of the canvas was now ringed by butterflies, with the heart of the painting empty. Greta wondered for a moment if they had finished and had no idea that they had only just begun.

Using pure vermilion, Vanlooch coated a brush and studied her nipples. 'Good. Good, nice and hard,' he said, and of course they were. Her bottom had been receiving so much interest, the darkened buds had sprung to attention. After painting her nipples with a generous layer of vermilion, he used another brush to coat the palms of her hands in pale green. Greta then had to do a sort of press up, supporting herself on her toes and lowering her breasts on to the top central half of the first set of wings. Her green hands with spread fingers made a pattern like the footprints of a bird as she repeated the exercise, the artist washing her hands and breasts between each print.

Her feet were next. He poured pale yellow into deep pink and blended a sort of amber colour. He pulled up a low stool for her and, as feet are so sensitive, she couldn't stop giggling as he slapped the mixture on her soles. As Greta made her way across the canvas, just below the butterflies, he rushed round to meet her, the stool in hand. He washed her feet, it was awfully biblical, gave them a fresh coat, and she set off again, her light touch leaving a faint trail like a memory of something and you're not sure what.

'What do you think?' he asked suddenly, staring at his work.

'Mmm, it's marvellous,' she replied and he smiled broadly as he turned her around, holding her in profile and running his hands over her sides, his palms brushing against her taut nipples.

'This is the important part,' he now told her, and bent

to pour gold paint into a fresh bowl.

Greta had to go down on her hands and knees to dip her hair into the bowl. She stood and while golden drips rained over her shoulders and breasts, he coated her entire body in twisting swirls of pink in various shades and it was just so amazing, so weird, she thought, because that very morning she had awoken like a giant raspberry ripple with Tara warm and sticky at her side. Tara was so delicious, so creamy, the memory made her insides turn luxuriously moist.

She was enjoying herself. It was fun being an artist's model and it seemed as if everything that had happened since she'd met Richard was connected; there was a pattern, however arbitrary, as free forming as Vanlooch's canvas, a sort of surreal play with each scene an echo of something else. Except Bill Longman, perhaps. That was just a blip, the exception that proves the rule.

Once Vanlooch had completed his work with the brush, layering her entire body in shades of pink, Greta rolled across the canvas. He scrubbed her down while the acrylic was drying and painted her again, changing the depth of colour, the paint swirls like a misty veil that blurred without ever quite concealing the configuration of angel's wings, the bright red stamps of her nipples, the pale green prints of her hands.

Vanlooch was getting excited, the paint going everywhere, over his face and hair, the floor, his white shoes, and Greta, being practical, couldn't work out why he hadn't worn an old pair. He went down on his knees and deftly applied a generous coating of nut-brown to her sticky pubes. The imprint she left on the canvas he assisted with flicks of a thin brush, making shadows, adding depth and contrast. She did it again and again, the browns and pinks and yellows building up in patterns that kept changing like the glass chips in a kaleidoscope.

'It's coming,' he said, as they stood back to wait for the paint to dry.

The sun was slipping over the rooftops across the river. It was warm behind the glass walls. The light was orange, the sky clear and cloudless. Greta studied the canvas and was surprised to find that within the storm of colour, the angel's wings, the brown triangles, the brilliant red dots from her nipples, the footprints and handprints, that from the pattern of swirls and abstract shapes the figure of a slender girl was emerging, shadowy and unformed, the mollusc from which the angels had flown, and if you half-closed your eyes they seemed to lift from the painting and hover in the still air.

Vanlooch mixed a bowl of white paint with a touch of brown and yellow, stirring the mixture with a spatula until it turned ivory, the colour of her skin. Greta then had to lay on her side, head up, back bowed, bottom pert, her arms stretched out, her legs behind her, bent slightly at the knees, her hair flying, her weight supported on her right thigh and shoulder.

'Hold it. You mustn't move,' Vanlooch instructed as he reached for the bowl of ivory.

He ran paint about her profile, the flicking movements with the brush giving an effect of movement, and when he was done she had to remain immobile, a marble statue carved in full flight. She was getting cramp by the time Vanlooch was ready to release her. He lifted her legs to one side, balanced her feet on the floor and pulled her up in one movement.

He spent a long time adding fine lines of ivory paint in what to Greta at first seemed pure whimsy, although a new shape, new life, was evolving from the figure of the girl, another incarnation. She couldn't yet make out what it was but it was exciting like being at a funfair and seeing yourself in the mirror maze, tall and short, fat and funny, as skinny as a thread, a child, an old woman, seeing yourself not as others see you but as you see yourself in your wildest fantasy.

Vanlooch was breathing faster, growing impatient.

'Now, lay down, lay down,' he instructed and Greta did as she was told, stretching out beside the canvas, resting on her elbows so that she could see what he was doing. This was art and important.

He took a clean brush, sucked the tip and slid it into her pussy. It came out slicked and silvery, so thick in juice she was embarrassed as she watched him applying her oils to the canvas, embarrassed and frustrated because she couldn't see the picture transforming, just his hand as he added highlights. He was an old-fashioned clerk keeping a ledger, her pussy an inkwell, dipping the brush in, teasing her fluids over the canvas and coming back for more. It tickled and she giggled. She lifted her bottom and opened herself wider. She was trying to draw the paintbrush up inside her, but the artist knew what he wanted and that was the milky sap that welled over her lips.

'Good, good,' he said. 'Nice and wet.'

Vanlooch was serious about his work. He teased the sticky stuff from her vulva and applied it pointillism style, stabbing the canvas with tiny dots, coming back for more. Greta became wetter, more animated. A long sigh escaped from her throat and, as she started to climax, Vanlooch loomed over her, eyes sparkling. He abandoned the brush and dipped his head between her legs. She trembled as she went into orgasm and he lapped at her pussy like a man finding water in the desert.

When the spasm ended, he grabbed a plastic cup and spat out her juices. 'Delicious. Delicious,' he said, rubbing his tongue over his teeth. He held the cup for her to see. 'Now this is *very* important: spit, don't swallow.'

She wasn't sure what he meant, but it all became clear as he lowered his trousers and she found his little soldier standing rigidly to attention.

Spit, don't swallow!

That's a first, she thought. She took him into her mouth and he tasted faintly of talcum powder. He rocked back on his size 7 white shoes, his knees were shaking and she had to grip his thighs to make sure he didn't fall over.

'Don't swallow,' she heard him groan and she thought he must have been saving it for a long time because after just a few moments her mouth filled with hot sperm. He pumped away like he was filling a car and when he had shed the last little drop she dribbled it out into the cup that held her pussy juice.

'We have created art, and art is life,' he said breathlessly, and they gazed down at their pale milky fluids.

The painter returned to his work. He took a new brush, made a small puddle with their essence and added a touch of emerald green paint. He looked back at her and after adding a speck of yellow to the pool what Greta saw on the canvas was a mirror image, a single shiny eye, her eye with long brown lashes, a look of surprise but contentment, a look of trust and wonder. He added glossy highlights from the cup of sperm, instilled energy, life, a universe exploding, transforming, being reborn.

The light outside was fading. Vanlooch lifted the canvas and together they carried it to the windows. He stood the work in landscape on two easels and as Greta studied the painting she was speechless. She had been surprised to discover the figure of a girl among the swirls of paint. Now she was impressed.

The human figure was still there in shades of pink, as were the butterflies on angel wings, a reference to change, to evolution, the palm prints and footprints fading as if left behind on the sand as another figure takes flight amorphously across the canvas, a mythical creature at full gallop: a unicorn, she thought for a moment, but there was no horn on its brow.

Then she realised: it was a flying horse. That's what Gustav had called her: Pegasus. And that's how Vanlooch must have seen her: that was her potential, not to be earthbound, but to take wing and fly with the stars. Greta was totally in awe, as were the people who stood at the Royal Academy years later, moved by the work, unsure what it was exactly, what it meant exactly, but knowing deep down on some primitive level that the painting was iconic, spiritual, eternal and deeply mysterious.

'It's a masterpiece,' she whispered.

'It's a start,' he said. 'Masterpieces take time.'

As Greta moved to one side to study the painting from a different angle, the glossy green eye followed her.

As she turned to Vanlooch, his mobile rang and he gave the machine straight to her.

'It's for you.'

'Me?'

'Hi, Greta.' It was Tara.

'How did you know I was here?' she asked. 'How did you get this number?'

'Guess who's waiting for you at the club?'

'For me?'

'Richard and Gustav,' she said breathlessly, and lowered her voice. 'They're absolutely gorgeous.'

'Richard and Gustav, there?'

Tara didn't answer. Richard came on the line and told her there was a car waiting outside and she had to come immediately.

'But I'm covered in paint ...'

'What colour?'

'What ... pink and white and brown and yellow, oh and red and gold ...'

'A rainbow girl. Come as you are, Greta May.'

And at that he hung up.

That was the game. The rules. The pact. It was such joy to hear his voice. His commands.

She was sticky, spermy, sweaty and with paint all over her body she looked like a fragment taken from the canvas. She dressed, Vanlooch waved without taking his eyes from the painting, and a mini-cab zoomed back over the Albert Bridge taking her to Hades in Mayfair where the two-metre tall doorman took a step back as if he was about to be attacked by a wild Valkyrie.

Greta understood why when she was ushered through to the dressing room where Tara was waiting for her.

'It suits you,' said Tara as she ran the zip down the back of her dress and hung it on a hanger.

Greta stood motionless, staring at her reflection in the mirror. Her hair was golden and stuck out in points like the Statue of Liberty and every inch of her body was covered in pink graffiti. She was a message from another dimension. Actually, she was a mess.

'You look like you've been having fun.'

'I've been painted.'

'So I can see,' said Tara.

Tara then explained that two girls were off sick and they had a party of very important businessmen in from the EU. Tara unhooked Greta's silver bra.

'This is your chance, Greta.'

And the penny dropped. She was expected to dance, and she had never done it before.

'No way,' she said.

'Richard suggested it.'

At that, Richard poked his head around the door and she was so pleased to see him.

'Break a leg,' he said, and left again.

'But what have I got to do?'

'Just wiggle about,' Tara replied. 'You dance around for a bit to get them excited, then you slip on to their laps and give them a good hard rub.'

'Is that all?'

'Don't stay too long on each one. As soon as you get the money, you move on.'

'Money?'

'That's why we do it, Greta. When they put the money in your knickers, that's the time to escape.'

Greta sighed. She had stage fright. It always happened. 'I can't do it, Tara,' she said

'I can,' Tara stressed in her competitive way and at that same moment Richard appeared back in the doorway.

He snapped his fingers. 'It's a go,' he said.

The music had started. She heard the speakers crackle to life and followed Tara in a daze through the dark corridor backstage.

And tonight for your complete pleasure we are proud to introduce Greta May. Let's give it up for our brand new performer, the beautiful, the adorable, the one and only Greta May ...

Greta was blinded by the crisscrossing beams of spotlights as she stumbled on stage. She was aware that out there in the dark people were clapping, which was always nice, and she could see the brass pole fixed to the centre of the stage.

The music grew louder, filling her head, running like creepy crawlies down her arms and legs. As the applause grew louder the butterflies in her tummy lifted on angel's wings and flew back to the canvas in Vanlooch's studio. She moved slowly at first, gyrating her hips and shoulders, holding the pole like a lover, running her crack up and down the slippery metal. The music pounded. She was on stage. She was performing, taking flight. She sucked her fingers. She massaged her breasts and pinched her own nipples until they hurt. Pussy was wet again and she heard the crowd roar for more as she slid her hand inside her pants.

The lights changed, pulsing like heartbeats. She could see the audience now, rows of men proffering money, £20 notes, £50 notes and euros in every colour. As she moved away from the pole, Greta noticed Richard in the wings behind a video camera. She looked across stage; there was Gustav with another camera. She was trapped in the crossfire, her every movement captured and she knew it was immodest but Greta loved seeing herself on film.

She danced to the front of the stage and the eyes of the cameras followed. She remembered the way Marley

Johnson had ripped her clothes off each night at the National and how the audience was always moved by the display. The lights were hot. She was bathed in perspiration. Her pussy was a lake. Her breasts were on fire.

And Greta couldn't help herself.

She couldn't stop herself.

She was a slut.

She wriggled out of her knickers and the men in the crowd came to their feet roaring and clapping as she discarded the little triangle of sopping cotton.

She was naked, covered in paint, sticky and sweaty. The men had fallen back into their seats, still waving their money, and Greta stepped into the arms of the first man at the end of the first row. He held her hips, he ran his arms up her sides and his cock sheathed in his trousers rammed at her slit. His eyes boggled. His throat opened in a roar and the next man was reaching for her, fondling her, touching her, grabbing her, wanking himself off. They were tossing their money on the stage like it was a tickertape parade.

Greta moved to the next man and the next, the first row, then the second. The lights were flashing as if it were a war zone, the music pounded hypnotically and the money kept raining down on the stage. One man with a big moustache and more innovative than his companions, turned her round and as he worked himself off against her arse she noticed the two cameras had moved like giant insects on tripod legs to the very edge of the stage and were capturing it all on film.

There must have been 40 men out there in Hades that night and Greta left them all with wet pants and suits covered in sweat, paint and pussy tears. Tara swept her money from the stage and Richard continued filming her as she retreated back into the dressing room.

Tara counted her money. There was £450 and €620.

'That's a fortune,' Greta said.

'That's how I get through university,' Tara told her.

The eye of the camera was moving between them, committing everything to film, and although subconsciously Greta was wondering why, what Richard and Gustav did with all that film, you are always high when you come off stage and it takes a long time to come down. During that time, Gustav appeared and the thought sailed from her mind.

Greta noticed Tara becoming all possessive. Gustav was smoking a cigar. He let out a plume of smoke and pushed his mop of bronze hair out of his eyes.

'Very good,' he said, studying Greta. Then he glanced at Tara. 'Shall we,' he added.

Tara gave herself a little shake as she tripped across the dressing room to join him.

Gustav looked back at Richard with a worried look suddenly clouding his blue eyes. 'You'll have to look after the shop for the next few days. The Americans are arriving and you know what they're like.'

'No problem,' said Richard. 'Go and do what you have to do.'

Richard glanced at Tara and Tara glanced at Gustav, and as Gustav glanced at her, Greta felt as if she was privy to a wonderful secret.

Tara flicked her hair over her shoulder as she span on her heels and followed Gustav from the dressing room.

'Where are they off to?' Greta asked Richard, although she had a very good idea.

'Questions. Questions. Questions,' he responded.

'Ohmygod, I forgot,' she said cheekily.

'Come, I'll take you home.'

'I ought to have a wash ...'

'Don't bother. I rather like you like that, all back to nature.' He paused. 'Are you a nature girl, Greta?'

'Not half,' she said, and he raised his eyebrows to heaven.

Greta dressed. They took a cab and Greta was thrilled

when Richard agreed to come in.

He inspected the flat, tut, tut tutting continuously as he did so.

'Looks like we're going to have to give you a few lessons in tidiness,' he said, and she felt ashamed because the flat was a disaster area.

'Oh, absolutely, Richard. That's *just* what I need.'

He glanced at his watch and Greta was bereft when she thought he was about to leave.

'You will stay,' she said.

'Not for long, I'm afraid. There's still masses to do.' He took her arm. 'Which little monkey house is yours?' he asked, glancing from the narrow hall at the two bedrooms, one on each side.

Greta led him into her room and it was nice the way he turned her round and solemnly undressed her. He fondled her nipples and ran his hand over her stomach, checking to see whether she had lost those few pounds, which she hadn't, of course, not with all the ice cream!

'Have you been a good girl?' he asked her, and she replied evasively.

'Well, I have done as I was told,' she said.

'Excellent. Now, you go and take a shower.'

She turned away, then turned back again. 'You will still be here?' she said, and he gave her one of his rare smiles.

'I'll be here.'

Greta showered as quickly as possible. She slathered herself in baby oil and found Richard propped up in bed reading Oscar Wilde when she returned to her room.

He pulled back the cover and she fell voraciously on to his sturdy erection. She licked the full length of warm, satiny soft skin from his balls to the crown, up and down, up and down, then took it deep into her mouth, pausing for air half way, then taking the rest down, down until the bulging tip reached the hollow of her throat. She moved leisurely like silk in a slow wind, caressing the tissue fine skin, rising up the shaft until just the head filled her mouth, sucking it hard, then descending again like a marvellous machine. Greta thought that if she were a Greek maiden being punished by the gods she would like to be condemned to be doing this and just this from now to the end of eternity.

Weird. When she was 17, a boy she had taken home from the disco had tried to stick his thing in her mouth while her dad was in the next room watching the late movie on TV. They had been kissing and groping and suddenly it was there, smelly with fags and cheap lager, probing at her open lips, and it managed to get between her teeth before she knew what it was. She bit down as hard as she could and the boy screamed and was rolling around on the floor clutching his wounded pride when her dad came belting in wondering what all the commotion was about. She just shrugged and he shrugged and she never knew for sure if her dad had guessed what had happened. Anyway, cocks in her mouth were a no-no.

Two years had gone by and now, Greta couldn't imagine anything more perfect, more beautiful, more natural. Richard's long, polished, glassy-smooth talisman was like a jewel, like a sculpture carved on another planet, and seemed to have been designed to slip into her mouth, her bum, her greedy wet pussy. He completed her, made her whole. Richard's cock was a deity from Olympus and she was his hand maiden, *his mouth maiden*. She worshiped the phallus.

Greta was getting emotional, frenzied, moving mechanically, covetously, and he stopped her, holding the side of her head and easing her gently away before his climax burst into her mouth as she craved. He kept a grip on his essence and spent ages licking out her two holes, his cunning tongue taking the warm juice from her pussy to oil her bottom. When his hard cock probed at the slippery pleats of her arse it slithered in painlessly, pressing through the tender walls to massage her singing

110

tingling clitoris. He moved without haste, bringing her along slowly, steadily, until she burst like a flower and Greta realised with immodest pride that this was her first anal orgasm. The first proper one. She panted like a pony and he turned her round and kissed her on the mouth.

This was the first time that Richard had made love to her without any slaps or spanks, and his black leather belt remained in the loops of his trousers. He kissed her eyes and kissed her seashell ears and when he got up to dress, he must have seen in the amber glow from the streetlight outside the wretched look on her face. He bent to kiss her brow.

'You are doing very well, Greta,' he said. 'I am going to be so proud of you.'

He left then, left her alone, her body pulsing blissfully, and she wondered what it was she was going to do to make him proud of her. Not that it mattered. She would do anything.

Chapter Ten – Il Duce

HOW DO YOU DRESS for a count? She was annoyed at herself for considering such trivia because one thing she did know was that you dress for the upper crust the same way as you would dress for Dirty Bill, whom she thought of as a good representative of the lower orders. Nobles aren't special, but she had to admit that they do make you feel special when you are in their company. Greta had met few knights of the theatre in her time. They were just like everyone else – they just had better diction and louder voices.

Still, a count! And an Italian at that.

She spent a long time in the shower washing off the last of the paint. She still had traces of yellow on the soles of her feet and had to balance on one leg to scrub it off. She warmed henna oil in her palms and smoothed it over her arms and legs, her sides and back, under her neck and into the hollow of her collar bones. The little bump of her tummy, which she considered totally sexy, was still putting in an appearance and her breasts had become quite a handful. They were just so *out there*, so perky and inquisitive, her nipples a deeper shade of red and so firm they throbbed for attention. She gave them a squeeze and suddenly remembered Tara Scott-Wallace tripping out of Hades with Gustav. The little minx still wasn't home.

Greta spent like *an hour* going through the skirts and tops in the two bedrooms. Girls tend to have heaps of clothes and they all get mixed up in one giant jumble sale, as Richard had noted with his tut tut tutting.

She closed her eyes and held her breath. It was *the morning after the night before.* Richard had made love to her like a hero in a story book, and while she had come to enjoy all the dares and derring-do, the trappings and thrashings, Greta felt like a new person, complete, invulnerable, contented. It seemed as if living inside her all these years, there had been a shop window dummy, a marionette on strings, a lifeless puppet filled with other people's thoughts and opinions, or having no opinions at all. She was the frightened girl who had run away from the theatre like poor little Orphan Annie. The girl had gone, waved goodbye from the deck of a ship sailing to the new world. She was a woman now. The strings guiding the marionette had broken and Greta had the feeling that she was becoming exactly who she always should have been. Confident. Compelling. Well-disciplined. She could see her profile in the mirror, everything rounded, soft, feminine. Greta adored her new life and realised with a stab of panic that she was totally, outrageously happy.

Ohmygod, the time!

Greta opened her eyes. She ran her gaze over the heaps of clothes and finally plumped for the demure but practical look and laid out a white bra and panties, a fitted, rather formal black skirt of the sort Miss Moneypenny might wear, and a white blouse that buttoned sensibly but left a hint of cleavage like a mystery or a promise. Finally, she chose the pink jacket she had once worn as a bridesmaid when Antonia from school married a South African old enough to be her grandfather and richer, she had whispered, than the man who stole the golden goose. In his honour, Greta put on a gold crucifix on a short chain and, before dressing, sprayed scent in the air and shivered as it rained in fairy kisses over her bare skin.

She painted her lips pale pink, brushed mascara over

her eyelashes and trembled with vague excitement as she recalled the all-knowing eye of Pegasus staring back at her from Vanlooch's painting. She was all the things he had captured on canvas, a butterfly girl on angel's wings, a renaissance woman bursting from the husk and transforming into something air-borne and mythical.

Madame Dubarry had been right. When this week was done, she would never return to the shoe shop again.

Under Tara's bed, she found the black heels she'd been searching for and concluded as she studied her reflection in the mirror that she looked every inch like the City girls who would come crashing into the tube rustling their newspapers at South Kensington.

She clickety-clicked her way along the pavement with the slightly puzzled look of a celebrity, something she needed to practise, and blithely ignored the builders emerging from a white van with gaping mouths and broken teeth. Did they really imagine the *'Bleeding hell, look at the tits on that,'* and, *'I'd give her one up the Khyber any day ...'* was going to win their way into a girl's knickers?

Greta weaved a path across the main road to the Underground and realised the moment the little bald man touched her derriere that he was bitterly disappointed. Everything was tightly tucked and neatly put away. His hands roamed her hip bones and across her tummy. He gingerly cupped her breasts when the lights dimmed and his hands fell away as they brightened again, the bulbs hissing, the rails screaming, the crowd squeezing them so tightly together she could feel his modest erection poking hopelessly at her thigh like an accusing finger.

She turned to face him. His head was just below her chin, his nose resting in her blouse. She slipped her hand down his trousers and his eyes went pop as she fished about for the little worm trapped in his Y-fronts. His lips parted and a tear jerked into his eye as it wriggled into her palm. She didn't need to move about. The train was rocking and rolling, nursing the warm croissant of flesh in intermittent jerks, and it was all going rather well when the driver slammed on the steel brakes and they were thrown apart.

A look of distress came into his features as he stumbled backwards over his briefcase. Greta was about to topple on top of him, but a steadying hand came to the rescue.

'Tut, tut, tut, tut, tut,' she heard and turned to the man with the bowler hat, another regular in their carriage. He was staring down at the little bald man as if at a football hooligan.

'Thank you,' Greta said.

'A pleasure, my dear,' he replied, and manoeuvred her away from the bald man as if for protection.

They remained separated for the rest of the journey and Greta gave her companions a little wave as she stepped out at Green Park. She set her long legs in motion along the platform as the train vanished into the tunnel and was aware of her reflection in the glass fronts of the advert displays as the escalator rose like a stairway to heaven. The sun outside was warming the pavement in Piccadilly and she hummed the music from Hades as she ambled through the jostling throng.

Life, she concluded, was more fun when you don't take it too seriously, when you just let things happen. She had once read on a birthday card the message: 'Be yourself and try to be happy. But first be yourself.' Greta considered it extremely good advice.

Madame Dubarry was sitting in the staff room smoking a cigarette with a gold filter ringed in red lipstick and stood to kiss Greta's cheeks when she entered. She studied her outfit.

'Very fetching,' she said.

'You, too. That's gorgeous.'

'It is a woman's duty, don't you think?'

'Women seem to have lots of duties,' Greta answered.

They both smiled. Greta watched the smoke rise in curls from the ashtray and did something so naughty she would think about it for the rest of the day: she took a drag from Madame Dubarry's cigarette and her head started spinning.

'I thought you'd given it up.'

'I had, no I have,' said Greta. 'I can resist anything except temptation.'

'You should always do whatever you feel like,' said Madame Dubarry and smoothed down the folds of her smart frock as if for Greta's benefit.

Madame Dubarry had only ever worn black suits, but the day before she had switched to white and this morning she was wearing a pink paisley A-line frock that fell an inch above the knee and showed her girlish figure to best affect. Her hair, always severely held in a French pleat, had been released and tumbled in raven's wing curls about her shoulders. Her eyes seemed brighter, glinting like black stones, and her lips were scarlet like a gypsy.

There was another change, too, and when Greta had first entered the shop it was several moments before she realised that soft music was issuing from speakers set up on the shelf behind the counter, and there was a stack of CDs next to a brand new stereo. It wasn't long before the bell was chiming and people were dancing across the burgundy carpet, slipping into new shoes and waltzing out with a distinctive red bag on rope handles swinging from their shoulders, the name of the store in gold lettering letting everyone know they were blessed with good taste.

'Sex and Strauss, it always works,' Madame Dubarry whispered during a brief lull, and then the bell was ringing again.

Greta heard Madame Dubarry laughing on several occasions and watched her become coquettish when a tall, elegant man made his way through the pattern of sunlight piercing the windows like a matador crossing the *sol y sombra* of the bullring. They spoke Spanish. The bullfighter bought two pairs of shoes and took Madame Dubarry off to lunch ... and it was only 10.30 a.m.

'You'll be all right on your own,' she said.

Madame Dubarry skipped along on tiny steps and Greta didn't get her break until four o'clock, when her boss returned with puffy eyes and a faraway expression.

'You look like you've fallen in love,' Greta teased.

'In lust, my dear, in lust,' she replied, and Greta understood exactly what she meant.

Madame Dubarry was aware that Greta had an appointment with Count Ruspoli, and as it was so late she gave her the rest of the day off.

Greta didn't want to be too early. Wasn't it a lady's prerogative to be late? She grinned and wondered what Richard thought of the old cliché. She was strolling along on her way to Pret, oblivious to the men taking note of her presence, but changed her mind and set off in the opposite direction. She made her way towards Soho and in Golden Square there was an internet café where she ordered sparkling water and went online.

She tapped in the word Pegasus and googled down the list. The flying horse had quite a history and was even a constellation with eight major stars; *more than Titanic!* Medusa with her snake hair and mesmerizing gaze was the creature's mother, born from her blood when she was slain by Perseus, which wasn't very nice but to be expected when you hang out with Gods. Poseidon was probably the father, which meant Medusa must have been playing the field, but Poseidon chose to ignore his equestrian progeny. It was said that one kick from Pegasus's hoof caused the spring of Hippocrene to gush from the earth and its flow was famous for inspiring poets. 'A muse. How lovely,' she whispered. Zeus lured the winged horse into a golden bridle and, once tamed and disciplined, Pegasus carried thunderbolts across the night sky.

Well, well, well.

Greta typed Count Leonardo Ruspoli in Google and was disappointed that there were so few references. She did learn that he came from a long line of Italian nobility with three Popes in the family and a wayward branch related to Machiavelli. Villa Mangia Baldini, his estate in Tuscany, produced Chianti and the count had business interests in the Far East. There was nothing personal, nothing to say what he was really like.

She finally put Greta May in the search engine and nothing came up at all.

Greta walked slowly back through Soho and made her way to the hotel, which was just around the corner from the shoe shop. The doorman turned the card she gave him through his fingers for several moments. He studied her legs and her cleavage, looking her up and down with the same louche impudence as the builders in their white van, and it occurred to Greta that someone should write a book or open a school to teach men how to behave in the company of desirable women. *I am a desirable woman*, she thought with sudden pleasure, and let the thought slip away in order to pursue her thesis. Men like Richard and Gustav, like Count Ruspoli, know exactly what a woman wants and needs and for those men women will literally bend over and give everything in the knowledge that what they receive will make them truly thankful.

'I have an appointment,' Greta said crisply, pointing at the pale grey card, and the man awoke as if from a deep sleep. He led her to an elevator set in a lushly-carpeted passage. He pressed a button, she stepped inside, and the doorman stood back as the doors whispered to a close.

The lift rose without haste and opened on the top floor. She stepped out into a vestibule filled with flowers and tall mirrors. The solitary door was large, highly polished and half open. Greta heard foreign voices as she poked her head into the room.

A man with a fierce moustache, and not dissimilar to Madame Dubarry's bullfighter, was directing three

118

women in pink gingham uniforms as they carried great platters of fruit from one side of the suite to the other. The count was in an armchair by the window reading *Corriere della Sera*, the shadowy light falling in stripes across his pale linen suit. He was wearing a dark blue shirt and no tie.

'Hello.'

He seemed surprised to see her and, as he stood, nodded his head in that old-fashioned way of men with good manners.

'Ah, you are early, I am so sorry, we have yet to finish.'

'Should I come back later?'

'Good heavens, no. Come and see the finishing touches.'

He smiled now, took her hand and led her to a marble bathroom that was totally huge and where, in the sunken jacuzzi, the three women were busy assembling from the platters of fruit the perfect recreation of an Italian villa with its formal gardens and surrounding tree-clad hills. Rings of pineapple formed six columns across a palladium façade that was pale pink as if caught in the setting sun and must have been assembled from a whole market stall of mashed strawberries and cream. There were lawns of kiwis dotted with apple sculptures, sprigs of mint like olive trees, an orangery of orange slices, a lemon grove, beds of dried raisins, banked hills of greengages and cherries, mangoes lined with banana stepping stones, a fruit miracle that could easily have been created by Archimbaldo, another Italian.

The work was almost done. One of the gingham maids added a pond of pale ice cream, 'Blueberry flavour,' the count whispered, and the woman slid out behind the man who looked like a matador and was in fact the count's equerry. Greta stared up at Count Ruspoli and he swept his hand through his leonine hair.

'I don't know what to say,' Greta said.

'You don't have to say anything.'

'But it's so ... so big.'

'It is a family conceit,' he confessed. 'An indulgence.'

Greta studied the fruit salad, an architect's model, moving slightly as the slices of fruit slid from position, and she remembered she hadn't eaten all day and was just dying to jump in which, she realised, was probably the point.

'It's hard to know where to start, I suppose,' the count said.

'It seems a shame to mess it up.'

'But lots of fun.'

He smiled and his whole face came to life. Greta thought Count Ruspoli was probably the most handsome man she had ever seen. His eyes were as blue as the summer sky in Italy and sparkled with little stars of light; his nose was long and forceful and Greta could imagine that nose getting up to all sorts of mischief; he had a square chin that balanced his lush sweep of hair, and faint shadows below prominent cheekbones. It was hard to pinpoint his age. He could have been 50, or much more, or much less. He was ageless, timeless, a figure from another time and place, the renaissance, the Middle Ages, the crusades.

'I'm going to jump in,' she said.

'As one should in all things.'

Greta undressed where she stood and the count held her clothes for her like an assistant in a shop. He folded everything neatly and placed her things on a marble shelf. He stood back to consider her body and Greta had the feeling that she was being appraised by a true connoisseur, an authority, an expert. There was nothing prurient or vulgar in his study. She could have been a painting by Rembrandt, a sculpture by da Vinci, a diamond at Tiffany's. He took her hand and she turned.

'*Buono, buono, buono*,' he mumbled.

If this had been a test, she thought she had probably

120

passed. Greta's nipples were tingling and she rolled them wantonly through her fingers. The count drew her hair over her shoulders to get a better view and she was overwhelmed with an odd mixture of shame and elation. She felt utterly at ease being naked, being assessed in this way. She liked it. She craved it. In fact, being naked seemed to be more natural than being dressed. Hadn't *homo sapiens* run around for millions of years without any clothes on? Had some rebel gene crept through from that time corrupting her hopelessly? A warm feeling ran up her spine and her tummy rumbled. She was starving.

The count took her hand and she stepped down into the hillside of greengages at the edge of the gardens. When she sat, the entire edifice wobbled and the multi-coloured fragments of fruit washed over her thighs. She slid a slice of kiwi into her mouth.

The count left the room and returned with a chair that he placed beside the bath. Greta noticed that he was wearing the brown suede loafers he had bought earlier in the week. 'Would you like a spoon?' he asked her. He had settled back comfortably in his chair and it seemed a pity to disturb him.

'I think I can manage,' she replied and popped a strawberry between her lips.

While Greta stuffed herself on fruit salad, the count watched with a delighted expression on his carved features.

Count Ruspoli was a man who had come to appreciate women *of a certain kind*, he told her, after a lifetime amusing women of *every* kind. He paused for a moment's reflection and Greta's green eyes were filled with wonder. She adored his voice and was content to listen as he unfolded the curious tale of his peripatetic and curious existence.

It had all started, he said, lowering his voice, at the age of 12 when the housekeeper's daughter hopped into his bed at the Villa Mangia Baldini to verify the legend that, like his father and grandfather, like Ruspolis through time, he was endowed as few men are endowed with a penis worthy of the epithet Il Duce. It is, he said modestly, as a tower, a lighthouse, a beacon in the dark ages, a wonder of the modern world.

As he was about to change after breakfast that day, the housekeeper came to his room in the tower and stripped him of his nightshirt as she had done many times when he was a child. Unlike her daughter, who had shown the natural reserve of a girl just turned 13, the mother was there that bright spring morning to pay homage to Il Duce, this genetic quirk, as he put it, this rose headed, marble column that, like a secret or an heirloom, had been passed down the generations. The housekeeper fell to her knees, took his growing erection into her mouth and sucked at the firm flesh until, the second time that day, his essence overflowed from a hungry orifice. Had she once serviced his father in the same manner? Undoubtedly. It was like the quest for the Holy Grail. Like being inducted into a clandestine sect.

The scullery maids and under-maids, the cook and her assistants, women from the village and distant villages, their sisters and cousins and nieces from neighbouring towns, their daughters, mothers and wives, grandmothers in black and girls in pigtails from near and far found justification day after day to make a pilgrimage to the villa to worship at this unending fount of elixir. It was believed among those simple people of Southern Italy that the count's sperm warded off the evil eye, cured infertility, soothed melancholia and restored youth. He was privileged that long summer to spread joy and jism among the womenfolk in the boot of Italy and was relieved at the age of 13 to be sent to the military academy in Rome.

Greta slid a piece of ripe mango between her lips during his brief pause and the count then continued in a softer tone. The legend of Il Duce was soon to follow him to the capital. Young girls would scale the academy walls to warm his bed with their perfumed flesh. Generals' wives and daughters, the titled ladies of the aristocracy, the matrons of the haute bourgeoisie and the female staff in every grand house were eager to pay their respects and, being a man of noble birth, he was obliged to acquiesce to their caprices.

'Noblesse oblige,' said Greta.

He nodded sadly. The count was pursued across Italy. He went to France to complete his studies, and on to Belgium, Holland, Germany and Hungary. He found no peace among the strict Catholic girls of Southern Spain and, once in a convent in Cadiz, the Mother Superior shed her habit and, bald as an egg, begged him to take her cursed virginity. He stayed at the convent of Our Lady of the Southern Cross for three long days and serviced 47 celibate nuns, the Mother Superior on six separate occasions. The last he heard, she had left the calling and was working behind a bar in La Calle de Los Pecados in Cadaqués, a fishing hamlet in Catalonia.

Upon sailing to America, like the Statue of Liberty, his reputation preceded him. Driven by the limp failings of their husbands, by that new world craving for old world debauchery, those Mayflower princesses and Southampton socialites cast off their bible belts and chastity belts to pay homage to his legendary appendage. Like the idol the carpenter carves from wood then bends down to worship, one touch of a woman's hand and Il Duce would rise like a deity to receive due veneration.

The count had left his DNA in 10,000 women and sired many of the sons of the noble families across the continent. In the next generation, he said with a dark smile, there will truly be a European Union. 'When you are born with great wealth and position, you can either devote yourself to gossip or set out to leave your mark on the world.'

His voice brightened as he explained that it was on this

fair isle of England with its seaside vulgarity and a fear of the foreigner that he was given the respite that allowed him to keep his vow and never again enter the orifices of another woman.

Greta had a lump in her throat.

'Oh,' she said, 'that does seem a pity.'

'If a man cannot keep his word to himself, then he is not truly a man.'

That sounded quite profound and Greta nodded thoughtfully. She couldn't help feeling a little sulky for she was as eager as those 10,000 women across the world to take a glimpse of Il Duce.

Count Ruspoli was silent now, one foot crossing the other, his long legs stretched out beside the jacuzzi.

'Why don't you hop in and join me,' she said. 'It really feels nice.'

'Would you like that?'

'Very much,' she replied.

He smiled and came to his feet. When he slipped out of his shoes, Greta told him to put them to one side so they didn't get splashed.

'Very wise,' he said.

He carried his shoes across the room and placed them on a shelf. He removed his clothes with his back to her and Greta admired his tall athletic frame, his wide shoulders and small waist, his round bottom. When he turned she held her breath. The legend was everything she had imagined. Il Duce was in repose, bobbing between his muscular thighs like a lion resting before the chase.

Count Ruspoli stepped in beside her. He slid forward and his big feet crushed the Villa Mangia Baldini, the pineapple slices went flying and a wave of strawberries and cream swept up her legs. Greta gathered up a scoop from the mixture and remembered that although the count had vowed not to enter his women, he didn't say anything about denying his divine creation from their mouths. She coated Il Duce in pink cream and it grew and grew as it

124

slid down her throat. She stopped for breath, licked it all over like a giant lolly and looked up into his eyes.

'Delicious,' she said.

'You're very good at it,' he remarked.

'I'm still learning.'

The count drew her up closer and ran his fingers over her lips. 'You have the most generous mouth I have ever seen,' he said.

She smiled. 'You didn't tell me why you made a vow not to enter any more women,' she said, and he smiled back.

'It ruins them for the future. Their husbands and lovers will never satisfy them and they spend their lives lost in memory.'

They were quiet for a moment. Greta was dreamily sliding the skin up and down the great rod of his penis. It was like a meditation, oddly comforting. It was like climbing to the top of a mountain and staring out at the universe. You know you are going to have to go down again, but that moment of being there is worth all the effort of the climb. As Greta studied Il Duce, she noticed around the base lots of scars as if someone had taken an axe to a column of marble and tried to chop it down.

'What happened?' she asked.

'Women have taken pleasure in leaving their mark with their teeth, some, as you can see, drew blood and left small wounds, a mark of pride, I believe.'

'Does it hurt?'

'There is no pleasure without pain, Greta May.'

'I know,' she said, and they nodded like two conspirators who have found each other.

She looked closely at the marks. Some had only made it six or seven inches down from the tip. Others were much further, nine and ten, and she dearly wished she had her wooden ruler from geometry for one set of teeth marks she thought was a good 11 inches down the column.

Greta climbed between the count's legs. The attention had made Il Duce grow and it poked at her like a cannon from a castle wall. She scooped up a handful of cream and coated the beast before taking the head between her lips. She sucked it for a few moments like a sweetie then took a breath before sliding her teeth down the shaft. She stopped again, wetting the mast with her tongue, taking a deep breath and going down, down, the cream easing the prodigy deeper into her throat. She thought she was going to gag, but stopped again and took air through her nose until the feeling passed.

The count remained motionless. This was her crusade, her joust with the eternal. She rocked slowly backwards and forwards, easing the head beyond her tonsils and down to the hollow of her throat. The grip she had on the base of the column told her there was still a lot more to go.

Greta took several deep breaths through her nose. She placed her palms flat on the marble outside the count's knees, she wedged her feet against the back of the Jacuzzi and, spiralling slightly, she lowered Il Duce down to the base. When she could go no further, when there was no further to go, and she had taken it all down her gullet, Greta bit the warm skin as hard as she could. She felt the count wince with pain but he didn't move. Greta kept her teeth locked down and only when she was sure that she had left her mark did she push back up on her arms in order to slide the sweet creature from her mouth.

They studied the marks together. The count had a look of astonishment and Greta couldn't help feeling proud.

'You have a divine mouth, my dear,' he said.

'Thank you.'

'I have the distinct feeling, Greta May, that you are going to be a winner.'

'A winner in what, though?' She was puzzled.

'Success, my dear, is the meeting of preparation and opportunity. The opportunity will come. You must be prepared for it when it does.'

Greta had the word *wow* in her mind but managed to stop herself saying it. She held Il Duce in her two palms and watched the tip growing fiery red as she nursed the great column up and down, up and down. She felt it throbbing as if it were about to burst and then it did burst in a vast creamy gush that covered her face and ran into her mouth and the count tasted gloriously of fruit salad.

Chapter Eleven – The Secret

GRETA WOKE EARLY THAT morning feeling refreshed and irrepressibly excited. She was naked as always under the duvet, the sun flooding the room and turning everything golden. She enjoyed nursing the slopes of her protruding hips and thought if she were a sculptor she would make marble mountains of her favourites parts, hip bones and shoulder blades, her plump sulky lips.

Her tummy was almost completely flat in this position and she caressed the indentation of her belly button because belly buttons are terribly neglected. Her pussy was waking, hungry for attention, but Greta decided it would be a good idea to make her wait. She was *so* demanding. Greta grinned and wriggled her toes and ran her palms up over her rib cage to cup her breasts. Her little pink nipples were fizzing and she squeezed them until they hurt.

There, now be good.

It was like the last day of school and after a shower she decided to dress accordingly. She pulled her old school uniform from the back of the cupboard. She beat out the creases with the flat of her hand and thought the blouse looked awfully sweet with its little Peter Pan collar. She looked at the green tartan skirt and thought: Greta May you are *such* a slut. 'You deserve a good smack.' Greta adored the word smack and said it again and again as she smacked her bare bottom: 'Smack. Smack. Smack.'

She held the skirt up to the light. Throughout the fifth year two things had been taking place simultaneously behind the backs of the nuns: as she and her friends were growing taller, surreptitiously each month they turned up the hems of their skirts. Greta was still growing. She was five feet eight-and-a half-inches in her bare feet and the tartan band of fabric barely covered her round bottom as she put it on.

She chose pink panties, a matching satin bra with plenty of lift and thrust and was absolutely certain the designers didn't make such gorgeous things not to be seen. Her white blouse barely met the waistband of her skirt and she almost gagged doing it up to her throat. The gagging feeling made her feel proud and wistful. Thousands of girls had left their marker on the count's column but none had done better than her.

Greta found a pair of white knee socks, pushed her feet into flat shoes and wasn't surprised that she couldn't do up the top button on her blazer. Hats like shoes create character and, when she popped her straw bonnet on her head, in the mirror's reflection was everything the neat clean schoolgirl ought to be.

She squeezed orange juice and was standing up at the kitchen counter eating a strawberry yoghurt from the tub when Tara wandered in all bleary eyed and wrapped in a mammoth dressing gown. She took one long look at Greta.

'You *are* debauched,' she said

'Thank you,' Greta replied and it made Tara smile. 'Did I wake you? I'm sorry.'

'No, it's all right. I've got to write an essay on divorce and the rights of women.' She waved her hand through the air as if at a bothersome fly. 'Don't ask,' she said. 'You don't want to know.'

Greta put the tub down and Tara approached shaking her head. 'Come here,' she said, and as Greta lowered her face Tara licked yoghurt from the corners of her lips, her pointy tongue darting between her teeth. She pulled Greta's bottom lip out with her teeth. She sucked it until it was gorged with blood and Greta remembered Count Ruspoli praising her generous mouth. Greta ran her finger around the inside of the yoghurt pot and manoeuvred her way through the folds of Tara's dressing gown. Tara had nothing on underneath and her sticky finger wormed its way between the pleats and folds of her hot vagina.

'We're going to have to have a big tidy-up, you know.'

'Why,' asked Tara petulantly.

'Richard said so. He's very strict.'

'So's Gustav,' Tara responded and blushed.

'Did he ...'

'I'm not telling you, Greta May. And don't stop, that's lovely.'

Greta turned her finger in a spiral. Tara was rocking back and forth, getting wetter, her face contorting. She went up on her toes and the big dressing gown slipped from her shoulders as she went into spasm. Greta ran her free hand over Tara's bottom and could feel the raised welts left from a thrashing.

'Did you like it?'

Tara was sighing through her tiny orgasm. 'It was lovely.'

Greta slapped her bum. 'No, that?' she demanded.

'No ... Yes ... No.' Tara had to think about it. 'I quite liked it when it was over. Everything sort of glows inside and when Gustav, you know, did it, my whole body melted and the pain went away.'

'I wish they'd told us about it at school.'

'You're getting totally gaga,' said Tara. 'What are you dressed like that for, anyway?'

'For fun. That's what life's for. That's what Aristotle said. Are you seeing him again?'

'Who?'

'Dhaaaa!'

'He gave me his phone number and told me I should call him this afternoon at *precisely* two o'clock.'

'Are you going to?

'Depends ... depends on how my arse feels.'

Greta turned Tara around and her friend let her study the six rosy pink lines that striped her bottom. Greta bent and when she planted a row of kisses on her cheeks she tasted of chocolate.

'I'm going to be left all alone,' Tara said. 'What am I going to do?'

'Stock up on Chunky Monkey,' Greta said and they laughed.

At least it was *her* turn to wash the sheets! Tara had been propped up in a bank of pillows reading a great big leather book when Greta arrived home gorged on fruit salad. Naturally, she had to tell her *everything* and Tara got so wet as Greta described the genetic flaw that runs through the Ruspolis she abandoned the law to feed her ice cream fetish.

Greta glanced up at the clock. It was time to go. Time was always in such a hurry and you have to rush just to keep up with it. She gave Tara's bum a slap, grabbed her satchel and ran out the door.

The builders in the white van were parked outside the same house and one of them dropped the bag of cement he was carrying as she passed.

'Fuck me! That ain't legal,' he said ...

... and his mate replied: 'It is if you don't get caught ...'

... and Greta had no idea what they were talking about.

Mr I Don't Know Who & Don't Want To Know Who was waiting at the end of the platform and his eyes bulged as she tripped along the concourse swinging her satchel. He was wearing a smart suit and had abandoned his briefcase for a silver case of the sort that photographers carry. Greta would soon find out why.

The train burst on to the platform, hissing and sweating, the doors opened and she followed the man to the far back corner. She remained with her back to him and the moment the train pulled away he lifted her skirt, took the sides of her knickers and eased them down from her bottom. His short fingers teased back the firm elasticity of her cheeks and a finger worked its way into her pussy. He was really taking the initiative and carried on manoeuvring his finger back and forth, making her wetter, even when the doors fizzed open at South Ken.

The stern girls and striped shirts rustled their papers, the carriage rocked, the lights flickered and the bald man wedged his silver case between her feet. Did he know it was her last day at work? The last day she would take this train? Perhaps ever! He must have prepared for it, planned his strategy. He climbed up on his case, giving him several more inches, and she felt his plumb sausage poke between her thighs.

Greta bowed her legs, moved up and down, up and down, the choreography of their movements allowing the little chap to pierce the mouth of her pussy and slip into the damp cavern within. She heard a slurping noise over the screech of the train wheels. She noticed the City gent in the bowler hat across the sea of people and could tell by the melancholic cast in his eye that he knew exactly what the bald man was up to and wished he had tried it on days ago. He wiped a tear from the corner of his eye and stared down once more at the *Financial Times*.

For Greta, this wasn't sex. It was just a bit of fun. She was being naughty and silly, dressed as a schoolgirl, a stranger's little cock sliding over her pink knickers and up her crack. At Knightsbridge the lights went out. He gripped her hips and jolted back and forth with gathering fury. She felt a dribble run down the back of her neck and a dribble slip down her thigh as he shot his load and withdrew exhausted.

Green Park. Mind the Gap.

Greta pulled her knickers up and the spunk leaked into the gusset.

'Thank you,' she heard him say, the only words he had ever said, and she stepped out of the carriage on to the platform.

Sticky stuff seeped over the insides of her legs as the elevator rose through the grey miasma underground and it was always a pleasure seeing the trees in the park opposite when she left the station. She was getting lots of lusty stares but pretended she wasn't as she strolled along in her school uniform. It was such fun being a schoolgirl again.

Greta remembered that last year at Saint Sebastian when they all went out on Saturday into the town dressed to kill in their skimpy clothes. The local girls with their piercings and bloated bodies, chain-smoking, eating chips for comfort, would go green with envy, their skinny boyfriends spitting and shouting vulgar things that made the convent girls shake their bony hips and look even prettier. It was curious to Greta that all the rich people she knew were thin and all the poor people she saw were fat.

It was when she was turning 16, during that last year at school, that she began to be aware of the boys in town gazing at her, measuring her breasts, the length of her legs, her tiny waist that she showed to best effect in skinny shirts and slippery hipsters. She had been picked for the lead in a Noel Coward play at the drama society and it was probably the combination of being on stage and being ogled by the chavs in town that persuaded her that her future was in the theatre.

Something had gone wrong.

And it was *all* her *own* fault!

It had probably been a mistake to move in with Jason Wise. He did make promises he didn't keep, that was true, it was true of everyone in the business, and although she had conveniently blamed him for her stalled career, she knew deep down that he wasn't responsible. Jason had actually managed to get her put up for several suitable roles and the fact that she was rarely asked back for a second reading she could only blame on herself, on her lack of presence, a lack of vitality, a lack of that essential, illusive, indefinable *je ne sais quoi!* And she didn't know what *je ne sais quoi* meant, not exactly, but she knew that at those castings she didn't have it. She had been too timid, too self-conscious. She had gone to play a role. Now she knew the trick. You just have to be yourself.

That's the secret.

Be yourself and try to be happy. But first be yourself!

Greta could hear squelchy noises as she tripped along Piccadilly swinging her satchel. She was shamelessly pleased with herself. She was certain every girl had fantasies about having sex with a stranger, having sex in public, having sex on the tube. She had lived all those fantasies at the same time and just loved the feel of the sticky liquids oozing out of her wet pussy as she turned into Bond Street. It was so great to be 19 in a new age when everyone was finally free to be and do whatever they wanted.

Madame Dubarry sniffed the air with appreciation when she entered the shoe shop and Bach was playing a sonata.

'Greta, how fetching.'

'It's not too short, is it?'

'Not for me it isn't.'

Madame Dubarry was wearing trousers for the first time ever. They were very tight across her pert bottom and fell in a saucy flare mid-calf. She wore a white blouse that was open sufficiently to reveal a good portion of her breasts peeking out saucily from a lace bra.

Friday was always busy and that morning they spent so much time on their knees they could have been penitents at Easter. They cooed like birds of paradise as people slipped into new shoes and fluttered their plumage whenever someone showed a second's doubt. They were whipped along on by Wagner and Mahler trumpeting from the speakers, the credit card machine pinged and the till kept up a ringing percussion.

Being secretly conservative, Greta at lunch chose carrot juice and sushi because that was the tradition at

Pret and then went on a long walk through Soho like a criminal visiting the scene of the crime. The Rastas were drumming and the Hari Krishnas were beating cymbals.

Hari Krishna. Hari Krishna. Hari Hari.

She half expected to see Dirty Bill when she peered into the pink aquarium of the sex shop but there was only a crowd of girls giggling as they poked each other with the electric dildos. She turned right and left and left and right but she never found the narrow street with the horse posts and the houses all leaning drunkenly together. She still missed her watch.

That afternoon they worked just as hard and that day they sold a record 137 pairs of shoes. Madame Dubarry looked watery eyed as the clock struck six and the last customer marched out with a red bag on long handles swinging from her shoulder.

'It's going to be so dull without you, Greta, what am I going to do?'

'Don't you have a new girl coming?' Greta said and Madame Dubarry patted her eyes with a handkerchief.

'That's true.'

'You'll soon beat her into shape,' Greta added and they both smiled.

Madame Dubarry became unusually coy. 'Greta, there's one thing I'm simply dying to ask, and it's so bad mannered ...'

Greta shrugged. 'I don't mind ...'

'Count Ruspoli ...' Greta waited. 'Is it true?'

She nodded her head. 'It's true,' she said, and Madame Dubarry closed her eyes and abandoned herself to her imagination.

Chapter Twelve – Bogwash

THE PINK LIGHTS AT Jasmine's made everyone look younger except Jason Wise, she reflected in a rare moment of malice. Show business was the ultimate vanity and at 42 he still hadn't been invited to direct his first film.

But of course I wouldn't, darling, even if they asked me.

Jason was standing away from the bar stroking his goatee with one hand, rolling his wine around the glass with the other. There were wisps of grey at his temples and the early signs of a paunch. The three men with him were leaning forward as if to gather in his words like desert people collecting the dew. Sitting on a stool swigging beer from a bottle was Marley Johnson, his black skin shiny as polished shoes, his face as open as a secret at boarding school. The other two were toffs in pastel shirts, the word *actor* spinning about their floppy haircuts in invisible haloes.

Jason turned as if with some sixth sense towards the entrance as she snaked her way through the amorphous throng towards them.

'Ah, the Fairy Queen has deigned to delight us with her presence,' he said and nearly spilled his spinning wine. 'God, darling, what have you done? You must be on the monkey glands.'

'I must be 19,' she corrected.

'How perfectly dreadful. White wine?'

She nodded and went to kiss Marley's cheeks. He

gazed appreciatively at her long legs below the tartan kilt, up over her cotton blouse with the Peter Pan collar, and when he reached her eyes, his brow furrowed as if he had a faint recollection of having seen her before but was unable to place where. There were lots of young actresses but there was only one Marley Johnson. He playfully flicked the strap on her satchel.

'So, girl, have you come from school or a casting?' he asked

'She's come from a shoe shop,' said Jason and Marley looked confused.

'Is that a new show?'

'No, it's where she sells shoes.' Jason gazed down at his own new loafers to make the point.

Greta turned her back and focused again on Marley. 'So, how are you? It's been ages.'

'It seems like for ever. Even longer,' he boomed and the toffs laughed.

Marley dropped a big arm around Greta's shoulders. He pulled her closer and she was embraced by the peppery cologne of his aftershave. Greta had a special feeling for Marley. After all, he had stripped her naked every night through 60 performances of *Let Thunder Roar*. It was like he was her first lover and you always remember the first. That honour had fallen in fact to a 16-year-old in the back garden one summer. It had lasted precisely two-and-a-half desperate minutes and had left Greta wondering what all the fuss was about.

Jason introduced the floppy hair cuts: Alex and Gregory, actors indeed; each kissed her perfunctorily and as Jason handed her a glass of wine she was reminded of the exhausted feeling that hits the company backstage after an uninspiring performance.

Men who mattered smoked cigars and did the business while girls perched on the arms of leather chairs like bouquets of flowers. Marley was assessing her with big doggy eyes and she found herself doing the same, watching his sensuous lips as he spoke, the muscles expanding and contracting under his white shirt. He glanced round at the girls fluttering their petals. There were corrugations lining his brow.

'So, you're not an actress then?' he asked and shot an accusing look at Jason.

'Marley, I was the girl you stripped naked every night at the National for six weeks.'

'And now you're all grown up,' he said. He gazed at her breasts pushing against the thin cotton of her blouse as if to revive his memory. 'What are you doing now?'

'I'm sorry?'

'What are you in?'

'She *works* in a shoe shop,' hissed Jason.

'Temporarily,' she said.

'Try saying that after a bottle of crème de menthe,' Jason added and the haircuts laughed again.

It was one of those conversations typical of Jasmine's. People wanted to know everyone else's business but were usually too busy to listen, and much too eager to tell everyone their own business. Jason refilled her empty glass.

Greta was dying of thirst and asked for sparkling water, drinking it down, one glass after another. Marley kept his strong arm about her and the boys talked the talk, the TV slot just missed, the soap that was coming up, the new casting agent, their headshots and long shots, the reading at Pinewood next week.

They fell silent and all heads turned as if in reverence for royalty as Tyler Copic strode in with a tall, thin donnish man 'from the Film Council', Gregory whispered, his voice rising like a ringing bell from the depths of his chest.

Tyler Copic threw up his hands as he ambled towards them.

He spoke in a low voice, deadly serious, a California accent.

138

'Two guys are sitting at the bar and one says to the other: listen, buddy, I didn't want to tell you this, but I went by your house yesterday and your wife was in bed with your agent.'

'*What*?' says the other guy. 'You mean *my* agent *went* to my house!'

They roared with laughter.

'Tyler, you old wanker,' said Jason, grinning, raising his glass. 'Wine?'

'Later, Simon hasn't got a lot of time,' he said, glancing at the don. 'Listen, what do you know about Lorca? My manager's reading that play, what's it called, *Blood Wedding*?'

'Not exactly your cup of tea. It's as old as the hills for one thing,' Jason told him.

Tyler shrugged. 'Sammy's an asshole. I just wish I'd get home early one day and find him in bed with my wife,' he said and they all roared heartily once more. He glanced at Greta. 'Catch you later,' he added and combed his hair back with his palms as he followed Simon into a vacant booth.

'Very good friend of mine,' Jason explained and Alex gave himself a little hug.

'I adored, just adored *Pay To Play*,' he said.

'What about *Streets*?'

'Wow.'

They fell silent and sipped their drinks like guests at a wedding after the newlyweds have driven away. Tyler Copic directed edgy, menacing films that people had heard of. His presence had given them a sense of identity. Greta had shared those feelings once and was glad she didn't have those feelings any more. She glanced again at the flower girls perched on chair arms and table tops and knew instinctively that you don't get work as an actress by hanging out, by showing your tits. You work when you know your craft.

The barman plunged another bottle of wine in the ice

bucket and they raised their glasses in a toast.

'To ...'

Jason couldn't decide what and they all stood there playing statues.

'Well?' Gregory demanded.

'To fucking.'

Marley roared and sprayed beer over Alex's pink gingham shirt.

'Bastard.'

Ghosts of blue smoke crossed the ceiling and Greta suddenly remembered that it had been a whole week since she'd smoked a cigarette. Well, except for that one puff. She made a promise to herself that she wouldn't break the rules again and, at that moment, while she was feeling contrite, she was sure she saw Richard at the top of the stairs, just a movement, a shadow, and he was gone. She swallowed her wine in one long gulp.

'I have to pee,' she announced and hurried towards the stairs.

The club was a maze of rooms like Russian dolls one leading to another, one inside the other, narrow corridors curving into flights of stairs that led like a drawing by Escher in circles to nowhere. The bar on the ground floor gave no indication of the size of the premises above and, as Greta turned into yet another corridor she imagined she must have walked the entire length of Dean Street. She was Alice spiralling down the rabbit hole and realised she was completely lost.

Richard was just a trick of her imagination and when she heard the sound of someone on the stairway behind her it was only Jason Wise.

'Ah, *there* you are,' he said.

Marley was following and the two young actors were looking nervous like first-nighters before the show.

Ohmygod, they're going to do me, she thought.

'I have to pee,' she said again.

Jason squeezed by her and opened the end door. She

140

glanced in.

'You're not serious?' she said.

'Greta May, I have never been more serious about anything in my life.'

He beckoned and she entered the men's lavatory, a white tiled space with the smell of pine and bleaching lights that gave her four companions the look of gargoyles with grinning carnival masks.

'You know, girl, all my life I've been looking for that mouth,' said Marley. 'That's one big mouth you got.'

'And no fillings,' she said.

'She's got a sense of humour.'

'That's not all she's got,' said Jason and the boys laughed again.

To complement her large mouth, Marley produced from his Levi's a large cock, not of the dimensions of Count Ruspoli, of course, but big in the normal scheme of things.

Greta watched with cold detachment. If you're going to get done, she was thinking, you may as well make the most of it. She'd had a sneaking suspicion when Jason Wise made her promise to meet him at Jasmine's that fate was being tempted.

Marley was rocking on the heels of his Cuban boots, his cock bouncing jauntily, and Greta was drawn to the shiny purple thing like a moth to the flame, a wave to the seashore, and ran her warm palm up its length to the big fiery head. The others giggled.

'Not so fast, girl. Not so fast.'

She had got carried away, drawing the loose skin over the shaft, watching mesmerised as the head vanished and re-emerged with each thrust. Marley eased down his jeans and jockey shorts and shuffled backwards into a narrow cubicle. He lowered the lavatory lid and sat, his cock rising like a pole over large hairy balls. Her school blazer was pulled from her shoulders. The floor tiles were hard on her knees.

141

'The tip,' he said. 'Slow now, there's no hurry.'

He pulled the tails of his shirt aside and made himself comfortable. Greta studied her subject for a few seconds and as she whisked her tongue over the fine indentation she realised that the top of his cock was the shape of a tiny bottom, the taut mauve skin rigid around two fine openings the size of the holes in a button. She flicked her tongue like a whip across the groove until the large hand buried in her hair guided her mouth down the pole, her hot saliva greasing the way. Greta went slowly up and down, up and down, keeping her lips slack, the movement of her tongue bouncing it playfully against the roof of her mouth.

Marley groaned. 'Get on down, girl. Get on down,' he cried, and held the side of her head in his hands, locking her there so that she became a machine, an air pump blowing him for all she was worth.

It was a relief on her poor knees when the weight was removed from them. Her tartan skirt had been pulled up around her waist. She went up on her toes, her feet left the ground and her smelly knickers were brusquely removed. She kept pumping away, slurping and sucking. She wiggled her arse because she had such a pretty little arse. She was so ashamed she was such a slut and pictured herself in the toilet cubicle sucking cock with three men looking up her pussy and the thought made her fidget even more.

She heard someone spit. She felt the moisture run through her cheeks of her bum and felt the pang of want course like an overflowing river from her lips gripped about Marley's cock to her dripping cunt. Her legs were raised, and one of them, Alex, or Gregory more likely, shoved into her wet slit with a careless thrust that took the wind out of her sails.

As she was lifted higher, Greta was forced further down the trunk of Marley's throbbing monster. Slowly like session musicians they found a rhythm, one pushing, the other pulling, and a stray thought struck her consciousness and what she thought was it was so much better being up here performing than down there in the bar talking about it.

Marley's purple helmet thrust her tonsils aside and she gagged as the silky head lodged at the base of her throat. She was jiggling her tongue, gasping for air, and the boy at the back was riding her like a jockey. Marley was thrusting his thighs up from the lavatory lid as he reached down into the deepest wells of his being and started to come.

The jockey must have felt the vibration at the other end like a charge of energy from Marley's exploding helmet, the hot spunk erupting like molten lava down her throat, through all the channels that led to her vaginal passage to engulf the eager prick prodding at her sopping entrails. Marley's come was like a frothing tidal wave, a come that just kept coming and coming, filling her mouth, her throat, her tummy and prodding at her swollen bladder.

Marley had drawn deep in the well and, before he finished, he withdrew from her inflamed lips to scribble his signature over her face, the creamy jism coating her cheeks, dripping from her gaping mouth, and falling in dollops to her white breasts below her blouse.

'You're the champion,' he said. 'You can suck cock for England.'

She didn't have time to say thank you. She was gasping for air as the actor bringing up the rear shot his wad and she tingled with an exquisite little spasm as her clitoris savoured a warm upsurge of pleasure.

Greta's cheeks burned under the coating of sperm. Her earlobes were scorched by friction, her knees were sore as she settled down on the white tiles. She didn't try to stand, or even look round. Alex in the gingham shirt sat on the seat Marley had vacated, his trousers about his ankles, his little pink sailor standing upright for inspection. She ran her large salty tongue down its length and his whole body

143

shook as if from a shot of adrenaline. It was tiny after Marley's colossus and she rolled it around her mouth like a lump of toffee. He was jigging about, but stopped suddenly.

It was the voice of God.

'Hey, you guys, is this gang busters, or what?'

It was Tyler Copic and they all laughed as if it were the funniest thing that had ever been said.

Alex carried on and she wiggled her little bum. Now, there were four men standing there scrutinising her dripping parts, the lips of her vulva rolled back like the peel of an exotic fruit, ripe and delicious, and she realised as her hand reached between her legs that she hadn't actually climaxed. Not really. A little spasm, nice though it is, isn't a full-on, wow kind of orgasm. With a long finger she stroked the flowering nib of her clitoris.

'Look at the dirty bitch, she can't get enough,' she heard Gregory say and the others chortled.

'You don't have to do that, honey,' Tyler Copic said. 'May I?'

'Be my guest,' Jason told him.

'Wow, you guys,' said Tyler with a sigh.

The aroma of men in rut was clammy in the windowless room, their lusty smell hotly seductive. Greta's skin was sheened in damp. She wanted to be free of her clothes and as if her guardian angel was on her shoulder listening to her thoughts, her school blouse was lifted up over her sticky body. Alex popped his cock momentarily out of her mouth and the little piece of clothing was discarded. Her skirt was removed and she wriggled her white bottom appreciatively.

'That's better, I like to see what I'm fucking,' Tyler said and there was the laughter again. Like schoolboys, she thought.

A tongue was licking her clitoris. It was Tyler's tongue and he had done this a million times, she could tell, slow but steady, firm but smooth, soft as a feather; he was a tongue artist and Greta loved to be tongued. Her stomach quaked. Ribbons of fire snaked through her insides and Tyler at the precise moment pulled out his Oscar winning member and slid it into the pool of Gregory's come.

'That's good, honey. Easy now. Easy as she goes.'

Greta was concentrating on her own pleasure, pressing up from the tiles to meet his languid thrusts, all those clever little pussy muscles clenching and releasing with swiftly growing contractions. He rode her in rhythmic, melodic, gentle movements, probing the pink walls and gossamer fabric of her body, each motion driving the cock in her mouth like a piston deeper down her throat. Time hung suspended as if she had plunged from a high diving board and was plummeting into a deep lagoon.

'Agh. Agh. Aghhh!'

It was her own voice. She released the cock blocking her vocal chords and screamed as she climaxed. Alex had got there at the same time and released his come into her open mouth. The American director, directing from above, drained his cock inside her and lowered her feet to the floor.

'Jeez, that was the first time I've come in ten years.'

Again the giggles. Alex was wedging himself back between her teeth and she milked his little pink cock until it ran dry. He held her there, not sure what to do next and she waited, aware there was more to come and she was ready for it. It wasn't just blood running in her veins. There was fire and passion, grit and brimstone. Once you give into your instincts, give in completely, there is no way back, no way of knowing where it might lead you. Greta had been suppressing this part of her personality. She was 19 and she loved fucking. She was born to be fucked. It was liberating to finally know it. She would pursue sexual pleasure no matter how extreme, how kinky, no matter what the fetish.

Alex was taking deep breaths like he'd just run a marathon. She felt a strange new heaviness somewhere

145

below her stomach and suddenly realised her bladder was about to burst. She went to speak but the moment passed.

A hand, Tyler's hand, she thought, was stroking her bottom. He was panting away like an old steam train going up an incline.

'... you blokes are something else,' he said.

Gregory had already shafted her but was ready for more, buoyed up by Marley's enthusiasm. 'That's one great mouth,' he kept saying, and she took Gregory's soggy cock into her cheek as he slid into place on the lavatory seat. She heard a zip unzip, loud in the confined space, like the rasp of dry chalk on a blackboard. Two hands jerked her knees wider apart and something sticky ran into her anus – soap probably, she'd seen a pump bottle beside the sink. It bubbled out of her with an obscene squelch and a stubby helmet started pressing at her pretty bottom.

'Come on. Come on. You love it.'

It was Jason Wise. So predictable.

'Ride her cowboy,' Tyler said. He'd got his breath back.

Jason drove his plump cock like a boy with a new car carelessly up her arse. He'd spent six months trying and now he'd finally managed it. She'd washed his socks and sucked his cock but this was all he wanted. If only all life were so straightforward.

Greta tried to put some effort into it but she was growing tired. Even excess gets excessive. Jason pumped away and her ears hurt with Gregory clinging on to them. Her body was a sponge dripping liquids, her own and everyone else's, her flesh burned and her jaw was beginning to ache.

She turned off her thoughts and, like a mouse on a treadmill, went through the motions, up and down the cock in her mouth, round and round the cock up her arse until Gregory managed another little squirt and Jason proudly removed his appendage and shot his sperm over

146

her back and down in a gooey trickle between the worn crease of her arse.

There was another still moment. Everyone was sated. Even her.

'You guys all done?' Tyler asked and there was no response.

'Yes, I rather think you have,' Greta replied for them.

'Cos you know, where I come from, you finish with a bogwash. It's traditional.'

Greta didn't know what a bogwash was but soon found out. Gregory stepped away. Her hands were quickly, roughly tied behind her back with the arms of her blouse. She was lifted again by the thighs.

Jason, she assumed, after buggering her, wanted to humiliate her even more. He pushed his soiled cock in her throbbing vagina and a hand gripping the back of her hair guided her head down into the lavatory. Someone hit the mechanism and she was plunged into the deluge. As she pulled backed, gasping for air, Jason Wise beat down on her pussy and submerged her once more below the gushing cataract.

She was terrified and amazed, a wave of contradictory emotions coursing through her, submission, arousal, humiliation, the thrill of the unknown. Being bound was strangely thrilling. She was an explorer exploring her unexplored self and she rose again, gagging for breath as the water refilled.

'You slut. You bitch. You slag,' Jason was saying, riding her for all he was worth, punishing her for something and she wasn't sure what.

The cistern burst into life once more and her head was lowered into the churning water. He pushed her down, deeper down. She couldn't breathe. Air fled in bubbles from her nose and mouth. Her heart was beating so strongly she could hear it hammering in her throat. Her ears pinged as her lungs were about to give out.

As she was on the point of drowning, of dying, Greta

reached a peak of sensation beyond the clouds, beyond her dreams. Her little body was ripped apart by the biggest orgasm ever, a vast, exploding, earth-shattering quake that surged and rippled through her body and gave her the strength to shake her hands free of her bonds. She clenched the side of the lavatory bowl and pushed back, driving up the shaft of Jason's cock, seizing the initiative.

Jason let go with a dribble of come and remained immobile, locked to her arse like a trapped dog. As the pressure lessened, her bladder finally gave way and Greta hosed yellow piss in a steady stream over his stomach, down his legs, his trousers and over his new shoes.

'... bitch.'

'Jeez, you can't get this on the porn channel.'

Jason shook himself free and Marley like a gent eased her shakily back on to her feet. 'That's some pussy,' he remarked as if it were separate from her, a car, perhaps, or a magic ring.

Jason was brushing at his clothes. 'Bitch. Bitch. Bitch,' he was saying.

'Hey, she's all right,' Tyler Copic said, friendly but forcefully. He was the movie director, not Jason. He looked at her. 'When you're in LA, look me up, eh,' he added, and she noticed the miffed look pass across the eager faces of Alex and Gregory.

Jason was wiping piss from his legs with a handkerchief. He looked like he had something more in mind, not that she could think what, but the others were satisfied and shuffled him towards the door as he zipped himself into his wet trousers. He looked back at her for a moment and she realised they had always been in competition and in this, the last round, she had a feeling she had won yet again.

Greta liked the sticky feeling in her sated parts and just dried her frizzy locks under the hand dryer. Her cheeks were pink like petals and her eyes were golden and sparkled with light. She found her knickers, zipped herself into her tartan skirt and buttoned her blouse. She slipped her arms into her maroon school blazer and in the mirror's reflection she had changed from everything the neat clean schoolgirl ought to be to what all the schoolgirls at her convent dreamed of being. Well, all the pretty ones!

As she turned away, the door opened.

It was Richard.

'I don't believe it,' she said.

'I'm sure you do.'

She smiled and he smiled and she liked his good white teeth.

'Are you ready to be carried off to the country?'

'Gagging for it,' she replied.

Chapter Thirteen – Marsham

THE ROAD SLIPPED BELOW the car tyres, the Range Rover rolling through the night like a ship at sea. The lights coming towards them skimmed over the windscreen and Greta felt safe, content, satisfied. Well fucked, actually, she thought, covering her smile with her hand. It had been an eventful week, what with one thing and another, and she was dying to see what Richard now had in store for her.

As she glanced towards him, he patted her leg.

'There's a bag in the back,' he said. 'You can put your clothes in there.'

He spoke in a matter-of-fact tone and she imagined they were still playing that game where she must ask no questions and it was best to just do as she was told. Her life before she met Richard had lacked direction. Now she could see signs for Canterbury and Dover. She was going somewhere.

'Shoes as well. You won't be needing them.'

'Is there a prize?' she asked in a faintly mocking tone.

'That all depends on you,' he replied.

Richard was always so mysterious it was exasperating. She unclasped her seat belt and reached behind her for the bag. Inside the bag, lying at the bottom, was a small maroon leather box. She looked at the box for several seconds and, when she opened it, her eyes filled with tears. Nestling in a bed of blue velvet was her Cartier watch.

She looked at Richard, then back at the box. She thought for a moment that he must have replaced the one she had lost. But how did he know? She hadn't told him. She hadn't told anyone. She had taken a shower in a stranger's pee and that's not really the sort of thing you go around bragging about, sordidly intriguing though it may have been.

The watch showed the same time as the car clock and even in the light of the passing vehicles she could see it was her own watch, not a replacement, but the one her father had given her, the same square face, the inlay of gold, the C on the clasp. She was aching to know how Richard had come by the watch, yet another part of her was enthralled by the mystery, by the flavour of not knowing. She held it to her lips.

'Thank you,' she whispered.

'I'll look after everything until you're ready.'

What did that mean?

What did it matter? She slid from her school blazer and folded it into the bag. She unbuttoned her blouse, pulled the sleeves from her arms and wrapped the material around the leather box to keep it safe. She unhooked her bra and dropped it on the pile before slithering her tartan skirt under her bottom. She wasn't wearing any knickers and assumed Jason Wise had taken them as a trophy. It was just the sort of thing he would do. She pushed her shoes down the side of the bag, pulled the zipper and placed it in the back.

Air from the vent was blowing up her legs. Car headlights scanned her body and she moved restlessly feeling ashamed with the smell of sex wafting from her skin. Five men had deposited their sperm in all her openings and mixed with her own abundant juices the scent was as piquant as a stable, a simile more apt than she realised. Greta's breasts throbbed, jerking faintly with the movement of the car, her pink nipples turning hard as they filled with blood. She was sure there was something

151

wrong with her. Just her nudity, just her own heady perfume, was enough to send her into raptures. No wonder Richard had sniffed her out on the tube.

She sat there nursing her nipples, her damp bottom slippery on the leather seat. Richard turned off the motorway into roads that narrowed into winding country lanes. She saw signs for Deal and Sandwich. The view of the fields was blocked by high hedgerows, the night growing darker, the stars more distant. He slowed almost to a stop before turning into an opening that was so constricted you would never find it unless you knew it was there. The bushes formed a tunnel, slapping the vehicle with vicious swipes as they passed.

The track was several miles long, almost impassable in places, and ended at a grassed square that reminded Greta of the film set for *Madame Bovary*, a TV two-parter in which as a milkmaid her entire dialogue had consisted of the single word *Oui!* The cobbled paths were lit by the glimmer of lamps that must have come from Victorian times and she wondered if they were powered by gas. There were a dozen cottages, squat buildings shaped like loaves of bread with thatched roofs and small windows shiny as eyes behind the flower boxes. They were candy houses from a nursery rhyme, or the house of the three bears that Goldilocks so unwisely entered – eating porridge and taking a nap, indeed! She shook her chestnut curls and felt a delicious quiver run down her back.

The pub was a larger building under the same nest of thatch. It was called *The Black Sheep*, the sign crudely painted and moving almost imperceptibly on big metal hinges. To her left, Greta could see a stone trough and, as Richard rolled to a stop, she noticed the place name Marsham painted clearly by the same naïve hand on a wooden board.

A man leading a horse across the square was approaching and Greta felt so humiliated sitting there with everything on show, completely exposed, and couldn't believe it when Richard lowered the electric window on her side of the car. She hid her own little triangle of thatch beneath her hands. The man leaned in, resting his arms on the window frame, and studied her dispassionately, clucking his teeth, his astute gaze moving down her body until they came to rest on her breasts.

'Evening, Mr Marsham,' he said as if addressing her blatantly erect nipples.

'Hello, Tom. Everything all right?'

'Everything is as everything should be.' He looked up at the sky and then back into the car. 'God's in his heaven and this is ...' he broke off and his face wrinkled with confusion. 'What day is it?'

Richard shrugged. 'Does it matter?' he said.

'Not to me.' The man grinned and glanced back at Greta's heaving chest. His nose was twitching as he caught the fragrance rising up through her fingers. 'You've got a ripe one here, I see, sir. Quite a handful, I imagine.'

'We'll soon break her in, Tom.'

'Oh, aye, I've no doubt,' he said and turned to the horse as it bucked, tossing its head. 'Come on, then, *whoa there*.'

The fly buzzing around the horse's eyes and mouth spiralled up out of sight and then with apparent determination shot through the window into the car and started bothering Greta. She waved her hands and it vanished into the back. She glanced again at Tom as he removed a sugar cube from his pocket and watched the horse lick it delicately from the palm of his hand.

Richard slid the car into gear. 'Let's make a start with the milking, shall we,' he said in a serious tone and Tom nodded.

'Aye, that'll do.' He appeared to pull at an invisible cap and continued towards the trough.

Greta glanced again at the sign for Marsham and then at Richard. His face gave away nothing.

He turned off to the right, passing the pub. Greta could see through the leaded windows lots of country types quaffing jugs of ale. The fly was crawling on her bare shoulder and she flicked it away.

'There aren't too many. You'll get used to them.' He patted her leg once more.

The track pushed through heavy wooden gates and beyond was a house on three floors, a welcoming light behind the windows. Wide stairs led between two columns up to the main door. She thought this was where they were going, but Richard kept on around the side of the building.

At the back of the house, at the bottom of a long dip, were various pens and outhouses, the moon silvering the rooftops and trees. The night had remained unseasonably hot, the moon three-quarter full and her body shone with a milky glow as she followed Richard across the yard. She could sense the tang of the sea, crisp and salty, not too far away, the smell of cut grass, everything growing and bursting with life. They entered a stable lit by a couple of low-watt bulbs, the smell of horses and fresh hay lush and familiar.

In the first stall, close to the door, was a grey mare with a foal no more than a few months old, its legs so spindly and fragile Greta wanted to take it in her arms for a cuddle.

'She's beautiful.'

'Yes, we're very proud of her,' Richard said and patted the mare. 'And you, too, Delilah,' he added, rubbing his nose against the horse's nose. It was a sweet gesture and completely out of character she thought.

Greta stroked the foal. 'What's her name?' she asked, forgetting herself, and he glanced up.

Above, screwed into the woodwork, was a brass nameplate with Delilah and, next to it, attached in a temporary way by a single tack, the brass disc contained her name.

Greta?

Her lip dropped. She looked back at the foal, at the name plate, back at Richard. That's not fair, she was thinking. She liked her name and he'd stolen it. He watched her, waiting for her to speak, but she showed great restraint in not saying a word.

'Here,' he said, moving to the next stall where a chestnut pony stared at her with big glossy eyes.

Her name was Thunder. Greta tickled her ears and the pony pushed into her shoulder. She rubbed its neck and felt in an odd way that she was being made to feel welcome.

The third stall was empty. The brass plate with the name Pegasus on the wooden beam above was so shiny it had obviously only just been screwed into place.

'Here we are,' Richard said, and patted her bottom in the same way as he had patted the flanks on the mare.

'But ...' She didn't complete her question. Richard pointed at the lens of a camera trained on the stall from a fixture on the roof and his look made it clear that this was not the time for questions.

On the shelf made from the cross spars supporting the back wall were five leather bands, natural in colour, each with a double buckle, a brass ring and the smell of new shoes. Greta remembered the girl in the video wearing exactly the same thing, the leather adornments and nothing else.

She kept still, aware of the camera as Richard buckled the straps in turn to her wrists, ankles and neck. He used a spring clip to connect a leather lead to the ring at her throat and connected the other end to a metal eye screwed into the side wall. When the job was complete, he didn't say anything, but ran his palms down her bare arms in the way a mother might her child, very expressive, and she felt oddly content to be in Marsham with Mr Marsham, even if it was all a bit weird. He pointed again at the camera.

'You do not have permission to remove the lead,' he said. 'It's strictly against the rules.'

With that he turned and made his way back through the stable, pausing to pat Delilah as if to say good night. He switched off the lights and Greta stood in the darkness wondering what to do. She gazed out, wondering if Richard was going to return, but he had left for good and the night was completely silent.

The stall was carpeted in fresh hay that prickled her skin when Greta lay down. She rolled into a ball, clutching her knees, but just as she was getting comfortable, she felt a tweaking in her bladder and panicked. She had forgotten to go to the bathroom and should have asked Richard when she had the chance. Now she didn't know what to do and just wished there was someone there to tell her. She was sure there were all sorts of rules but he had told her just one: you do not have permission to remove the lead.

She pressed the spring clip at her throat. The faintest touch and it opened. She could slip away for a few minutes. It wouldn't do any harm. She glanced at the silver eye of the camera and imagined Richard watching her on a monitor somewhere in the big house.

Greta thought if she used all her willpower she could hold it until morning, but the more she thought about it, the more urgent her need to go. The pressure was building like the tide against a sandcastle, pressing in, lapping in waves at her insides, squeezing her intestines. 'I can hold it. I can hold it,' she said, and she said it because she knew she couldn't.

She writhed and wriggled. Straw slithered up her nose and up her bum. She was naked, her pubic hair no longer a silky fleece but a matted nest. The sperm coating her thighs and slicked through her bottom had dried, the odour of sex clinging to her like a beast in rut. Greta was irredeemably debauched and dirty and Richard knew what he was doing keeping her tethered to a lead in a stable. He was right. She knew that. But she couldn't hold her bladder a second longer.

When she finally squatted down at the back of the stall it was such a relief nothing happened. She pressed and pushed. She flexed her muscles, gave her bum a wiggle, and then it came gushing out of her, a single torrent of steamy urine that soaked her feet and wet the straw and dribbled down the insides of her legs. She had been gritting her teeth, holding her breath, and now she let the trapped air out in a long sigh. There's nothing like a really good piss, she thought, and grinned with satisfaction when she remembered the look on Jason's face when she peed over his new shoes. Greta wiped away the last drips with her fingers and was tempted to give her clit a little time but not with the camera so brazenly watching.

She settled down in the straw and through the open door could see the sky pierced by stars, the moon slipping behind the horizon. Greta had no idea of the time but was happy that Richard had found her wristwatch. With that thought in mind, she slipped into a deep sleep and her eyes only opened to the sound of the cock crowing.

Greta wasn't sure where she was for a moment. She stretched her limbs and, as she rolled over, the lead jerked the leather collar and she was fully awake.

Daylight was giving colour to the interior of the stable and as Greta stood, shrugging off the stiffness in her legs, Tom came bowling in whistling to himself. He wore a plaid shirt with a stained waistcoat, his hands thrust in his trouser pockets. He had long exaggerated sideburns, a mop of curly hair and was a good deal younger than Greta had first thought. She was a bit disappointed that it wasn't Richard who had come to wake her, but Tom gave her a dimpled smile as he approached and she felt oddly contented.

'You're up then, are you.'

She nodded.

He unhooked the lead from the stable wall. He turned her round, brushing the straw from her shoulders and back. 'Got to keep you looking your best now,' he said and made particular effort with her bottom, his fingers sliding roughly into the crease.

She followed him outside where a golden Labrador sat on her haunches waiting. She sniffed Greta thoroughly and, when she was satisfied she was no threat, she turned her big watery eyes on Tom.

'There you are, Grace, you look after her now, there's a good girl.'

He patted the dog's head and she walked along beside Tom, her gait slow and steady, identical to her master. Greta found herself ambling along the same way and felt silly.

Across the yard, bad-tempered hens were stamping noisily around their enclosure, waiting to be fed. The peacocks in the adjacent pen sang out shrilly, fanning their tail feathers in displays of male vanity. 'Don't mind them, missy,' said Tom, pulling at the lead, and she trotted along behind Grace.

At the furthest distance from the stable, the brick shed was occupied by five goats, a big billy goat with curling horns and aggressive beady black eyes, and four nanny goats huddled together in one stall as if for protection. What struck Greta was the smell. Unlike horses, goats had a strong, sour odour and inside the barn it made her tummy churn.

It didn't seem to trouble Tom. He was still whistling the same tune. Grace sat obediently in the doorway watching, and Greta noticed that another camera was recording her every move. It made her self-conscious at first but it wasn't long before she forgot it was even there.

Tom collected a low, three-legged stool and a metal bucket that was so clean she could see herself vaguely distorted in the reflection.

'Have you done this before?' he enquired and she

wasn't exactly sure what he was asking but she was sure that whatever it was she hadn't, not without any clothes on anyway.

She shook her head.

'You'll soon get the hang of it.'

He sat her down on the stool, spread her thighs and pulled the rump of the nearest goat towards her, inserting the animal's udders in her uncertain fingers.

'Squeeze and pull,' he said.

She squeezed and pulled, and nothing happened.

'Like a bellows, evenly, slowly.'

She tried again and the goat shrieked and kicked its hind legs. Tom spanked the animal's backside.

'Come here. Like this,' he said.

But he didn't demonstrate on the goat, he demonstrated on Greta. He took her breast in his weathered hand, squeezed from the undercurve in an upward motion, pushing the flesh towards her nipple, which he now took in his free hand, rolling it between his fingers in such a way that she half expected to see a stream of liquid flowing from her breast.

'You got it now?' he asked, and she shook her head.

You are such a slut, Greta May. Such a slapper. You're incorrigible.

'Not quite,' she said, shamelessly proffering her untouched breast.

He leaned over, squashing the taut flesh, rotating the teat until it tingled and the bottomless reservoir inside her leaked, drooling creamily between her legs. She panted for breath.

'Are you ready now?'

She swallowed hard and nodded.

Greta tried again and this time it worked. A jet of translucent milk squirted from the goat's udder, hissing as it hit the sides of the metal bucket, and she was thrilled she could actually do it. The animal wriggled uneasily, then settled back and, like her, enjoyed the sensation, pushing its hot udders into her hands. Greta pulled and squeezed and squeezed and pulled, first one, then the other, each squirt strangely sensual. It was like a cock shooting its load and she blushed she was so ashamed of herself.

When the bucket was full, Tom took it and emptied the milk into a large vat.

'And the next,' he said.

He stood behind her making a roll-up as she edged the stool beside the next goat, plopping her bottom down and starting again. She squeezed and pulled, the warm milk spewing into the bucket, a fine spray coating her cheeks and hair. The ripe smell of goats and hay and Tom's cigarette was hypnotic, invigorating. Greta felt mediaeval. She could have been a milkmaid all her life and thought how much better she would have played her scene in *Madame Bovary* if she'd had more experience, how the actress is born from experience and passion and suffering. She glanced up momentarily at the camera.

Tom emptied the bucket and she worked on number three, the smallest of the goats, a chocolate brown creature with pale nervous eyes. It fidgeted and kicked, squirting Greta's chest, the warm liquid dribbling down over her belly into her pubic hair. She was growing stained and smelly, her body wet, sticky, perfumed in goat's milk.

'Always a bugger that one,' Tom said as he took the bucket. He emptied the milk into the vat. The Labrador watched his every move.

Tom leaned down to return the bucket and twiddled her nipple affectionately. Greta moved the stool beside the last of the goats, a tall, dignified animal aware of what had to be done and determined to make the most of it. The nanny goat had learned that her purpose was to be used as nature intended, and Greta felt as if she had made a friend when the milking was done and the goat turned awkwardly in the confined space to lick her cheek.

Tom emptied the bucket. The camera hummed, turning on its axis as Greta went to join him. As she crossed the barn, she entered the billy goat's line of vision and it rose on its hind legs, bucking on its tether and snapping its teeth. He could smell the milk on her and in this place he imagined all the nanny goats belonged to him. Greta froze, covering her breasts, her mouth open, her will consumed by the beast's savage lust.

'Bloody devil,' Tom yelled, raising his hand in a threatening gesture that made the goat back away. 'Never mind him, girlie,' he said, yanking her lead.

The billy goat stayed in its stall, hissing and drooling, kicking its cloven hoofs against the woodwork. Greta glanced over her shoulder, the brute's black eyes gripping her in their lurid gaze, and only when Tom tapped the side of the vat did she pay attention. Her heart was pounding, her breasts rising and falling.

Tom watched, an indulgent smile on his lips. 'Now then,' he said, adding a crumbly white substance to the vat of milk before handing her a long wooden paddle. 'That's the live culture, work it in,' he instructed. 'Nice and easy.'

Greta stirred the milk, turning the paddle using her two hands. Tom reached for a jar and added two tablespoons of powder.

'Vegetal rennet,' he told her and he glanced momentarily at the billy goat as she looked up. 'Everything organic, girlie,' he added.

They moved to the side wall where the scrubbed counter contained rolls of muslin and numerous knives and tools.

Greta was studying one of the cheese moulds when Richard stormed into the barn with such a furious expression even the he-goat stopped bucking against its tether. Richard was wearing breeches, a full white shirt and in his hand he carried a riding crop which he used to slap the side of his black leather boots. His hair seemed more lush, and his blue eyes sparkled with fury.

Ohmygod, it's Heathcliffe, she thought.

'If you wouldn't mind,' he said softly, in his nice voice, turning and marching off.

Tom followed, grabbing Greta's lead, the Labrador joining the parade, the peacocks calling, the hens squabbling. Delilah and Thunder were tied to the rail marking the end of the yard and they turned to watch their progress. Richard strode into the stable and stopped at her stall. He kicked randomly at the straw.

'You'd better get this cleared up,' he said, directing his instructions at Tom. Greta opened her mouth to say something but nothing came out. When she noticed the bowl with cereal and a big glass of orange juice on the table at the end of the stable she realised she was hungry. It had been left for her and just seeing it placed there so carefully made a tear jerk into her eye.

She glanced back at Richard. Passion has a dark, violent, tumultuous side and Greta saw its face in his features. She gazed at him, trying to make him look back at her, but he turned on his heels and marched out. They followed him to the fence where the horse and pony were tethered. Grace barked, a short, sharp bark of uncertainty.

'Shush, there, shush,' said Tom.

Richard was standing at the low gate. On the wooden posts there were four hooks, two at the bottom on one side, two a little higher on the other. Richard threw a horse blanket over the top of the gate and Greta didn't need to be told what to do. She had made a mess of her sleeping quarters and deserved to be disciplined. Tom spread her legs and Greta wasn't completely surprised as she bent forward that the rings on the leather straps around her ankles and wrists fitted exactly over the hooks.

She made herself comfortable, her breasts hanging low on one side of the gate, her spread bottom on the other, the taut smooth plain of her hips tapering to her waist. At the top of her thighs her vulva pushed out from the curly dark hair with its ferment of semen and goat's milk, the sun reaching parts of her body that before had always been hidden. Richard ran the side of the crop between her gaping lips and she could see the leather slicked and shiny as he took it away.

She wondered why there was a delay and, leaning forward to peer between her legs, she observed Tom making his way back laden down with a tripod and digital camera. He gave them to Richard as if with distaste for such gadgets and Richard focused the lens directly up her bum. She gave it a wiggle, even though she knew full well that you should never react to the camera.

The Labrador silently watched, its pink tongue lolling from its mouth. The horse and the pony seemed to have lost interest and gazed into the distance as if in anticipation of a gallop across the fields. Greta lifted her head. The long meadow dipped and then rose steeply to a knoll of trees, the blue sky beyond. Except for the hum of insects, the air was still and she could think of nothing more splendid than her own submissive body displayed for punishment on a summer's day in England. Her bottom was open, winking lasciviously, her labia throbbing, moist with the ooze of feverish arousal.

'Six each, I think, Tom,' she heard Richard say, and a shiver ran through her.

'Yes, that should do it.'

Richard began. She glimpsed him for just a second before closing her eyes. He had been slapping his palm with the riding crop and now brought it down with a heave across the bare cheeks of her trembling buttocks, the pain of that first lash painting a red line across the firm silky flesh. She opened her mouth to howl and her voice vanished in all that space. The dog barked, softly, deep in its throat, and she heard Tom shush her again.

She tensed up and the second stroke wasn't as painful as the first. She howled anyway. It was expected. She pushed her bottom up to meet the third, absorbing the stroke, transmuting the pain inexplicably into pleasure. Richard paused for a second. Tom blocked her view but she was sure he was adjusting the camera. He returned, swiping the air with the crop and the sound was worse than the lash of it crossing her skin.

She clenched her muscles once more and her hips jerked involuntarily as he administered three strokes in quick succession, three lightning strikes so quick she had not been expecting them. One, two, three, swish, swish, swish, and the fire raged across her flesh raising crimson welts so immaculately painful it was both a surprise and a relief when Tom suddenly tossed cold water from a bucket over her jutting backside. She imagined this was how they did things in the country and was glad of a moment's repose while Tom took the crop and Richard fussed again with the camera.

Her bum still blazed. Water dripped from her pussy and ran down her legs. She had taken six strokes with a riding crop and closed her eyes tightly as Tom stepped up to apply the second set.

'Are you ready, girlie?' he said.

But it wasn't really a question. The crop came down like the strike of a red hot sword, like a hammer against an anvil, cutting deep and sending waves of pain down her legs and up her arms, so fierce she almost pulled the hooks from the fence posts. Richard was broad and muscular. But Tom had a countryman's strength and seemed to relish his task, the crop meeting her scolded flesh in a fresh wallop that made liquids spring from her nose and eyes and tortured pussy, a great seepage of spittle, sweat, drool and tears. Her clitoris was sparkling, obtruding from its cowl of pink inner lips, the channel of her pussy slippery wet, warm and creamy.

Number two. Number three. Number four. Number five. The same pause in between, the same solid whack that numbed her and sent her body into wild shuddering spasms. Her eyes were glued shut; her breath was laboured. She was counting the strokes off to herself, biting her tongue, howling like a beaten dog, like a lost soul, her insides turning, her body smelling of goats and sperm, running with sweat.

The sixth came down like its five companions. Her arse was a roaring fire but the pain like a breaking wave rolled over the flames in a steamy crescendo like nothing she had ever known before, her body erupting in a strange ecstasy that left her slumped over the gate spent and delirious. She didn't scream, she didn't howl, she felt the contractions pumping out her orgasm and the feeling was luxurious.

Tom brought it to an end with another bucket of water, tossed at her rear as you would pitch water over two mating dogs, and she thought she would have a word with him about that at the appropriate time. Richard was behind the camera, recording everything and she felt so comfortable stretched out she was almost sorry to be unhooked from the fence posts.

She turned. Richard was walking away. He climbed on the grey mare and rode off without looking back.

Chapter Fourteen – Wildchild

TOM STOOD THERE, HANDS resting on his waistband, a look of admiration about his leathery features.

'You did all right,' he said, taking her lead, and the faint air of pride she felt made her breasts swell as she followed him back to the stable.

On the shelf was a wooden pot in the shape of a barrel with brass rings and an ill-fitting lid. It contained a sticky unguent that Tom scooped out and slapped over her bottom, working it in, running his fingers into the crack. The fiery glow soon faded and, when he was satisfied, Tom did something she had not been expecting: he planted a kiss on each of her bum cheeks and she thought what is it about men and arses? They want to kiss them, lick them, spread them wide and, most of all, they want to spank them. Wallop them. Give them a good thrashing. They want to see a girl's buttocks glowing pink, striped in red weals and slicked with moisture. Then they want to kiss them and lick them and nurse them with creams, preparing them for another spanking.

Weird. But at least she had learned her lesson: no more peeing in her own bed.

Greta squirmed, arching her back, deliberately pushing out her bottom, but Tom had done with her bum for now and produced a broom of the sort witches fly around on in fairytales. His glance along the stalls made it clear that she was to sweep out the entire stable and she took a deep breath as she set about the task. Her body after the thrashing was damp and the dust coated her skin in a fine gritty layer. The flies were devils buzzing around her wet parts and no matter how many times she swatted them aside they made their way back again.

Tom left with Grace trotting along at his side, and returned carrying a fresh bale of hay on his shoulder. He had taken off his shirt and the waft of male sweat was so heady it made Greta's breasts noticeably perky. She watched him break open the bale with his bare hands, muscles rippling, his stomach flat above a broad belt and she remembered her first taste of leather gagged and tied to Richard's bed. She cast her mind back and it seemed like a lifetime ago.

Greta worked methodically, starting from her own stall, then moving into Thunder's stall, which was rank with pony dung and she thought that was unfair because it was much messier than her own. Greta – Greta the foal, that is, not Greta the girl – watched, fearful and fascinated as she swished the broom around its legs and the animal did a little dance as if she were playing. Greta put her arms around its neck to blow in its ears, the baby nuzzling all furry and warm against her shoulder.

'Come on, girlie, no rest for the wicked,' said Tom.

He was following behind, spreading fresh hay in the stalls. She worked faster, flicking the broom in the corners and sweeping the pile out the door to the wooden container at the side of the building. There were two scoops with short handles like dustpans, and although she was careful lifting the soiled hay, flecks of dung turned to pale streaks on her arms and chest. She tried to brush it away but that only made it worse.

Grace had followed her out of the stable and as Greta watched her quaffing water from a bowl, she ran her tongue over her own parched lips. She rubbed her tummy when it rumbled. She was dying of thirst and starving hungry. She had milked four goats, shed simply gallons of liquids being cropped and worked up a sweat sweeping out the stable. Greta watched the Labrador as if in a trance

167

and only came to when a cart rumbled noisily into the yard. The driver teased a whip over the flanks of a sleek golden brown mare clopping along the path.

'Whoa, there, whoa,' she heard, and at that same moment Tom appeared at the stable door. He didn't speak, but indicated with his thumb and she hurried back inside.

Tom was setting her food down on the floor. She wasn't sure why the plate and glass had been moved from the table; why the spoon had been taken away. She didn't really know why she'd been thrashed, aside from the general obsession with her bottom. Richard must have known she would need to pee when he secured her to the leash and what it all suggested was that she should just accept everything and see where it led her.

Tom collected a brown glass bottle from the shelf and shook out a yellow pill with V400 on the surface. He placed it between her lips and she swallowed it down with the orange juice; at least it was in a glass, and she couldn't recall anything ever tasting quite so delicious.

Bits of dung where she had tried to wipe her body clean clung still to her fingers and although it was tempting to pick off the strawberries and mango arranged on the top of her cereal, she chose instead to go down on her hands and knees and sucked them up between her teeth. The cereal was awash in goat's milk and she lapped it up with her long pink tongue. Each mouthful was so yummy she wanted to bury her face in the bowl and did just that, chewing and licking at the same time. Tom watched and when she was finished, he patted her head and she gazed up at him with big green eyes full of contentment.

He didn't say anything, but tousled her hair and then led her out to where the cart had stopped by the gate at the bottom of the yard. It was stacked with turfs, row upon row crammed tightly together and taller than the tall man waiting there with an unlit roll-up jammed between his teeth. He was a younger version of Tom and wore a leather waistcoat over his bare chest, grass-stained jeans and boots.

Greta had completely forgotten that she was naked and didn't feel at all self-conscious as the man watched her approach, his grey eyes running over her curves, her legs, her breasts standing out from her chest, the pink buds smugly rigid. Grace was trotting along at her side and Greta enjoyed being out in the fresh air with the sun warming her skin.

'This is the first lot, then, Tom,' the driver said and lit his cigarette. His eyes still on Greta although the inspection wasn't at all like the lustful stares of men on the Underground, more a countryman's regard for a prize pony.

She flicked her mane obligingly and he grinned.

'Don't know why he don't just seed it,' said Tom in response, gazing at the turfs.

'Ours is not to reason why.'

'Aye, Alex, ours is ...'

'... to go and have a pint ... or two,' said the younger man, interrupting. 'Bradley's just opened the bar.'

'So there's more to Alex Caldwell than meets the eye, is there?'

'You ain't seen nothing yet,' the younger man said and ran his hand through the coins in his pocket.

Greta looked from face to face. Their words sounded oddly like dialogue. She didn't speak. This was role play, it was amusing, and she kept up the game when Alex stepped down from the cart, bent over and slapped his hands, calling her to him.

'Here, girl. Come on now.'

She bounded over, Grace still at her side. Alex stroked the dog before turning to her. He twisted her nipples, as if testing them, and she let her tongue hang out obligingly. He ran his hand through her bush, then rubbed the tips of his thumb and first finger together.

'He's found himself a nice wet one,' he remarked, glancing at Tom. Alex ran his fingers under his nose and then slapped her backside. 'Bit of a pong though, you want to give her a wash down.'

'Aye, it's the goats what does it.'

Tom secured the mare while Alex lowered the tailgate at the back of the cart. Greta noticed another camera set up on a tripod behind the fence.

'Where does he want this lot then?' she heard Tom ask.

Alex gestured towards the fence. 'Piled up here for the time being.'

Tom turned to Greta.

'Neatly, now,' he instructed. He unhooked her lead before glancing back at Alex. 'I'll just get little Thunder inside, she gets skittish in this weather.'

'You spoil that pony and you'll ruin her,' said Alex.

But Tom just waved over his shoulder and ignored the remark.

While Tom was leading Thunder back to the stable, Alex filled a bucket of water for the mare. He stood back and watched Greta climb the cartwheel, her legs like scissors opening and closing. He then collected another bucket of water which he placed beside the cart in the shade.

Greta was tapping her lips with a fingertip, considering the ranks of folded turf and, when Alex stood up from setting down the bucket, he was at eye level with her bottom. He held his palms as if in front of a fire before rubbing them together.

'Lovely. Nice couple of loafs fresh from the oven,' he said and sniffed the air. 'Delicious.'

She smiled. He was funny and had a twinkle in his eye.

Tom was on his way back. 'What about that pint?' he called and Alex patted his pocket once again.

The men delayed a moment, studying her as scientists would a chimp. Greta leaned forward to balance herself, spread her legs across the width of the cartwheel, and hoisted one of the turfs on to her shoulder. She climbed down, supporting the roll of earth with one hand, and carried it to the fence. As she went back for the next one, the men lost interest and ambled off down the lane. Grace lumbered along behind them.

Greta repeated the action, stepping up on the cartwheel, shouldering the next turf to the fence and going back again, the work so bracing after the months in a shoe shop she enjoyed flexing and stretching her strong young muscles. The turfs were dry, but her body was bathed in perspiration and the earth turned sticky. Smears of mud slicked her shoulders and arms, her chest, it ran between her breasts, the soil clinging to the creases around her joints and crumbling into her grubby pubes, the verdant smell adding to the whiff of goat's milk and her own orgasm under the crop.

She paused to think about the thrashing and had absolutely no idea how it worked, how two men flogging her most intimate parts should produce such deep and abiding satisfaction. Such strange pleasure. Just thinking about it made the flame of arousal flare up in her once more. The breath caught in her throat. She turned her nipples between her thumb and finger and a trickle of sweat ran down her back. Her hair was hanging in knots, her face was streaked and the unguent leisurely applied to her tanned arse was varnished in a fresh layer of mud that drew out the sting. She was naked, natural ... 'I'm organic,' she declared with a grin, a part of the summer setting. She felt as if she belonged, that she was a piece of a puzzle slotted into the appropriate place.

Greta gripped her hands behind her back, stretching every tendon, the cute lip of flesh on her tummy growing flat and muscular. At the beginning, carrying just one roll of earth had been as much as she could manage, but with the turfs within reach on the back of the cart, it was just as easy to carry two, the stack as it grew taller beside the fence giving her an air of purpose and satisfaction.

Not that she was in a hurry. Greta had no sense of time or urgency. She had no appointments. No clothes. She was at one with the rhythms of nature. Even the camera was as much a part of the landscape as the trees on the hillside. The peacocks were still fanning out their feathers and the mare was patiently regarding the view across the fence. Greta admired her nobility and calm. She remembered hard-working, long-suffering Boxer from *Animal Farm*. If all the creatures had behaved with equine dignity and selflessness, the revolution would have succeeded and they all would have lived happily ever after. Horses, she concluded, were simply the best of all animals.

Greta stroked the mare as she gazed across the meadow. There wasn't a breath of wind. Even the magpies on the barn roof had no energy to fly, and the insects had lost the will to be irritating. There was silence except for the hum of the earth, the turning of the sky.

She glanced along the path. The village was hidden from view. No one could see her. Tom had tossed the lead over the side of the cart. She could cross the fields to the sea, walk the coast until she arrived at Dover or Deal. They couldn't be far. If she wanted to go there was nothing to stop her and it struck her that it was the last thing on her mind. She was there in Marsham, collared and mud-caked, strapped and stripped of her own free will. She was where she wanted to be. Ever since she was little, Greta had felt the need to run to the mirror for reassurance but that cruel dependency had gone.

A smile crossed her lips as she considered how far she had come playing the role Richard had created for her, how far and how quickly. There was a part of herself, deep and dark, a tiny seed in a dry fibrous husk that had been thirsting for moisture. Richard must be an Aquarius, she reasoned, the water bearer. He had awakened her thirst with a mysterious elixir. The seed had burst from its wrapping. It was growing, spreading its wings and she wanted to fly high in the clear blue sky and reach the heights of her nameless desires and fantasies, play Richard's game until she won the prize.

Greta's throat was suddenly parched but she decided to finish stacking the remaining turfs before rewarding herself with a drink and worked harder, the sweat pouring from her, coating her entire body in mud.

The water in the bucket beside the cart was crystal clear, sparkling now that the sun had shifted the angle of shade. She stared at the high piles of turfs and wiped her palms on her bottom. She cupped her hands, but realised as she was about to lower them into the water that they were ingrained with dirt. It crossed her mind to tip a little water out and wash her hands, but it was easier to go down on her knees, lean over and drink from the surface. She was a wildchild and she loved it. She lapped at the water and it seemed to taste so much better this way, on all fours. She submerged her face and swallowed in great gulps, dipping her head deeper into the bucket as she drank.

She drew back, tossed her hair, the drips glistening like jewels in the sunlight. She stretched on her toes, supported her weight on her hands and wriggled her bottom as she dipped her head below the water. It was so divine she stayed there, holding her breath, and didn't hear Tom and Alex returning from The Black Sheep. They had stopped to watch her and when she became aware of their presence she felt a flash of embarrassment that she masked behind a smile, staying in character.

'Very nice,' Tom remarked.

'Can't think of anything more gratifying,' said Alex, 'than the sight of a healthy young creature with its 'ead in a bucket.'

She was on all fours, covered in mud, warmed by the sun, her hair standing out like a haystack. Alex approached and brushed water from her cheek. She nuzzled his leg and felt him stiffen inside his blue jeans. She pushed against the swelling flesh like a pony pushing at a door and he stroked her hair, delaying the moment until it was just too much for him.

'Here we are then, girl. Here it is.'

He unzipped his pants and unveiled a long, hard cock faintly tasting of beer and bar smoke as it slid between her lips. She ran her mouth down the shaft, in and out, flicking the tip with her tongue, and down again, taking its length deep into her throat because she knew the deeper it went the more they seemed to like it. She bit down gently with her teeth. She felt the tremor run through his thighs and then she felt something else.

Her bottom cheeks were being spread. Tom stuck a finger through the sticky ring of her arse, worked it in and out several times, then replaced it with the probing head of his throbbing member. He lifted her thighs, pushed in hard, filling her back passage right up to the cervix, and being there in the gorgeous weather with a cock in her mouth and another up her arse just seemed like the most natural thing in the world.

All the water she had consumed had irrigated her vagina and as the urgent vibrations pressed down on her clitoris she began to turn liquid and her muddy body went into spasm.

Ohmygod, I'm coming. I'm coming. Fuck me. Fuck me. Fuck me rigid. Ohmygod.

She rocked back and forth, sliding her mouth down Alex's shaft, pushing back into Tom's erection. Alex started to come and grabbed the back of her hair. He rammed the trunk down her throat and the taste was soursweet like warmed goat's milk when his sperm washed over her taste buds. Tom, too, was reaching the critical moment and pushed deep into her arse, coming copiously and slipping out slowly on a sloppy tide that ran into her pulsing pussy. Her stomach muscles clenched and her climax burst from her like a cork from champagne.

'*Ohmygod,*' she gasped as Alex pulled out of her mouth and she felt a wave of pleasure and a jot of irritation because she had abandoned her role and spoken.

Tom had lowered her thighs and, still on all fours, she observed Richard strolling unhurriedly across the yard, not looking at them, but scrutinising the neat towers of turf.

'Nice job,' Richard said, speaking to Tom, who nodded in agreement as he hooked his withering cock back into his pants.

'Yep, all done, Mr Marsham,' he answered. 'We were just going to get on with the cheese.'

'So I see.'

Tom laughed.

'In a manner of speaking,' said Alex.

'I'm going to have a spot of lunch, Tom,' Richard then said. 'You can send Pegasus up when she's finished.'

'Aye, right you are.'

She was disappointed that Richard didn't even glance in her direction and then, to make it worse, he put his arm around Alex and moved him to one side.

'So, how are things going?' she heard him ask, but didn't hear Alex's reply.

Tom clipped her lead back in place, the strap dangling. As they were crossing the yard, Richard called.

'You should give her a wash down, Tom, you know what old Bradley's like.'

'Aye, I do an' all,' he replied, and the two men exchanged knowing smiles.

Tom continued and Greta followed in a carnal haze. She was sweaty and sensuous, but the serene feeling that had taken possession of her turned to terror as she entered the milking shed and the billy goat charged, looming up with obscene longing, and it was only the tether at his throat that prevented it seizing her in a satanic embrace. Tom grabbed the cheese paddle and went on the offensive, and the he-goat kept struggling, trying to get at

175

her. Greta was shaking with fear, rooted to the spot, her hands covering her pubis, the goat leering with unruly lust at her muddy body.

'Down, down, you filthy beast,' Tom yelled, striking the goat with the paddle until it dropped down on all fours and backed away spitting and stamping. 'If we didn't keep him the ladies wouldn't give milk, see,' he explained. 'Come on, girlie, I won't let him near you.'

She edged her way back to the milk vat, her hands trembling as she gripped the sides.

'Just life on the farm, don't let it get the better of you,' Tom said, and he wasn't gentle, just matter of fact, and she glanced over her shoulder at the billy goat, its black eyes glassy and malevolent. It hissed through its teeth and Greta hissed back.

Tom tapped his fingertips on the rim of the vat and she did her best to concentrate. The goat's milk now had the consistency of jelly and as Tom stirred it with the paddle it solidified, turning thick and buttery. He cut squares of muslin and showed her how to line the moulds. Using a curd knife, Greta drew curls of the creamy stuff from the surface and patted it down into the muslin, working it into the edges as you would fill pastry with cooked apples for a pie.

They emptied the moulds from the previous day, turning them over, slapping the bases, and producing small perfect wheels of goat's cheese a bit smaller than the Dundee cake her old nanny used to give her when she was a little girl. The cheese was soft still to the touch, but the rind was darker and was beginning to harden.

While she continued to fill the moulds, Tom placed the finished wheels in a basket. 'Off they go to market in a week or so,' he said, and placed the basket on a shelf. He brought one of the matured cheeses back to the table and cut off a thick wedge for her. Greta took a bite and it was so scrumptious she realised even her taste buds had come to life.

'Nice?'

She nodded vigorously.

'Come on, keep going,' he added and she scraped the thickening curd a little at a time into the mould.

Greta turned instinctively at the renewed outbreak of hissing behind her. The goat straining at its leash was intimidating, but what made it all the more humiliating was that her breasts were firm and it was her own ripe aroma that was intoxicating the creature.

'Don't mind him, girlie, his bark's louder than his bite.'

She took a deep breath and carried on filling the moulds before Tom placed them on the shelf. Billy goat gruff was kicking its devil hooves against the barn wall and Greta for some reason suddenly remembered a fat girl named Rachel Gold whose father practically owned Yorkshire and whose court at the convent consisted of all the plain girls who loathed all the pretty girls.

Greta at 14 had grown tall and shapely with breasts that encouraged the nuns at Saint Sebastian to cross themselves every time the buttons on her blouse popped open. Rachel bullied Greta persistently until one day in the showers after hockey, Greta grew so tired of her horrid comments she waited until the girl was in mid-flow and shoved a bar of soap in her open mouth. Rachel went berserk and charged, but Greta like a matador stepped out of the way and Rachel fell skittering over the wet tiles. She stood, snarling as she took a breath. She slapped Greta across the face and Greta slapped her back. They went for each other, two naked girls like two rabid dogs and kept fighting until the games mistress pulled them apart. Greta had scratches down both arms, teeth marks in her neck and a black eye that turned purple, green and yellow in the coming weeks, a trophy she was proud to display for all to see. Rachel Gold may have got the better of her in the fight, but she never bullied Greta again.

Greta turned and snarled at the billy goat. The creature

kicked its heels and strained at its leash as if Greta had thrown down the gauntlet and he was ready for the challenge.

When the work was finished, they left the barn and went back out into the hot sun. On the side of the building was a tap and a galvanized pail that Tom filled. He unhooked the leather lead and hung it on a nail.

'Stand back, girlie,' he said and when she did so, he threw the water over her.

He repeated this several times and she stood there dripping as the mud turned slippery on her white skin. Grace chased in circles, the peacocks hollered, and Tom collected a sponge which he used to wipe her down more thoroughly, dipping the sponge in the pail, sloshing water over her shoulders and back and down her legs. He teased the sponge into the caverns of her ears, scrubbed her underarms and worked through the cheeks of her tender bottom. He ran the sponge under the tap, wringing it out several times, before squeezing clean water through the open lips of her vagina. He was careful with the most intimate places and Greta, with eyes closed, learned the lesson of the tall nanny goat and gave herself fully to the sensation.

Tom filled the bucket with fresh water, tipped it slowly over her head, then rubbed the drips away with the palm of his hand. He looked closely at her bottom and Greta turned to do the same. It was a field of pink with fine crimson lines like one of the paintings on Gustav's wall.

'There, you'll do,' he said.

He went to get her lead but as he was about to put it on, she took it from him, folded it in loops and slipped it between her teeth. He grinned and shook his head. He was about to slap her bottom but changed his mind for some reason and she was both pleased and disappointed. She liked Tom and nuzzled his cheek to show it. He was looking at her as if she were a cryptic clue in *The Sunday Times* crossword, then turned her around and pointed up the path.

'That way,' he said, and she trotted off with the lead all wet and leathery in her mouth.

It had been nice being all lathered in mud and it was nice being clean again. Alex and the golden mare had gone, the turfs were ranged in neat piles and she was pleased to have done such a good job. Greta slowed to a walk. It was hot. Her skin was damp. She could smell the woody scent of her underarms. Her breasts seemed fuller, solid on her chest, the areolae and nipples baby pink. Her pubes were silky and her long mane lay down her back, the sun picking out threads of gold.

With the exception of the set for *Madame Bovary*, the village was unlike any place Greta had seen before, the cobbled paths and horse trough, the tall birch shading the corner of the square, the little houses with shiny windows belonging more to a picture book than present day. She looked round for a camera; she was sure there was one there somewhere. Her eyes rested on the sign: Marsham, and she remembered Mr Marsham was waiting for her in The Black Sheep.

He was sitting alone and the way he was tucking into the big plate of roast beef and Yorkshire pudding made Greta imagine it must be Sunday, although she was sure it was only Saturday. Old-fashioned farm tools filled every inch of wall space and on the beamed ceiling horse brasses hung on belts of black leather. A man scraping out the bowl of his pipe and a woman who seemed vaguely familiar were sharing a table and the big, bearded fellow she assumed was Bradley watched her enter as if he didn't fully approve of naked girls in the bar.

She let the lead drop from her mouth into her hand. Richard crooked his finger before patting the stool at the end of his table. She sat, hands in her lap, watching for each little emotion his face might reflect. She liked Tom but it was from Richard that she desired approval. Being exposed while everyone else was dressed reminded Greta of Richard's dominion over her, his power to give her pleasure or pain, or to take them away. He carried on eating and the smell of the food made her mouth water. Finally, he picked up a potato and fed her from his fingers. He shared the rest of the food that way, feeding her with titbits of meat, some sprouts and carrots. Gravy ran down her chin and, as he was wiping it away, the woman from across the bar paused on her way to the bathroom.

'Don't spare the rod, Mr Marsham,' she said, shaking her head.

'Indeed not, Mrs Maddox.'

Mrs Maddox!

Greta couldn't believe her own eyes. She knew she had seen this woman somewhere before but it took several moments before she remembered that Mrs Maddox was the tweedy woman who had made her bring out every pair of shoes the shop possessed before buying some cute kitten heels and a pair of pointy sling backs.

You're going to do very well, very well indeed.

Greta recalled the odd phrase. She remembered the plotter's look she had exchanged with Madame Dubarry and the way she had pinched Greta's cheek until it hurt.

Now she pops up in Marsham chatting with Mr Marsham while Greta sat there naked with gravy on her chin. It clearly wasn't a coincidence, Mrs Maddox being in Marsham, rather than the gravy on her chin, or her being starkers for that matter, and Greta that moment felt like a little fly, a little flying horse, caught in a sticky intriguing web.

The thought was frightening and exciting. She had been cast in a role, a major role, as far as she could tell, and she intended to give it her absolute best.

Mrs Maddox looked Greta up and down for a long time and then turned again to Richard.

'She's a fine, strong thing, let me have a look at her.'

She hoisted Greta up from the stool by her armpit and

turned her around. She felt the muscles in her arms and legs. She pressed a finger into the soft flesh of her bottom, making a dimple, the pink flare turning white and then growing pink again. She nodded with approval and ran the side of her hand between her legs, see-sawing slowly back and forth and then removing her hand slicked with a thick creamy coating.

'Don't spare the rod,' she said again, and continued into the bathroom.

Chapter Fifteen – The Beating

GRETA WATCHED THE LAVATORY door close and turned to Richard with big puppy eyes he had no difficulty reading. She had consumed a bucket of water and was literally bursting. Lines creased his brow like sheet music, and she just had to sit there gritting her teeth and squeezing her legs together under the table.

He finished his drink in a leisurely swallow, stood to attach her lead and told Bradley to put lunch on his bill.

'Always a pleasure, Mr Marsham,' he said.

At that point, Mrs Maddox appeared, brushing down the pleats of her skirt.

'Come along then, girl, don't just sit there,' she said, chivvying Greta towards the door with brisk little taps on her bottom.

After the pub's cool interior, it seemed hotter outside. Richard paused to savour the taste of the day, his gaze wandering lazily about the square. Marsham was like a painting by Constable, a place on the borders of imagination. It wasn't that time had stood still, the Range Rover parked some distance away was testimony to that. No, time was played out in its own unique space, as in a film, especially with the cameras peeking out from every corner, yet all magically real, no set designers, no make-up, no costume.

They set off towards the tree in the far corner of the square, the strap hooked to the band at her throat held loosely in Richard's hand.

'Lovely weather, Mrs Maddox,' he said.

'And no good will come of it, you can rest assured.'

Richard glanced at her with a barely visible smile and her voice darkened.

'It awakens the passions,' she added with a severe sniff of her long, pointed nose and Greta wondered guiltily if the broom she had used to sweep out the stable belonged to Mrs Maddox.

They reached the pool of shade below the tall birch and Richard jerked the lead to pull her closer. When he opened the clip they gazed at each other for just a moment and the blue of his eyes were like chips of sky. He didn't say anything. He didn't need to. Greta could read him as well as he could read her. They were connected like sound and its echo. Like a key and a lock. Those who grow through discipline are in constant search for the person, perhaps the one person, from whom discipline will complete them. It is a happy marriage.

Greta lowered her eyes. There was a prickling in her armpits. The sense of humiliation and her need for approval were conflicting emotions, but the feeling in her bladder was stronger than both.

'Come along, girl, we haven't got all day,' Mrs Maddox said and tut tut tutted to herself. 'You don't have to ask me what this one needs ...'

Her voice trailed off.

Greta was squirming with embarrassment. Being naked had become familiar. It seemed right and proper. But not this, she thought, not with people watching. Her tummy was clenched tight. While she delayed, she heard the pub door open and glanced behind her. Bradley and the pipe smoker propped up the doorway like a pair of statues. To make it worse, if it could be worse, a tall man had appeared and was standing behind the horse trough, a leather boot propped on the stone rim. His face was shadowed by the brim of his straw hat, but Greta was sure she knew him from somewhere, from that other world in the past.

Mrs Maddox was fanning herself and panting. 'It's rather too hot for me just standing here,' she complained, and Richard lightly touched Greta's elbow with the tips of his fingers.

She swallowed and, taking a deep breath, moved towards the tree, where she squatted down, knees spaced out, her toes curling into the grass. She closed her eyes and the golden stream of urine that came splashing out of her sounded like a roaring wave in the still afternoon, a downpour, a waterfall. She peed like a pony, a huge puddle engulfing her feet and spreading beyond the shade below the tree. It was horrible and wonderful. She had a deep craving to be naked like this, to be displayed, her breasts ripe and voluptuous, her legs spread, a veil of warm steam rising to her nostrils as sour and sensuous as goat's milk. She ran her tongue over her dry lips and opened her eyes. Mrs Maddox had drawn so close, the puddle was about to reach the toes of her polished brown shoes and the woman stood back shaking her head with incredulity.

'Well I never,' she said.

Greta gave her hips a wiggle to shake herself dry and was sure she discerned about Richard's features an air of pride and that made her feel better. The pub door slammed as Bradley and his customer returned to the bar and the tall man sauntered off below his straw hat. Richard turned and Mrs Maddox strode along at his side, fingers knitted below billowing breasts that shuddered with vexation as she reminded him that she knew a thing or two 'about this sort of thing'.

'All knowledge is valuable, Mrs Maddox.'

'Mr Marsham. You don't spend a lifetime in correction management without learning a thing or two about human nature.'

'That aspect of human nature, Mrs Maddox. Are we not multidimensional?'

'Young girls are young girls, sir, and what they require

is discipline.'

'That's what my father always said.'

'And your father was a man who knew about such things,' she said darkly, and added, 'God rest his soul.'

Mrs Maddox glanced back at Greta, scampering along, naked as a flower and furtively brushing away the last warm drips of wee leaking down her legs.

They had reached one of the cottages and continued on a stone path that passed through a mature garden to the open doors of the workshop at the rear. The man bent over his desk drawing in a sketchpad looked up through spectacles clipped to his nose and Greta tried to remember the special name for those glasses but her mind was wandering and her eyes were glued hypnotically on the vast rump Mrs Maddox transported beneath the stretched pattern of squares on her woollen skirt.

The man stood, stooping to peer over his spectacles. He looked to Greta like a quiz fanatic who spent hours between the dusty pages of old encyclopaedias, his pale eyes tired, his body loose in his clothes like a stuffed toy with half the stuffing knocked out of it.

'Well, here we are,' announced Mrs Maddox.

The man flapped his white hands. 'My dear, are you hot?' he said. 'Can I fetch you a glass of water?'

'If I need water, William, I can fetch it myself. Let's get on with it, shall we.'

She took her husband's seat at the desk. Mr Maddox bowed in that old world way that reminded Greta of Count Ruspoli. 'Mr Richard,' he said. 'How nice to see you.'

'Mr Maddox, always a pleasure.'

'Indeed, sir,' he said in reply and, hands now gripped behind his back, he turned his attention to Greta. 'Now, let's see what we have here.'

He moved around her, his gaze running over her body as if he intended measuring her and, weird she thought, that's exactly what he did do. He took a tape measure from a drawer, dropped it over his neck like a tailor and led her with a delicate touch to the wooden contraption a bit like a gallows attached to the wall. He lowered the top beam to the crown of her head and stood on tiptoes to read her height.

'Five feet nine and ...' he hesitated. 'Nine-and-a half inches.'

Mmm, I've grown an inch!

Mrs Maddox started making a list with a pencil. Mr Maddox moved Greta to one side and, with the light behind her, she had a better view of the workshop, the walls lined with glass jars full of clips and flanges, the workbenches stained with dye, leather hides in rolls like carpets in a showroom. Greta liked the look of the tools wedged in leather loops below the shelves, ancient awls and chisels with shiny edges and wooden handles.

Mr Maddox glanced at his wife before chastely moving the tape around Greta's breasts. '36 and ...' he hesitated again and Greta took a big breath. 'And a half.'

Mrs Maddox tutted with apparent outrage as she wrote it down.

Greta's waist was just over 24, her hips were 34.5 and she felt faintly gauche that her figure didn't match the symmetry of the girls in magazines with their flawlessly regulated curves. Mrs Maddox was agitated no matter what the measurement. She wrote it all down on a list with a good deal of sucking on the point of the pencil and Greta recalled vaguely that at school they said the habit gave you lead poisoning and made you stark raving bonkers.

Mr Maddox ran down her inside leg ... 33 inches; across her shoulder blades that were sticking out *like the wings of an angel*, and she didn't hear the measurement because Mrs Maddox was tutting so loudly it sounded like a swarm of midges were tapping against the windowpanes. Her feet were size 7, and Greta was mortified because she only took a 6 and didn't know if she had always been fooling herself or whether her feet had grown to balance the immodest fullness of her breasts. They were throbbing, tingling, swelling before her eyes, the roundness lifting them from her chest like gifts crying out to be cupped in open palms, the pink buds peeking inquisitively up at the ceiling. Greta May, you are so wanton, she thought to herself, and couldn't resist squeezing her nipples for just a second to take away the ache.

Mrs Maddox observed this impertinent behaviour and sat back to savour the sadistic implications of the situation, the naked submissive girl feeling guilty for touching herself and eager to please after her shameful display peeing in the village square. It was hard for Greta to believe that she'd done such a thing, but she couldn't have waited another second and the image of herself squatting there with a golden lake spilling out from between her gaping legs was even at that moment so awfully arousing.

Mr Maddox climbed up on a stool, his chalky hands fluttering about her like a moth's wings. He measured her neck as if for a string of pearls, her head as if for a hat, the distance between her eyes for a costume mask, and the width of her wide mouth for what she had no idea. Finally, he took up a pair of scissors and cut a lock of her chestnut hair which he tied with a pale blue ribbon.

'All done,' he said, stepping down.

He removed his glasses to rub the blood back into the pinched spot on his nose; *pince-nez,* she remembered, and smiled to herself.

'Grinning now, is she!' said Mrs Maddox.

Richard had remained motionless in the shadows and Mrs Maddox glanced in his direction as she stood and gave the pad with its list of measurements to her husband.

'I'll just be a few moments, Mr Marsham. You're not in any hurry?'

'Not at all.'

She waved a stern finger at him and repeated her earlier piece of advice. 'Don't spare the rod,' she said and Greta swallowed as she watched the woman bustle out through the door leading into the house.

Richard ran his hand through his curls as he crossed the room. He flicked through Mr Maddox's sketches, commenting favourably, the older man shrugging modestly. They ignored Greta and she stayed as still as a shop window dummy, exposed and luminous in the refracted light knowing what was to come, not its precise nature, but the general area to be uncovered. Actually, she thought, it is uncovered, her pink bottom so precise and perfect in two matching and inviting globes. Greta felt certain that if this bottom belonged to someone else, she would want to spread it across her knee, explore all the crevices and pleats and then give it a good walloping.

The men were facing away from her and she cupped the two round cheeks in her palms. They were warm still from the earlier tanning, creamy like extremely expensive knickers, the skin firm, but mobile, each sphere like two parts of an opened peach. Her hands were brushed by the kiss of silken hair as they slipped over the sweet loop of the undercurve. Like a blind person reading braille she ran the tips of her fingers over the uncelebrated arrangement of sensitive curves and hollows where her bottom met the tops of her thighs, neglected for its sheer proximity to the little star of her anus and the exquisite slit of her vagina, but glorious nonetheless.

Greta grew moist touching her bottom, her vulva pressing through her closed thighs, rosy pink, the pink of a momentary flush and gleaming like a ripe quince hanging from the branch of a tree. Bottoms were made to be seen, and Greta understood as Mrs Maddox marched back through the door that they were made for spanking. The big woman strode straight out into the garden wielding a cane with a curved handle, slashing the air like a practising swordsman.

'Here we are then,' she said, and the sweat on Greta's back turned cold as she imagined the cane's hot icy tongue searing into her yielding flesh.

The two men paused in the doorway and watched Mrs Maddox carving another slice from the still air.

'Just here will do. I like a bit of space.'

Richard wasn't smiling. He looked serious, but in an apprehensive way and Greta wanted to do her best. She followed him outside. The sun was relentless, baking her skull, drying her damp back. Mr Maddox clipped his glasses back on his nose and stood at Richard's side bent like an old tree.

'Don't just stand there, girl.'

Greta stepped forward. There was a patch of grass among the rose bushes and rhododendrons where Mrs Maddox was waiting, the pale cane flexed in a bow between her two hands.

She looked Greta up and down, at her pert breasts, the peaks outrageously firm like udders. Her ribcage was trembling with the beat of her heart, her back firm, slightly arched with the pride Mrs Maddox intended to beat out of her. It was degrading to be standing there like this, like a slave girl in some primitive market, yet the waft of her arousal was unmistakeable and she clung to the small pleasure of knowing that she, or more precisely her pretty bum, was about to be exposed to Mrs Maddox's lurid voyeurism.

Mrs Maddox addressed the men. 'I'm rather old-fashioned in my way, no props, no benches, just a piece of leather if you please, William.'

'Leather, Henrietta?'

She drew breath and didn't answer.

Mr Maddox went scurrying back to the workshop and Mrs Maddox hung the crook of the cane over her arm before taking Greta's nipple in a vicious, vice-like squeeze that drove the air from her lungs.

'We'll soon have you in shape,' she said, and moved to

the other little bud and gave it the same savage twist.

Mr Maddox returned and there was a look of smug satisfaction in his wife's eyes as she grabbed the piece of leather from him and ran it across Greta's mouth. She rubbed it back and forth until her lips parted and Greta choked on the tart animal taste as her teeth opened and the leather wedge came to rest against her tongue. Mrs Maddox stood to one side.

'Right, over you go. Legs spread,' she said. 'Come on further than that. Hands on ankles.'

Greta got into position, her body bent in profile to the men.

'Now listen. I'll say this once: you do not move unless I tell you to move. And no whimpering if you don't mind.'

Greta took a deep breath, muscles flexing, bottom forced out, the crease opening like the covers of a book.

Mrs Maddox nursed the two soft cheeks, then slid her hand in the yawning chasm between. Greta tried to control herself. She squeezed her eyes shut and she really, really tried. She wasn't turned on by this dreadful woman, quite the reverse, but her body had a mind of its own, it was greedy, obsessive, a complete and utter tart. Greta was centre stage, the centre of attention, stark naked, her bottom displayed like a work of art, the puffy swollen lips of her vagina revealed in the most humiliating way. Her hips moved involuntarily, gyrating gently, her engorged labia drawing the woman's fingers in a vacuum through the soggy opening. The woman responded, rubbing her fingers carelessly over Greta's sex and the drool oozed over her hand.

'Look at this,' she said bitterly. 'She's sopping wet.'

Mrs Maddox ran her prodigious nose over the drawl then dried her palm over Greta's side. She stood back. She swished the air, once, twice, three times. She then rested the cane across Greta's buttocks, choosing her spot, measuring the distance. She was panting like a steam engine, pumping herself up. Greta felt the pale instrument slide from her flesh, it rose into the air, then came down across her sugary cheeks like a blade of fire.

Nothing had prepared Greta for this. The pain was electric, excruciating, consuming. It was how she imagined childbirth but worse. It was like giving birth to a cloven-hoofed devil and the satanic gaze of the billy goat crossed her mind like a shadow. Tears fell from her eyes, snot from her nose. She rocked back and forth, trying to keep balance.

'Keep still.'

And she tried to keep still. She tried to absorb the pain. She tried to imagine she was someone else, or somewhere else. The leather bit between her teeth grew slimy and she dug in harder as she felt the line being measured once more, the cane lifting into the air and coming down on her damp body like a flash of lightning. Greta wanted to cry out and she just chewed down harder on the foul piece of leather. She could do this. She could take six lashes from Mrs Maddox. She could take 12 if she had to.

Greta held her breath for number three, the blow cutting across the first two as if Mrs Maddox were creating a design, the points where the lines intersected sharp stabs of agony on a field of pain. Greta was dazed. She tried to keep count and lost count. There was a fourth, a fifth, randomly placed, scribbling stripes of red graffiti across her tender flesh. She was learning the difference between the cane and the crop, the touch of leather and the flat of the hand. And she learned, too, that where pain can produce pleasure it can also produce just more pain. The pain was a forest fire, almost removed from her, like something seen from a mountain top, a distant event.

She opened her eyes and caught a glimpse of Richard. He had folded his arms together, one hand raised to hide his mouth. Old Mr Maddox was staring at the ground and the sound of the cane beating the air once more made

Greta close her eyes and steady her legs, the hot wand of fire blazing a new trail across her bottom.

Mrs Maddox changed the line of attack and slashed the cane down across just one of Greta's cheeks. She did it again, aiming at the same spot and Greta was sure she had gone beyond six and was grateful that the worst was over. She had passed the half way mark. Richard would be pleased. Greta took one more across the right cheek and Mrs Maddox took her fiery instrument of torture around the other side in order to concentrate on the left, the angle taking the cane across Greta's side in a place where there is less cushioning and the agony is multiplied.

Was that nine? Or ten? She didn't know and it didn't matter. The cane cut an arc through the motionless air and uncoiled again like a dragon's tongue across her young body. It was a different sort of pain now, outside her experience, a burning like acid that moved below the surface and into her thoughts. She was a new person, an object to be used, flogged at will, humiliated and abused. She was Richard's toy. She was his slave and he was her master. She understood that. Mrs Maddox wielded the pale yellow cane, but she was Richard's tool. Greta was being punished for something and she didn't know what but she knew she must deserve it.

There was a pause, brief but discernible. Greta was sure this was the end. Just one more. I've taken 12 strokes with the cane. I've done this on my own. She hasn't got the better of me. I've done this for Richard.

Greta gritted the leather wedge and screwed up her eyes. The cane came down like the blade of a guillotine and Greta stood there bent over, her bottom and sides screaming, her hands wet where they gripped her ankles, her long locks of gleaming chestnut hair sweeping over the grass between her legs.

'A glass of water, if you please, William,' she heard

Mrs Maddox say, and Greta straightened her back with a feeling of gratitude.

The woman stood back half a step. 'I thought I told you not to get up,' she said, her mouth twisting in anger. 'Just behave yourself, girl.'

Greta stared into the woman's eyes and read her thoughts. It wasn't over. It had only just begun.

'Did you hear what I said?'

Mr Maddox was hurrying back, the glass trembling in his hand. Greta looked pleadingly at Richard. He looked away and she bent to take a fresh grip on her ankles. She felt the cane in repose on her bottom and big tears leaked from her eyes as she chewed down on the leather bit. She listened as the woman gulped down water and the drop that fell on her bottom added an extra touch of cruelty.

Mrs Maddox gave the glass to her husband. She took a breath, sighed with satisfaction and sawed the cane across the tops of Greta's legs. She drew back and brought it down, the cane stinging the air before cutting a crimson line into the thin white flesh. That's one, Greta thought. The second moved further up, lacerating the tender place where the thighs and bottom meet.

Sweat seeped from Greta's every pore, down her back and into her hair, over the curve of her breasts and settled in tears on the peaks of her tingling nipples. Her vagina was moist from fear and her throat was parched from sucking the wedge of leather. Her mind was beginning to wander and she remembered being a little girl chasing a puppy through the garden. She wasn't wearing any clothes and she couldn't remember why.

The cane carved its path across the undercurve of her cheeks. Greta felt its weight lift away and when it came back down it sliced like a knife across the soft petal lips of her pussy, raising a faint spray that evaporated in the warm air. Greta had a momentary vision of her name in lights, totally out of place. She saw the piece of leather fall from her mouth and the pain was so intense, so terrible, so unbelievable her little body took control. She heard a single word ...

'Enough.'

And the world went dark.

Chapter Sixteen – The Golden Bridle

WHEN SHE OPENED HER eyes, Greta wasn't exactly sure
where she was. The light seeping through the grey slates
of the roof was speckled in dust and for just a moment she
thought she was in the dirty attic in Soho where she had
followed Dirty Bill.

Her body throbbed with a dull ache. She could smell
witch-hazel and as the odours of the stable drifted over
her senses the cock crowed and she was fully awake.

Her back was sticky with sweat. She pushed the
blanket to one side and the strap pulled at the ring
connected to her choker as she rolled on to her knees. She
stood, flexing her shoulders, stretching her spine, every
movement sending a burning sensation across the
damaged skin of her raw buttocks. She must have fainted,
she realised, and was deeply ashamed. She had been
determined to take everything the cruel woman could
give, to learn from it, to learn about herself. She had
failed on the first day.

If it was the first day? It seemed like for ever. Even
Tom's whistle as he made his way towards her stall had
the familiarity of time and she turned automatically so
that he could brush the straw from her back. He did so
with great tenderness. It was Tom she thought who had
probably cared for her damaged bottom.

He went down on his haunches for a closer look.
'There, not too bad,' he said.

She turned with tears misting her eyes. He unhooked

her lead and attached it around his waist. Grace was waiting for them outside and licked her ankles before they crossed the yard to the shed. The hens were clucking boisterously, the peacock feathers gleaming like opals in the sunrise.

Tom smoked and a feeling of calm came to her as she squatted on the low stool among the goats, the smell oddly soothing, the milk hypnotic as it splashed into the bucket. She moved deeper into the stall, among the skittering hooves, pulling and squeezing each set of fleshy udders, and the goats responded with a generosity even Tom noticed as he took the full buckets to the vat.

'You see, girlie, they've found a soul mate,' he said and she turned with a small smile. She wanted to please.

The chocolate goat showed more patience, although again the first nervous spray coated Greta's face before they found their rhythm. The tall friendly goat Greta called The Lady pushed eagerly into her hands and milking her had all the intimacy as if she were touching a part of herself.

The billy goat was kicking its heels and reared up as she made her way to the cheese table.

'Get back in your hole,' Tom roared and the he-goat bared its teeth as it hissed at her. The dog barked and the nanny goats trembled on their skinny legs.

Greta did her best to ignore the commotion and didn't notice the camera above turning on its axis as she placed the three-legged stool back on the shelf where it belonged. There was work to be done. She wanted to get it right. She watched closely, stirring the mixture with the paddle as Tom measured out the live culture before adding it to the vat. The he-goat was leering at her and as she glanced over her shoulder she had a terrible vision of Mrs Maddox reshaping the air with her pale yellow cane.

The curd had to mature but there was always something to do. The hens had to be fed, greedy things that stamped over her bare feet, the peacocks with their silly displays, their feathers tickling her thighs as she moved among them. She watched Richard ride over the fields and had a dim recollection of a girl with auburn hair riding a pony in a video. She had thought that's what she would be doing when they set out from London.

She drank orange juice and ate plates of muesli with fruit. The stew in the evening was always packed with fresh vegetables grown on the farm and she ate with her own wooden spoon. Every day she took her V400 pill; that first day when she'd climaxed so greedily under the crop she had wondered if the V stood for something other than vitamin, but after that day many days passed and she was neither beaten nor aroused.

Most of the time she was sticky with goat's milk and streaked with mud. The animals on the farm accepted her moving about them with a tolerance that at first seemed surprising and then became natural. The afternoons were hotter than she had ever known in England, but the faint breeze drifting in from the sea brought with it promises of new worlds and faraway places.

Alex arrived each day with a fresh load of turfs. While the men sauntered off to The Black Sheep, she would unload the cart and was steadily transferring the rolls of earth two at a time up the low rise beyond the paddock. Her shoulders were strong. Like iron hammered for a sword blade, the beating had made her stronger. She unrolled the turfs and laid them out, knitting them together, the soil coating her body and making her feel at one with the earth.

Tom and Alex would return carrying a board and while they pressed the turfs in place, she dragged the big hose from the barn back up the hill, the reel unwinding like the line on a kite. The new turfs had to be thoroughly soaked twice a day and already they were binding and growing greener.

The task seemed as if it would take for ever but, suddenly, the hillside was bristling in a carpet of new grass as green and shiny as her eyes. Alex brought a stack of boards on the cart and she watched bewildered as the men assembled a grandstand with a canvas roof and triangular pennants in red, yellow and blue.

A week must have gone by. Perhaps two? Time was different now. She was different. The shadow of her old self had been beaten from her. She had stopped being Greta May playing a character and become the character Richard had pictured and Vanlooch had painted. She was Pegasus. The name was on a brass disc above her stall. She lived in a stable with Delilah, Thunder and a little foal named Greta.

She could hear the chime of church bells when she awoke that morning and thought it was probably Sunday. The sun had lifted over the horizon and she found hanging from the side of her stall an intricate set of leather straps joined by brass rings and shiny buckles. The straps were golden in colour and smelled of polish. She was still studying the strange artefact in the morning light when Tom bowled in to administer the usual brushing. He inspected her bottom.

'Fantastic. Good as new,' he said.

He brushed down her thighs, around her knees, down her calves. The fine hair on her body had softened, grown translucent and slowly vanished. The dark patch of her pubic hair was perfectly shaped, a well defined triangle, and silky soft. Her skin was the same even colour, pale bronze, kissed by the sun as she went about her daily chores. Her hair gleamed and fell in abundant coils to the pit of her back. The little curve of her tummy that she had once thought so sexy had gone. Her stomach was flat and muscular from carrying all those turfs, her breasts standing out firm and shapely from the fine lattice of her ribcage. She had always wanted to be considered a great beauty and thought it was beauty that made you a success in acting as in life. She didn't think about those things now. She was flawlessly herself and that was enough.

Tom hooked her lead about his waist and they crossed the yard with Grace trotting along behind them. The goats had grown greedy for her touch and the milk they gave more copious. The he-goat that morning was more animated than ever and violated her with its penetrating gaze, its tongue hanging lustily from drooling lips, its devil hooves beating a death knell against the woodwork as she prepared the cheese for market.

When she left the goat shed, Richard was in the paddock with Thunder connected to a long rein and trotting in circles. Tom went off to get a fresh bale of hay and, as she watched Richard at his task, it occurred to her that no one would ever beat a pony. They are sacred. They know how to behave. They don't require the rigours of discipline just the patience of training. A pony is everything a girl could be if she really tried. It was something to aspire to. Life was a constant process of change and transformation. Only when you surrender your will to the flights of destiny do you break from the shell of a chrysalis and enter the fragile perfection of a butterfly. Well, a pony, she thought. She admired Thunder's arched back and long proud neck, her fine, tapering limbs, the way she moved so elegantly, lifting each little hoof and flexing her legs at it fell again to the earth. Richard was flicking at the ground with his whip, but its tongue never touched the pony.

He caught her eye and when he smiled she felt warm all over. It was the first time Richard had glanced in her direction for so long she wasn't sure what to do. She took a step forward, then stopped as it dawned on her that the convoluted set of straps hanging in her stall had been made by Mr Maddox especially for her.

During this moment of confusion, Richard nodded his head and she rushed back to the stable.

Tom was cleaning out the soiled hay. It was her job to do the sweeping but the little wave he gave her made it clear that he would do it today. She clutched the golden straps in eager fingers but no matter which way she turned them they didn't make any sense at all. She glanced up as a long shadow shot thin as a needle across the barn floor. In his loose white shirt and polished knee-boots and tight britches, with the sun behind him, lighting his features, Richard had never been more striking.

'Come, come,' he called.

She hurried to him with the golden bridle and he eased it over her head. He removed her collar, slid it through the straps and did the collar back up again. The bridle buckled at the back of her neck. A bit connected to two brass rings slipped into her mouth and the blinders that partially covered her eyes accented her forward vision, her view of the future.

'Perfect,' he said, and she knew he was pleased.

They left the stable and crossed the yard to the fence. When she climbed the low gate, she noticed the four hooks screwed into the fence posts, waiting for her if the need arose, and she had a feeling that they would never be used again. At least, not by her.

Richard connected the reins to her collar and she trotted around the paddock in orderly circles, slowly upping the pace, her thighs stretching and getting a proper work out. She had built up her upper body carrying turfs, but her legs could still do with some work. Richard flicked at the earth with his whip, the beat helping her keep rhythm. While she was learning how to move gracefully, Tom saddled Delilah. Richard climbed into the saddle and she ran at his side, up the hill to the grandstand and down over rolling meadows carpeted in bluebells and daisies that descended to the sea. Richard galloped across the shingle beach and stopped for her to catch up.

He didn't need to say anything. Words had become unimportant. They were joined by something primitive and esoteric and loads of fun. She ran out into the sea, chopped through the waves and swam in the cold water.

Her body felt clean for the first time since she'd arrived in Marsham and her hair was glossy as it dried in the afternoon sunshine. Richard trotted back to the paddock and she kept pace with Delilah all the way to the stable. After she had brushed down the mare she tucked into a bowl of stew with noodles and beans and couldn't recall ever eating anything quite so delicious.

That night, Greta had the dream where she saw her name in lights and was wide awake in the pre-morning chill, listening for the cock crow and watching the light filter through the roof. She couldn't wait for the new day to dawn. She did her work, and Tom was saddling Richard's horse by the time she had scrubbed down the cheese tools.

She watched Richard ride up the rise as she was leaving the goat house and felt a stab of disappointment. It was only a game. He was teasing. He glanced back with a grin and she had to sprint as fast as she could to catch up with him.

He slowed at the crest of the hill and, when she reached him, he flicked his whip at her bottom which of course made her run faster. When they reached the beach, he rode across the shingle and she followed him around the curve of the bay to the stone lighthouse on the headland. The shingle cut her feet to ribbons but she was determined not to stop and the salt water when she swam in the sea healed her wounds in no time.

The soles of her feet toughened and it wasn't long before they didn't hurt at all. She flew across the fields like Pegasus and swam in the sea like a fish. It had been freezing that first day but the cold and the heat don't bother you if you have the discipline to bare them. Her skin darkened and turned golden brown. Her limbs shone like they'd been polished, her muscles grew strong, and she could see great distances with her eyes focused through the blinders. Most days she wore the golden bridle. She was getting used to it, but liked the freedom when she didn't wear it at all. She remembered that time, it seemed ages ago, when she enjoyed being naked in the market. Now, she couldn't imagine there was any other way to be. Clothes would just be so silly.

It was on a particularly hot afternoon with the bridle left in the stable that she followed Richard at a leisurely pace along the beach to the lighthouse. They rounded the point for the first time and turned up a winding path to a field she had never seen before. It was partially hidden by coarse grass and a rambling bush with blackberries beginning to ripen among the thorns. She hurdled a low fence behind the mare and followed Richard up a steep rise to a tree-covered knoll where he came to a stop. They were on the rim of a valley shaped like an amphitheatre with a row of oaks like sentries on the far side. Richard patted Delilah's neck as he gazed into the distance.

Insects hummed in the still air and a pungent, familiar odour reached her senses, a smell she associated with the farm rather than the fields. She stepped forward and could see on the far side of the copse a dozen or so nanny goats, the four she thought of as old friends, and several more gathered in the shade nibbling around the tree roots.

She thought it would be fun to see her friends from the goat house and, with Richard giving Delilah a well-earned rest, she made her way through the trees towards them. The Lady baaed fretfully as she approached and the rest of the herd joined in, as surprised to see her away from the milking shed as she had been to see them.

They were looking beyond her, down into the valley, and as she turned she saw the billy goat as he saw her, her naked body polished like copper, gleaming against the pastel landscape. The he-goat seemed to have been waiting there for her, that this meeting was destined, inescapable. The goat remained motionless, a patch of black with curling horns like daggers. The creature brushed the grass below a cloven hoof and pinned her with its onyx eyes. She was frozen to the spot like a terrified rabbit, her knees shaking, her full breasts trembling, exciting the beast.

It took a few exploratory steps and stopped. It was gauging the distance between them. Cold sweat crept down her sides like a living creature. She glanced back towards Richard but he was out of sight behind the trees. She looked back at the fence. The billy goat had taken another few steps towards her. The nanny goats were getting skittish. She thought about taking off and running back the way they had come, but the he-goat was fleet of foot and would catch her. She looked for a stout stick to defend herself. There was nothing. Her lead was wound twice around her waist. She unclasped it and tested the leather, pulling it taut. There was nothing else.

The he-goat had moved to one side, as if to cut her exit to the gate, and she stepped out of the shade to meet it, moving cautiously down the slope, circling the beast as it circled her. As she left the trees, she noticed Richard. He had tethered the mare and was standing in the field, watching her. Their eyes met and he took a hand from his pocket to brush back his dark curls.

She looked back at the billy goat. Now that she had determined to take on the creature, the shaking in her legs had gone. She was a strapping muscular girl, 19, as strong as she would ever be. She stared into the beast's black eyes. It scuffed the grass, preparing to charge, a bull in the bullring, and she was the matador. The goat's pink tongue hung through its yellow teeth. It hissed at her and she scuffed the grass, copying its action. The movement made the animal lower its head and finally it charged, drool slipping from its mouth, its horns glinting in the sunlight.

She stood her ground, feigned moving one and moved the other as the goat was about to strike. It charged again and again, and each time she moved away, and each time the beast grew more furious. He was the hunter. She was the prey. He was in rut and she had been chosen. She was sweating and the smell of her sweat intoxicated the creature.

She knew it was only a matter of time before the billy goat struck her down. She needed a new tactic. She moved closer, inching towards the animal, closing the distance between them. When it charged, she went down on her haunches and dived out of the way at the last moment. The goat turned and reared up, goring the side of her thigh below the hipbone. She fell forward on her hands and knees, exposing herself fully. Smelling blood, sensing victory, the beast nudged her legs apart and roared in triumph as it prepared to mount her from behind.

With its forelegs in the air, the goat had lost its edge. She turned in one swift movement and wound the strap around its leg, just above the hoof, and tied a knot in the leather lead. The goat butted her, bruising her shoulder blades, its forelegs sliding down her back, its hooves scratching her skin. But she took the blows, she gritted her teeth against the pain and wound the strap round its other leg.

The he-goat was spitting, its saliva sliding over her bruised flesh. She pulled the strap tighter and used all her strength to push the animal on its side. It spat and hissed as it toppled over. She swung on to its back and it bucked, trying to toss her off, but she hung on to its horns. It struggled on to its feet, but she clung on as it hobbled along, his back legs locked, tied by the leather strap. Finally, the beast fell, crashing to its side. She stroked its head to pacify it.

The animal's breathing became even, as did her own. The gore on her leg was painful and she watched with disbelief as Richard yanked off his shirt as he approached and tore the white fabric into strips. He licked the blood from her leg and, as he bandaged the wound, she looked down at his pale body and realised he was all skin and bones. While life on the farm had turned her into a strapping, healthy girl, Richard had grown lined and gaunt. He released the goat from it bonds and, though the animal looked shamefaced for a few moments, it quickly revived its sense of purpose and went chasing after the herd of nanny goats on the far side of the trees.

Richard took her into his arms, it needed all his strength, and carried her back to the mare. He placed her into the saddle and they walked back to the beach where he slowly removed the bloody bandage. She swam in the sea and the cold salt water cauterised the wound.

Chapter Seventeen – Deconstructing Greta

NEXT DAY, THE BILLY goat remained cowering in the corner of his stall and drew back as if into its shadow when she entered the milking shed. Greta was sure she could discern a vague look of satisfaction in the beast's black eyes and realised all it had ever wanted from her was a show of discipline.

'Look at him, gentle as a lamb,' said Tom as he swung the three-legged stool from its place on the shelf.

The nanny goats gave more copiously than ever and, after the milking, Richard was waiting for her by the fence. Delilah was saddled and he held Thunder's reins loosely in his palms. He was slapping the side of his leather boot with a crop and she wondered for a moment if she had been disobedient and was going to get a beating.

Tom led her out to the paddock. He removed her lead and it came as a complete surprise to Greta when he cupped his hands and swung her up on to the pony's back. Even Grace was knocked for six. The Labrador remained stock still watching with a confused look in her big doggy eyes and then ran along behind her as Greta pressed her knees into the pony's ribs and followed Richard out of the paddock into the field.

She adored the feel of her breasts bobbing up and down, her pussy opening like a sea shell as she slid back and forth over the pony's back. It was the first time Greta had ridden for ages but it is something you never forget and riding bare back came as naturally to her as sitting naked beside Richard in The Black Sheep while he had his lunch. Greta wasn't sure at first whether this treat was a reward for trouncing the billy goat or whether, as she came to suspect, it was all part of the master plan.

It is fortunate that young healthy flesh heals quickly and in the coming days while the wound on her thigh was mending, every morning after the milking they rode for hours over the fields and along the coast. The mare was much faster than the pony but, no matter how hard Richard rode Delilah, Thunder kept up, forcing its spindly legs to keep pace, the perspiration rising from her coat, her mouth frothing with the effort. Greta hung on for dear life and came to admire the pony's courage and stamina.

One day they took the path along the shingle and out to the lighthouse. They turned towards the rambling blackberry bushes, jumped the low gate and stopped in the shade of the trees on the lip of the amphitheatre.

'Come on, fast as you can,' said Richard, and took off.

He was grinning, his dark hair flying behind him as they chased the mare down into the valley and up the steep incline that led to the row of oak trees on the other side. She was wet and sticky with a ripe pony smell when he lifted her down from Thunder. They made their way through the oaks and came to a halt above a long meadow that sloped down to a manor house with marble columns across the façade.

'Marsham Hall,' he said, but she wasn't listening.

She stared at him for just a moment then turned her attention back to the meadow.

Greta could see in the distance a girl harnessed to a trap with a man clinging on to the reins in the seat behind her. The trap was golden like a chariot, so was the girl. Like a goddess. A primitive deity. It was a scene from Greek myth and she just wished she'd paid more attention during classics at school. It's true what they say: education education education. Her heart was drumming and a tingle of anticipation shot up her spine.

She glanced again at Richard then back at the goddess. She was running so fast her toes barely touched the ground, her breasts pushed out like the figurehead on the prow of a galleon, the chariot bouncing over the grass in such a way that it constantly seemed on the verge of toppling over, but the man swayed from side to side in such a way that it never did. The sight was oddly moving, the naked girl soaring like the wind, free as a bird, the green hills bristling with trees, the sky above blue and cloudless.

The trap came closer before veering off. Greta first recognised the man; it was Gustav. When she saw that the girl straining in the shafts was Amber, everything that had happened since she first met Richard fell into place like the pieces of a puzzle and she could see the whole picture. It was like looking at a surreal painting and understanding the meaning. She glanced at him now. He smiled but he didn't explain. Richard never explained. But next day after her work a shiny green trap made of fibreglass was standing in the paddock waiting for her. She was so anxious to give it a try her breasts prickled and she had to give them a good hard squeeze to calm herself down.

Richard watched approvingly as he slid the rings on her wrist-straps over the hooks on the shafts. He attached reins to her bridle and climbed into the seat. She took a firm grip on the rubber sleeves that fitted over the shafts and took off up the hill, her shoulders tensing, her thighs straining, her muscles stretching. Ten weeks in Marsham and she was as strong as Boxer in *Animal Farm*. The bit in her mouth gnawed at the tender flesh of her inner cheeks when he wanted her to move right or left but the whip wedged in the shaft at his side remained where it was. He never used it, not even in fun, and she missed the feel of the lash on her bottom. Isn't that what bottoms are for?

She didn't ride Thunder any more but like the pony she tried her best to show the same resolve and resilience, the same good nature. She ran faster every day, pulling the trap behind her and Richard steered her over narrow tracks, through gnarled ancient brambles, across the shingle and up the steep hill to the field overlooking the sea where they would come to a rest like climbers on the roof of the world.

Greta drank water from his cupped hands and she would squat to pee because she knew it was something he enjoyed. She was completely herself with Richard. He had taken her to the limits of her fantasy. She had thought once how being a pony was everything a girl could strive for and now she intended to play the role to perfection.

She was up before the sun and milked the goats in darkness. Tom said he was going to deal with the cheese by himself and when he told her to trot over to the Gate House she couldn't believe her ears.

It was the first time she had been inside the big house and the feel of the Persian carpet beneath her bare feet was so soft it tickled. It was Mr Maddox who had opened the door for her and when Richard poked his head out from another room he held his nose and grimaced.

'What a pong,' he said. 'Do the best you can.'

'Aye, aye, skipper,' said Mr Maddox.

Richard was only wearing pyjama bottoms and the sight of his scrawny chest with all the ribs sticking out made the breath catch in her throat. He really had lost a lot of weight and she had more than a sneaking suspicion that he had been starving himself for her. As she'd grown stronger towing the trap he'd grown thinner to lighten the load. Their eyes met for a moment but then he closed the door and disappeared.

She followed Mr Maddox up the wide stairs. Something was happening. Something big. Everybody in those last few days had been rushing about as if on government business and she wished she wasn't always the last to find out what was going on.

Mr Maddox led her into a bathroom where the shiny porcelain and white towels seemed like objects in a dream after the simplicity of her place in the stable. She spent ages in the bath and watched the windows glow orange as the sun came up. Mr Maddox was as formal as always, the perfect gentleman, and when she stepped from the bath he avoided her blatantly erect nipples as he rubbed her down with one of the big fluffy towels. He was unable to conceal his erection tapping on her leg like someone at the door eager to get in, and she did the only thing a girl could do and released it from the constraints of his grey flannels. She sat on the edge of the bath and Mr Maddox sighed like an old steam engine as he slipped into the soft tissue of her succulent throat. His withered cock became boyish again and when his sperm stroked the roof of her mouth it had the oddly familiar taste of goat's milk.

'Oh my. Oh my,' he sighed and she drained his cock like she was sucking the dregs from the bottom of a bottle of carrot juice through a straw at Pret.

She tucked the little thing back in his trousers and Mr Maddox's hunched back seemed much straighter when he reached for what looked like a doctor's bag standing on the chair in the corner.

He watched as she perfumed her parts and coated her body in baby oil, running her long fingers over every crevice and crease, into the crack of her bottom and down between her toes. Mr Maddox removed from the bag a set of leather straps that she stepped into before he buckled the belt at the base of her spine. Where the straps ran under her bottom there was a metal fixture. To it, Mr Maddox attached a chestnut pony tail and when she fidgeted it bobbed jauntily behind her. He had made the tail for her, matching the colour from the lock of hair he'd taken that day she had been beaten so cruelly, the last time she had been beaten, she realised, and the thought brought a rare smile to her wide lips.

She sat in the chair and Mr Maddox groomed her hair,

combing it in the same style as the tail. He tied curls on the crown of her head with green ribbon that glowed like her eyes, like neon, like the pony trap. He buckled her into the bridle, then attached a silver disc to her choker with her stage name: Pegasus.

The steam coating the mirror had gone and she studied her reflection for the first time since she'd arrived in Marsham. Staring back from the mirror, and she made the observation without vanity, was a golden being carved and flawless, the bow of her back in harmony with the lush roundness of her bottom, her full breasts perky and sweet, the verdant garden of her pubic hair soft and curly after the bath, smelling fresh without the whiff of the stable. Her wide shoulders were toned and muscular, her long, strong limbs perfectly formed. Even the battle scar left from her fight with the billy goat had faded. Like Amber, she had become a mythical creature. Would she become a legend?

Mr Maddox studied her studying the mirror's image and did something so moving she would remember it when it mattered most. He took her hands between his palms, looked up into her eyes and squeezed her fingers. 'Today you will defy gravity,' he whispered, and she noticed in the corners of his eyes tiny tears magnified by the glass of his *pince-nez*.

Richard appeared in the doorway. It was time to go.

During all the weeks she had been in Marsham she had never seen more than a few people in the village and couldn't help feeling skittish when she looked out at the crowds pressing across the green. Garbled messages roared from big loud speakers and when she heard a gunshot she would have bolted had Richard not been there, his hand moving to stroke the curve of her back.

She took a deep breath, tossed her mane and followed him down the steps from the Gate House.

There were butterflies in her tummy and she flicked

her long lashes as if by the movement all the crowds would flutter away. She remained a pace or two behind Richard and the people as they crossed the green drew to one side with what she thought were admiring glances. With every step she grew more assured, her eyes focused through the blinders, her chin high over her long neck, her movement a study of elegance and grace. She swivelled her hips and tossed her tresses. Her hair gleamed like polished leather, the sun picking out golden threads in her chestnut curls.

The square was crisscrossed with bunting and ringed with market stalls selling costumes and uniforms, whips, canes and objects so strange she had no idea what purpose they could possible serve. The speakers blared and the magpies looked furious striding over the thatched roofs of the cottages. A naked man tattooed from the crown of his head to the soles of his feet was tattooing a serpent on a girl's leg, its jaws opening over her shaved mount. She wanted to watch but remembered that day in Camden Market when Richard kept hurrying her along and now she was a well-bred girl who didn't need to be told.

She saw a nanny dressed as Mary Poppins pushing a pram with a man in a nappy sucking a dummy. There was a submissive on all fours yelping like a dog while his partner beat him with the lead. They were enjoying themselves. People were trussed in chains and zipped into rubber, just their eyes peeking out. A naked woman strapped into a quivering dildo passed by on the arm of a man with so many piercings he looked like a giant pincushion. Many of the men wore tweeds with flat caps and binoculars hanging from their necks. But just as many were clad for S&M, leathered like Hell's Angels, like sailors, like cowboys, and when she heard two men in big hats speaking in a slow drawl she picked up on their Texan accents and recalled Gustav long ago in Hades telling Richard the Americans were coming.

Men, it occurred to her, were attracted to the theatrical

and, while many were costumed, the girls were naked, the way girls like to be, their bare feet on the grass, their breasts bobbing, their bottoms tanned and proud as they moved through the throng. She adored being naked, it was the most natural thing in the world, and was happy that day to see so many girls who thought like her, who dressed like her.

There were girls in collars and leads; girls in ballgags and masks; two girls looking magnificent in red headdresses yoked together in a wooden carriage; so many girls with bushy tails harnessed to every conceivable type of wagon and cart. Horses were tethered outside The Black Sheep where men quaffed jugs of ale and around the green traps rumbled over the cobblestones with girls between the shafts, some of those traps merely functional, others to the delight of the crowd performing bizarre erotic acts as they clip-clopped over the path.

Mmm, she thought dreamily, I wouldn't mind having a go at that.

Greta took a deep breath and enjoyed the country air, the musty tang of sweat and ponies, the gleam of varnish on the polished carts. There was a whole universe of disciplined girls and trainers, masters and slaves, sadists and masochists, people who had slipped out of their shells and were living their fantasy. She wet her dry lips with her tongue and, as she gazed about her, she wondered if there could be a greater pleasure than being there that August bank holiday in the sunshine.

It was a day never to be repeated. As she had moved on from the shoe shop she would move on from Marsham. Richard would sniff out other girls with the same insatiable hungers. Girls are volcanoes, throbbing with life, and inside them, under terrible pressure, is a bubbling lake of frothing jism, a fount of juicy pleasure that can only be soothed in endless orgasms. It just needed the right master or mistress to come along and release the safety valve. Richard had known her needs from the very beginning. He had pulled back the veil on her hidden yearnings. He had revealed her true nature and nature is destiny.

She wanted to reach for his hand but that would have been out of character. She fought the impulse. She shook her curls and wiggled her bum. She was naked. Her breasts tingled and her tail bounced along as she walked. There was a sheen of sweat coating her flesh and, though the crowds had made her as nervous as the magpies when she had first glanced out from the Gate House, now the men and women enjoying her nudity elicited a pleasant dampness between her legs. Could you go into orgasm just by people looking at you? She thought you probably could.

As they crossed the green they passed stalls selling saddles for ponies and saddles for girls; thigh boots and stiletto heels; restraints, strap-ons and toys; there was a hot dog stand, a coconut shy and her heart skipped a beat every time she heard gunshots ring out from the rifle range. Who in their right mind would want to shoot a little duck, living or made of metal?

She had thought briefly of the shoe shop and it seemed as if her musings had the power to bring her imagination to life as Madame Dubarry turned from a stand selling girl-brasses and stopped them in their tracks. It was hard at first to believe her old boss was there at the fair, but she noticed a twinkle in Richard's blue eyes and, of course, nothing that happened with Richard ever really surprised her.

Madame Dubarry was wearing a red leather cat-suit that clung to her curves and revealed her perky white breasts in front and the pale domes of her bottom behind. She was accompanied by Mrs Maddox, a sugarplum fairy in floating chiffon and the infamous kitten heels. The women trained their eyes on her in silence and at first Greta didn't notice that standing behind Madame Dubarry, tethered by a lead, was Bella, out of school, out of her clothes and learning the art of discipline. Her skin was china white with a newly minted glow and the neat tuft of her pubic hair appeared like the shaded area in a drawing. They didn't speak, but she could tell by the look Bella gave her that she was enjoying her summer job.

'Ladies, good morning,' Richard said.

'Good day to you, Master Richard,' said Mrs Maddox.

'Magnificent, sir,' said Mrs Dubarry, her eyes running over Greta as if she were about to commit her to canvas.

'It took some work, I can tell you,' Mrs Maddox muttered, and she glanced back at Bella as if to size up her bottom for a good beating.

Mr Maddox must have returned his bag to the cottage and was hurrying through the crowds towards them. He was breathless and took his glasses off to mop his brow with a handkerchief.

'You'll kill yourself one of these days, William, dashing about,' cried Mrs Maddox, the great edifice of her chest heaving with agitation as she spoke.

'Not at all, dear. I haven't felt better for 40 years.'

Mrs Maddox's breasts wobbled to a halt as she traced her husband's gaze to Greta. He was considering his handicraft, inspecting her chestnut hair, her pretty tail, her green eyes matching the ribbons in her hair.

'You've done a marvellous job, as always, my dear. We're all very proud of her.'

'Yes, we are,' he said.

Mrs Maddox took a sugar cube from her pocket. As she slipped the cube between Greta's lips, she ran her fingers between the cheeks of her bottom. 'I do declare she's wet,' she said in a stage whisper and Bella fluttered her long eyelashes.

Greta had hated Mrs Maddox after the beating but now she knew it had been for her own good. If life at Marsham was a play, the beating had been the end of the first act. The last act was about to begin.

The women wished Richard luck. He inclined his head

in his gentlemanly way and they continued their journey, out of the square to the path that led to the fields.

There were four girls racing that day. They were just ahead of her and, as she watched them climb the hill, the task Richard had set her was suddenly daunting. These girls were at their peak, toned, groomed and formidable, the embodiment of perfection: Simba, the Lion, tall and black with powerful legs and pink ribbons woven through her dreadlocks. The Valkyrie, trotting along beside her Viking master, tassels dancing from her ringed nipples, her blonde mane falling to her bottom. Then there was Amber, the beautiful girl who had impressed her so much when she had seen her in the video; she was even more beautiful in real life.

Greta remembered Gustav's doubts about her that day when he checked her teeth and Richard must have read her mind. He slowed his pace and drew closer to whisper. 'You just have to go inside,' he said and tapped her temple with his finger. 'All the answers are in there.'

But where are all the questions?

Chapter Eighteen – Defying Gravity

IT'S NOT EASY BEING a pony girl. And it's not for everyone. You have to become the character, immerse yourself in the part, commit every fibre of your being into the qualities and behaviour the role demands. It is a long climb up a dark stairway and you go a step at a time fighting floods of little doubts as you reach for perfection. Confidence is an invisible suit of clothes laid out at the top of the stairway and once the naked girl slips into the magic suit she can do anything, be anything, perform any role.

Were these thoughts running through her mind as she wandered along behind Richard? Well, sort of. They were thoughts that had occurred to her sporadically through the weeks of her training and she wondered, too, where it was all leading. Today. The big day. Of course. But what then?

What then?

She pushed the thoughts out of her mind. They say in show business it's not what you've done but what you are doing. It's not what you are going to do, but what you are doing now. She flicked her mane and bobbed her tail. She was impatient to get going but knew there would be another delay when she saw Gustav up ahead, chatting to the Texans, holding court, booming in his big voice.

Richard came to a halt, reticent and boyish as he swept back his hair with his palm. Greta remained respectfully in her place behind him as they pushed out their hands with the aggressive formality men display when they meet. Richard shook them in turn. Gustav studied her briefly before looking back at his brother.

'Good morning,' Richard said brightly. 'Lovely day for it.'

'Lovely day for lifting wallets,' Gustav replied, and the Texans laughed.

One of the Texans was extremely tiny, especially for a Texan. He was dressed as a jockey in black silk with shiny boots and a little cap. He had a big grin and bad teeth. 'Didn't know you had so much sunshine in this country,' he said in a squeaky voice.

'You'd be surprised what we have in this country,' said Gustav. He turned to Richard and added. 'May the best man win.'

'May the best *girl* win,' Richard replied.

'I am in no doubt about that,' said Gustav with a little laugh. He tapped his breast pocket and Greta wasn't sure whether he was tapping his heart or the wallet he was certain he was in no risk of having lifted.

'You know, Lord Marsham, we say in Texas, pride comes before a fall.'

Gustav dropped his hands into his pockets and looked down at the short Texan. 'We say in England, Mr Kane, confidence is what confidence does.'

'That's a new one on me,' said the jockey.

The other Texan, the tall one, said nothing. He had been sizing up Greta as the others spoke, his gaze swivelling up the hill to Simba, his steed. She was loping along, her eyes shifting left and right like a lion in the forest. The Americans had every reason to feel confident. Simba was six-and-a-half feet with broad shoulders and the long stride of a Masai warrior. She was black as ebony, as the Valkyrie was ivory white, like yin and yang, like piano keys, the girls the same size, toned and determined. Amber, too, was tall, as tall as a tree, her eyes glassy with resolve and self-knowledge.

Poor liddle Pegasus. She felt her heart pounding in her

chest and was suddenly bored with listening. Loud voices made her skittish. She wanted to run, run over the fields, run as far and as fast as she could.

The Viking was wandering back down the hill towards them and joined the men. He shook hands with Richard and the Americans, then lowered his shoulders fractionally as he greeted Gustav. Gustav had the same penetrating blue eyes as Richard but was older by several years and his aura she could now define by the little word *lord* in front of his name. It did strange things to people. It made women curtsy and grown men go weak at the knees. It didn't affect her. She was playing the pony and nothing more was demanded of her than she play it to the full.

Richard turned and shooed her away.

'Off you go, Pegasus,' he said, using her pony name. It was time to get into character.

She trotted up the incline passing the crowds making their away from the green to the grandstand. People who had already taken their seats took note of her gait and made marks on their betting cards. The other girls were ahead of her and the punters had done the same as they cantered by, judging their strengths and weaknesses, their form. It was only for fun but money would change hands that day and everyone wants to be a winner.

Before the big race there was a pony show, fire-eaters and a dancing dwarf with a bear who played the harmonica; perhaps it was the other way round? There were prizes for the most illustrious tattoos and outrageous costumes; there were feats of weight-lifting using clitoral and penal spikes, mud-wrestling and a wet T-shirt contest because even with so many bare breasts on display people want to see more. Breasts are adorable. Addictive. Hypnotic. Greta's were all tingly and when she gave them a squeeze the people in the crowd put their hands together in a round of applause.

A tent had been erected behind the grandstand and when she trotted through the flap the other girls were limbering up. Simba was down on her haunches stretching one long ebony leg, pumping up the muscles. The Valkyrie was touching her toes, up and down, up and down, taking swift shallow breaths, filling her brain with oxygen. Amber was as still as a statue, palms together above her head as if in prayer to some sky god, graceful and otherworldly.

She's the one to beat!

As the words ran through Greta's mind, Amber opened her eyes and they shone through the blinders like coals in a furnace. Greta tried to smile, not easy with the bit between her teeth, but Amber's eyes pressed shut again and she slipped back into the ether. She's a *Method* actress, Greta thought: she's thinking herself into winning.

Four traps made of fibreglass stood glimmering in the shadows, one black, glossy as oiled flesh, the name Simba in white on a narrow plate below the seat. The golden chariot sparkled like champagne, Amber across the back in black. The Valkyrie was spelled out in yellow on scarlet red, the colours of the flames in Valhalla. Finally, the furthest from her, stood the neon green trap with Pegasus glinting in gold between two wheels with shiny silver spokes.

While Greta was doing a few toe presses, the riders ambled in with set jaws and thin lips. All the handshaking and bragging had come to an end. This was serious business.

Richard took her hand and led her to the trap. She really would have liked a good hard slap on her bare bottom but her bottom remained firm, perky and unpunished. Richard was in deep thought. Before attaching her to the harness he turned her towards him. He took hold of her hipbones as if they were handles on a lawnmower and stared into her eyes through the blinders.

'You remember what I said?'

She nodded.

He tapped her temple and she felt panicky. This was important to him. It was more important to Richard than it was to her. He leaned forward, sucked her bottom lip and, when he let go, he was staring into her eyes.

'Don't race. Pace yourself,' he said, and slapped her bottom, a gentle slap but it was better than nothing.

She backed into the pony trap. He connected the rings on the shafts to her wristbands and the reins to her bridle. She could hear announcements over the speakers, a muffled voice that became clearer as they rolled out of the dark tent into an August sun so bright and blinding it was like a spotlight in the theatre. Gustav was in the lead with Amber; he was Lord Marsham, after all. The Texan named Mr Kane followed, the tiny man bobbing in his seat behind Simba, the lion so big she could have devoured him in one gulp. Greta was ready to go and should have been next, but the Valkyrie nudged her out of the way and the Viking squeezed through the gap.

'Whoa there,' said Richard. 'Take it easy.'

She followed behind and hoped the order in which they left the tent wasn't an omen.

As the traps rumbled into the midst of the crowd the people came to their feet clapping and cheering. She was so proud to be there, so grateful, and felt sure that in all the world there could have been few sights more charming than four naked girls trotting along the way nature had secretly planned.

To race any other way would have made no sense. Clothes, after all, are merely an option. Girls are at their best naked: nature's best design shown to best affect. As their legs stretch their bottoms roll like the motions of a clock keeping universal time, their breasts dance this way and that way, free as little birds, their shoulders glide like the wings of angels and their tails flow luxuriously behind them. She was in no doubt that it was a sight once seen would never be forgotten and to be there, to be a part of it, was as humbling as it was exhilarating. To be a pony girl

221

requires obedience and discipline. But most of all, it needs the confidence required to be a great performer.

There was a crowd opposite the grandstand on the freshly laid grass; the grass that she had laboured over. People waved flags and wet T-shirts; the fire-eater breathed out a jet of flame; cameras were flashing, videos whirred. The sun was high and her skin was bathed in a sheen of sweat. The names of the ponies blared from the speakers. She followed the other three traps as they trotted through the cheering ranks, their voices growing in volume with each announcement. They turned in neat circles beyond the grandstand and the people roared with approval as they trotted back again.

Was she surprised to see Dirty Bill standing at the starting line with a starting pistol shoved in the pocket of his yellow waistcoat?

She put the thought out of her mind and concentrated. She was leaning forward, toes on the line, hands tight on the rubber grips, her lungs working like well-oiled bellows as she took deep breaths, in through her nose and out through her open lips. Her breasts juddered with the beat of her heart and she would have given them a squeeze for good luck but her wrists were manacled to the fibreglass trap.

'Whoa there. Whoa there,' Richard was saying, his voice like a mantra, calming her, controlling her. He felt as light as a feather in the seat behind her, a mere shadow of the man who had fucked her mercilessly on the floor of his apartment before she had even told him her name. How did he know it was just what she'd always wanted?

No time to ponder. The Valkyrie was beside her, teeth gritted, her blue eyes cold as icecaps. The Viking was standing in his footrests. He was lashing the air with his bullwhip and the people cried for more every time the leather sang out. They were playing to the crowd and the Valkyrie got the biggest roar of approval when she opened her legs wide and hosed out a long stream of golden pee.

A giant egg-timer had been set up at the end of the grandstand and when the last grain of sand fell into the vacuum, Dirty Bill raised the starting pistol above his head and the birds in the trees took flight when he fired in the air.

They were off. Off like the wind and people ran along beside them as the girls jogged along the straight. The course was wide at the starting point and the four traps remained abreast as they started to go down the hill: she had learned not to gather speed on the declines or the trap runs away with itself. A sharp bite from the metal bit in her mouth reminded her to pace herself, save her energies for going up the rise on the other side. The traps ran on bicycle wheels, but brakes were not part of the design.

As they hit the lowest part of the decline the girls gathered speed and the people running with them gave up the chase. The far side of the valley was steeper. The race was on. The Valkyrie ran Pegasus off to one side, the second time she'd done that, and the Viking's whip stroked the Valkyrie's back as she began the tough climb upwards beside Simba. Amber was on the far side, farthest from her, and took the incline at a different angle: Gustav knew these hills and knew what he was doing.

Simba and the Valkyrie stayed breast to breast all the way up the hill and, as they reached the crown, they gathered pace on the long meadow leading to the coast road. Greta had taken the hill without difficulty but the two big ponies gained ground on the flat. The Viking loved his bullwhip and she could hear its lashes crackling through the air. Mr Kane was standing in the stirrups and the sound of the lash must have been hypnotic because he joined in, beating Simba's muscular shoulders until she found an extra spurt and shot ahead.

The Viking wasn't to be out done. He laid a few punishing stripes across the Valkyrie's back and when she caught up to Simba, the two drivers got in such a frenzy the lashes from their whips went every which way including each other. It was a scene from *Ben-Hur*, the men standing in their stirrups, legs spread, whipping the ponies, whipping each other, the girls frothing at the mouth as they gathered speed.

The path that led down to the shingle beach was up ahead. There was only room for one trap on that path. The Viking and the Texan were fighting to take the initiative. Their whips flayed the air and as the entry to the path came into view, they turned again on each other. The whips sang out once, twice, three times, then went silent as the leather tongues enwrapped each other in an embrace.

As they tugged them apart, they dragged on the reins, the bits cut into Simba's cheek on the right, the Valkyrie's on the left, and the girls were spitting blood until the whips unwound, the steeds running off the hillside to allow Pegasus to slip through the gap first with Amber close behind her.

Richard kept her on a tight rein; she had lots more in her and didn't know why he was holding her back. Before she had reached the end of the path, the other two were back in pursuit and on the shingle, Amber glided by like a hare racing a tortoise.

'Easy now. Easy now,' Richard was saying.

The shingle was biting her feet. Sweat ran off her body. Her jaunty tail and her mane in green ribbons were shiny as silk flying behind her. Her legs felt strong. Her back felt strong. The sea air was an elixir she drew into her lungs. She felt as if inside her there was an egg and from that egg some strange mysterious force was breaking through the shell. She kept her eyes on Gustav's broad back above the seat of the golden chariot and closed the gap with Amber as they turned towards the stone lighthouse.

'Easy now. Easy now,' Richard kept saying.

He had faith in her. She had to maintain faith in him.

The equilibrium he had needed to guide her and allow her to become all she could be without frightening her away was as finely balanced as a watch-spring. It is something primitive, primordial, intuitive, like a gift for line or an ear for music. She had thought of herself once as a musical instrument. Richard had played her like a virtuoso on a Stradivarius.

She was the best she could be. But was it good enough?

Amber was gaining ground on her again and Simba was already snapping at her heels. She tore through the gate between the brambles and almost immediately Simba eased by on the hill that led to the knoll of trees above the amphitheatre. The Valkyrie drew alongside and she could see the pink weals etched on her white back.

Is that what she needed, a good beating?

She imagined the taste of leather on her soft flesh and kept pace with the Valkyrie all the way up the hill. The Viking drove the red chariot straight into the trees behind the jockey, behind Lord Marsham. Richard peeled off to the left and, like a yachtsman tacking into the wind, leaned out at an angle as the right wheel on the trap left the ground. They curved precariously around the crest of the hill, the trap teetering on the edge of calamity, and emerged ahead of the pack as they plunged down the meadow where she had fought and defeated the billy goat.

Pegasus reached the bowl of the amphitheatre first and on the steep climb up to the row of big oaks, Simba and the Valkyrie pulled ahead again, sweat pouring off them like mini-monsoons, their riders thrashing at their bottoms, the sound like hands clapping as one whip followed immediately after the other.

She had ridden Thunder up this hill many times and the chestnut pony always kept pace with the mare as if her very life had depended on it. She gritted her teeth and did the same. She made her legs into pistons. The stitches like a snake in her gut uncoiled and the green chariot behind her suddenly felt lighter as she stayed right behind the two leaders all the way up the hill.

'Steady now. Steady now.'

They charged through the trees. She caught her first glimpse of Marsham Hall, the white columns sparkling, the long narrow windows mirrors of midday sunshine. They were half way. Amber glided by her and she was last again as they raced down the long meadow.

She ran through cowpats that splattered her legs, through shallow pools churned up from the leading traps and felt refreshed as the mud rained over her body, her thighs, her breasts, her cheeks.

Simba and the Valkyrie were neck and neck. Richard had driven her on a curving angle over flat grassland and she had a good view of the stretch of rutted land ahead of them. The little Texan was sitting back, hanging on to the reins. Simba was leaping like a panther over the gullies, but suddenly the wheels on the black trap hit a high ridge and Mr Kane went flying through the air. Like a riderless horse in a race, Simba ran on, but then wheeled round and went back for her jockey.

The Valkyrie galloped ahead, the Viking's long blonde hair dancing behind him. Amber stayed close and, as they went through the gate leading to the courtyard, Pegasus curled in behind the other two. A group of people was on the steps at Marsham Hall and they shouted their encouragement as the traps skirted the house and raced to the narrow track that led back to the village.

With its mature trees and overhanging branches, the track was a passage between two worlds, one slick and glossy, the other ripe with the smell of flesh and leather, and the people who lived in that slick modern world would never be aware that the other world existed. Sweat poured down her back and into her bottom. Her breasts bounced, beating time. The foliage slapped her cheeks and the ground underfoot was slippery with old leaves. She could see cars racing by on the country road, all going far too fast for anyone to glimpse the other world, the unforgettable site of three naked girls harnessed to pony traps running through the undergrowth like fawns in a tapestry.

The trees thinned out as the track turned towards Marsham. The Valkyrie had pulled ahead in the tunnel, but as they left the shade of the trees, she seemed to lose her balance on the curve and Amber drew level, the two sets of wheels almost touching before the golden chariot slipped ahead.

Pegasus felt the reins rise and fall with a slap on her back. She took a firm grip on the shafts, took swift intakes of breath through her teeth, and as she raced by the Valkyrie on the next curve she could see the girl was spent, her face distorted with the effort. The Viking was standing, lashing the air with his whip, but the Valkyrie dropped further back.

They reached The Black Sheep and the magpies on the roof let out a screech as they took flight. Men quaffing beer drained their glasses and ran with the pony girls as they crossed the green, turned into the farm and chased up the hill. Amber was pulling further ahead. The green trap felt heavier now and she understood why Richard had starved himself. He had done this for her, just as she was doing this for him.

The grandstand came into view at the brow of the hill. She could see the pennants waving. Hear the cry of the crowd. She felt the reins on her back, the bite of the bit between her teeth. Gustav was lashing his pony, the sound of leather scolding the still air, but Amber maintained the same pace like a mill turning with the flow of water or the breath of the wind.

The speakers were screaming. *Amber Pegasus, Amber Pegasus. The Valkyrie's crossing the green with Simba closing the gap. But it's Amber from Pegasus. Amber from Pegasus.*

She could see Dirty Bill in his yellow waistcoat, a

stopwatch in his hand. The people were pressing forward, narrowing the space into a funnel that drew them towards the finishing line.

And it's Amber from Pegasus.

She drew level with Gustav and saw the look of astonishment in his blue eyes. He stood in the stirrups and Amber's faultless features twisted in pain as the whiplash uncoiled across her rump.

It was unbelievable. Mr Maddox had told her she would defy gravity that day and his words ran through her mind as her feet left the ground. *I have thunderbolts in my veins. I will make my Zeus proud of me. I can fly.*

Chapter Nineteen – Duende

IT CAME AS NO surprise that Dirty Bill was Lord Longman, the environmental spokesman in the House of Lords. Count Ruspoli *was* Count Ruspoli; Greta knew the legend and had left her mark on its foundations.

Henrietta Maddox had discovered as matron at a well-known school that girls reach a state of grace when their bottoms are properly disciplined and had brought her zeal to Marsham. Tom and Alex had grown up in the village. Both had travelled, followed other paths, new callings, but what work could be more rewarding than life on the farm with Lord Marsham?

Greta wasn't keen on all this *lord* business, but did approve of tradition. Some hazy daguerreotype photographs of girls in harness dating from 1840 show Marsham Hall in all its splendour and in the main salon, eight etchings from 1723 show girls in activities in which she had become familiar, sweeping out the stable, milking goats, riding bareback, being strapped to a whipping stool for a spanking, the girls naked, naturally, the prints in superb condition. While the rest of the world was becoming bland and predictable, Gustav and Richard were loyal to the customs of their forefathers. Their mother had been an opera singer with a love of Mahler and Wagner, thus their names, but it was their father who had prevailed in their education.

Greta was pleased to see Bella getting a head-start for the following year's event and thought of the girl as her protégé. Greta was now a member of a special club and felt honoured to introduce others to their world. Tara Scott-Wallace was another candidate for discipline and Gustav planned to initiate her into the game now that she had finished her degree. After all that hard work a girl needs a gap year and what better way to spend it than naked in the country pulling a pony trap?

It was nice being a winner, of course, but when you win something, you lose something, too. She would lose Richard's guiding hand, the bite of the bit in her cheek, the reins on her bare shoulders, that uninhibited acceptance of everything. The discipline she would require in her career would have to come from within. There would be no safety nets, no chastisement, no spankings, except for pleasure. She was herself again, but more so, more self-confident, the complete Greta May.

She was dressed in green silk with emerald earrings, Jimmy Choo shoes and the little Cartier wristwatch she had lost in Soho and Richard had been looking after for her since her arrival in Marsham. She had grown to love the village and that night it had never looked prettier. Wooden boards had been laid over the green and strings of pink lanterns hung from the trees. She danced in Richard's arms. She danced with Dirty Bill, as she would always think of him. She danced with Count Ruspoli and he told her that she had awoken something in him that day in the marble bath and he had since given up his vow of celibacy. That made her feel proud.

Greta was momentarily disappointed that Jason Wise wasn't present, if only to gloat, but he had only ever played a minor role in her training and it was Tyler Copic standing with Richard at the edge of the square considering her thoughtfully as she glided towards him.

It was straight to business. Very American. He was casting *Blood Wedding*, the Lorca play he had talked about that night in Jasmine's. They had signed a *big name* for Leonardo. He wanted her to read for the part of the Bride. 'The bridegroom is a glass of clear water but the muddy river of the Bride's past flows through her veins,' he said, and it sounded like a review, like a calling to something inside her. It was the role Greta had longed for without knowing it. She was whisked off to London next day and the following week was in rehearsals.

It was a new interpretation of the play, the work Federico Garcia Lorca would have written without the strict censorship prevailing in 1932. Set below the fiery furnace of the Andalusian sun, through long days of rural tedium, it is the story of the Bride's irrepressible desires and secret passions. When she bolts with her first love Leonardo on her wedding day, the guests track down the lovers and kill them. Why would people do such a thing? Because they ran off? No: because they were caught *in flagrante*. They were caught fucking in the forest and that's what Greta May brought to the stage, that commitment, that passion.

Every night and two matinees at the Almeida, Leonardo stripped her white wedding clothes from her damp body and they performed with such ardour the play was a sell-out and moved to the West End. Other stars, bigger stars, queued up to join the cast as Leonardo but it was the name Greta May that topped the bill in tall letters that glimmered in lights over Shaftesbury Avenue. It made her heart skip every time she saw it.

It was live sex on stage that made Greta May a sensation. Many came to hear her joyous screams as the pink gash of her wet pussy is finally gratified, but they left the theatre in their hordes with moist eyes and moist parts and the knowledge that what they were witnessing was the birth of a true talent. Shooting around her theatre commitments during the 18 months that the play ran in the West End, she did two low-budget English films. The first bombed. The second, a horror spoof called *Zombie Queen*, went mega in America and Hollywood came calling.

Greta often thought about the cameras constantly

turning while she was in training on the farm. Three years later, Marsham Hall was burgled and the film came to light. Still pictures of her as a pony girl appeared in the press and someone made a fortune flogging video cuts on the internet. The controversial new standards of public behaviour laws in America resulted in two lucrative contracts in Hollywood being withdrawn, but Greta's name shot to the top of the A list in Europe. She won best actress at Cannes for her role in *Stolen*, the story of a slave girl's escape from people smugglers, and returned to the London stage to take the lead in the courageous new version of Shakespeare's *Macbeth* by the same writer behind *Zombie Queen*.

Tara had lap-danced her way through her finals at the LSE and left with a first. The girls moved to a new flat in NoHo where they installed the largest Jacuzzi they could find and employed an understanding char to take care of the ice cream sheets.

When her busy schedule permits, Greta wanders through Camden Market on a Sunday morning in the hope of catching a glimpse of Richard and Gustav taking new girls through their paces. What is it about Camden that makes you want to take your clothes off?

Life as an actress is demanding, but Greta makes sure she always has a few days off at the August bank holiday to attend the pony races. Richard had told her once that one day she would demand to be naked. He was right, of course. She wears a mask now she's a celebrity, but that feeling of freedom when she steps naked into the crowd at Marsham reminds her what it is like to be completely alive.

Greta was never quite sure how she had managed to win the race against the odds that day, but as she worked at her profession she came to see that to be a great artist – painter, writer, musician, flamenco singer, actress, pony girl, to be great is to find something inside that can't be seen or described. It is a subtle, mysterious power: the power to cut the strings of our earthbound existence and defy gravity. Lorca called it duende. Greta May has duende.

THE END

Also by Chloë Thurlow

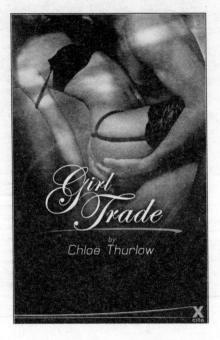

She feels wicked, liberated, daring. And bored. But her adventure begins on holiday in La Gomera, when a rugged beachcomber removes the leather thong from his neck and binds her hands behind her. Crossing oceans and continents in a nether world of smugglers, arms dealers, and pirates, she becomes the adored but captive jewel of the tough inflexible men who make a living in inhospitable landscapes. On hot afternoons on long days without number, she dedicates herself to the pleasures of sex in all its shapes and forms. She learns subservience. She becomes the perfect concubine. The perfect lover. She becomes *Chengi* – Girl.

ISBN 9781907016417   £7.99